Shadow at the Morgue

A SPENCER & REID MYSTERY
BOOK ONE

CARA DEVLIN

First Cup Press

Copyright © 2025 by Cara Devlin

All rights reserved.

No part of this book may be reproduced in any form or by any electronic or mechanical means, including information storage and retrieval systems, without written permission from the author, except for the use of brief quotations in a book review.

Any references to historical events, real people, or real places are used fictitiously. Names and characters are products of the author's imagination.

Edited by Jennifer Wargula

ISBN paperback: 979-8-992305708

Also by Cara Devlin

The Spencer & Reid Mysteries
SHADOW AT THE MORGUE
METHOD OF REVENGE

The Bow Street Duchess Mysteries
MURDER AT THE SEVEN DIALS
DEATH AT FOURNIER DOWNS
SILENCE OF DECEIT
PENANCE FOR THE DEAD
FATAL BY DESIGN
NATURE OF THE CRIME
TAKEN TO THE GRAVE
THE LADY'S LAST MISTAKE (A Bow Street Duchess Romance)

The Sage Canyon Series
A HEART WORTH HEALING
A CURE IN THE WILD
A LAND OF FIERCE MERCY

THE TROUBLE WE KEEP

A Second Chance Western Romance

Chapter One

London
January 1884

The dead bodies in the room didn't bother Leonora Spencer.

She'd grown accustomed to corpses over the years. The unending rotation of them being carted in and then out of her uncle's morgue had become a predictable, almost natural routine. They weren't a bother, and rationally, there was nothing to fear from them. It was the living who could be unpredictable and thus, dangerous.

That was never more apparent to Leo than when a man burst through the doors to the Spring Street Morgue's postmortem room and brandished a pocketknife.

Alone for the last half hour and left to the unenviable task of closing the incision on the final examination of the day, she had heard the bell signaling someone's arrival in the front lobby and thought of two things: she'd overlooked locking up the morgue when her uncle, Claude, retired home for the evening; and she was about to be discovered working on one of the corpses.

Leo froze with the curved needle, threaded with black catgut, in her hand. "Sir, you must leave. We are closed for the day." She wasn't sure how to address the fact that he held a knife, so she chose to ignore it.

"Give over his bag," he ordered.

A stained, gray kerchief covered the bottom half of the man's face, presumably to protect his identity. However, his eyes were a startling cloudy blue, nearly the color of well-established cataracts. A sharp widow's peak speared the center of his high forehead. He really ought to have worn a hat to conceal those distinguishable features, though Leo didn't think it wise to point that out.

"You'd like this gentleman's bag?" She gestured toward the naked corpse on the autopsy table. "I'm afraid that isn't possible. As he was found in curious circumstances, an official death inquest was ordered, and for the time being, his possessions are the property of the Metropolitan Police."

Remaining calm was the only way to handle distraught and unruly family members, gripped by grief—and sometimes an excess of liquor. This wasn't the first time one had stumbled into the morgue in such a state, but they didn't usually brandish weapons or cover their faces like housebreakers. Leo returned to her task, piercing the ashen skin of the corpse's chest with her needle. She hoped it would put off the intruder and convince him to leave.

"I don't give a damn about that. Give it over. *Now.*"

His shout bounced around the high, beamed ceilings of the room. Once a vestry for St. Matthew's Church, it had been transformed into one of the city's rising number of morgues. The stone floors and walls kept the vestry cool during the summer months and even more appropriately chilled during the autumn and winter. The only renovations to the building had been to erect walls to create a back room, some storage closets, and a receiving lobby, the latter of which this kerchiefed man had stormed through on his way into the postmortem room.

The leather bag in question was on a table next to Leo, as was the dead man's folded clothes, his shoes, and a worn, felt bowler. Nothing among the contents of the bag, which she had already thoroughly documented, pointed to the corpse's identity. As with all unidentified bodies, he'd been tagged as John Doe. And since the middle-aged man had been found sprawled in a street with no obvious wounds, a postmortem had been ordered to determine how he'd died. Her uncle had found evidence of a pulmonary embolism. Tragic, but nothing criminal.

"Are you family? The police would like to know his name," she said as she pulled the catgut through the skin.

Claude had made the customary opening incision earlier, cutting from throat to pubic bone, and he had performed the postmortem, as he had countless times during his career as an assistant city coroner. Lately, however, handling the curved needle and making neat stitches had become a challenge for him. More and more, Leo had started to take over the suturing required at the end of the postmortem. When his tremors acted up, it could be difficult for him to make clean incisions too. But while she preferred closing to opening, especially when it came to making the coronal incision at the scalp, Leo would assist however Claude needed her. It wasn't as if she hadn't learned the essentials of the procedure over the last several years she'd been allowed into the postmortem room. In fact, she'd become quite good at it.

"Shut your mouth and step away," the intruder ordered as he took a few advancing steps.

Leo rested the needle on the dead man's chest and did as she was told, though she was more annoyed than afraid. If he had wanted to hurt her, he would have done so by now.

"Very well, take it then," she said.

In truth, it didn't matter. While Claude had been removing and examining the man's organs, she'd gone through the bag and detailed every item in the possessions register. Officially, that was her job. That, and typing up death inquest reports for Mr. Pritchard, the deputy coroner, to bring to inquests at the coroner's court. She also greeted those who arrived to identify the bodies and oversaw their collection, either by family members or a funeral service.

Even if she hadn't already written down the contents of the bag, Leo would have been able to do so now, in meticulous detail. Her memory was such that she could view something once and then flawlessly recall it again, even years later. Her perfect memory came in quite handy at the morgue. She could accurately recall everything from the pattern of a dress on a body that came in months back, to the exact amount of money in a coin purse written into the possessions register, to the finer details of a death inquest she had typed last summer. It wasn't as though she could memorize whole books, word for word, but short passages were simple. She could recite details of newspaper articles she'd read long ago, memorize numbers effortlessly, and right then, she could easily picture the several mundane items within the bag the intruder had demanded. She couldn't comprehend what he might want with them. They certainly weren't worth all this trouble.

The kerchiefed man plucked the bag from the table, then looked around the postmortem room at the half dozen tables within it. Two were occupied by white-sheeted bodies. One was a man killed during a mugging, whose multiple knife wounds had been sufficient evidence for cause of death. The other was a young woman in her twenties, crushed beneath the wheels of an omnibus. Neither required postmortems.

The intruder pointed with his knife toward the open door of a supply closet. "In there," he said gruffly, and Leo's stomach dropped.

"I really must object. Take the bag and leave. I won't try to stop you."

"Get in!" He advanced again, the slip joint knife pointed toward her abdomen.

She gritted her teeth, her chest growing tight, but again, conceded. Arguing with a desperate man holding a weapon would be unwise, even if being shut into a darkened space made her skin crawl and pulse race. The door slammed behind her, and the snap of the padlock sealed her fate. Expensive chemicals and tools were stored upon the shelves, so Claude had Leo lock them up each night. The key for the padlock was in her skirt pocket. A lot of good it would do her now.

"This is unnecessary!" she shouted as the man's boots scuffed across the stone floor. He didn't sound to be leaving, as she thought he would. Surely, he'd penned her up in here to prevent her from running out into the street and calling for help. As the morgue was but a stone's throw from Great Scotland Yard, the headquarters for the London Metropolitan Police, a constable or two would have certainly heard her shouts and investigated.

Come to think of it, this man had quite a lot of impudence to be robbing a place so close to so many officers of the law.

She pressed her ear to the wooden door. He was lingering about the postmortem room. But after a few protracted moments, his footsteps carried back toward the lobby and then disappeared entirely. He was gone.

And she was still locked in a closet.

Leo tried to breathe evenly and focus on the strip of light coming in at the base of the door. She didn't like confined, dark spaces, and for good reason. Though to think of those reasons now would only hasten the panic already threatening to paralyze her. Instead, she thought of her larger problem: the body of the John Doe, still lying half-closed on the table. It would be a disaster if anyone were to come into the morgue and find him like that, for it wouldn't take much to conclude that the young woman locked in the supply closet, wearing a canvas apron, was the very person who'd been in the middle of a postmortem closure.

Should Mr. Pritchard or his superiors, or anyone at the Yard, learn that she'd been helping with such tasks, her uncle would lose his position as assistant coroner in a blink. It wouldn't matter that Claude had the favor of the illustrious Chief Superintendent Gregory Reid—or rather *former* Chief Superintendent Gregory Reid. Allowing a woman to perform any kind of surgical operation on a body, living or dead, would be beyond the pale and grounds for immediate dismissal. If that were to happen, Leo wasn't sure what she or her uncle would do, especially now that Aunt Flora was unwell.

Like the tremors diminishing Claude's skillful hands, Flora's mental fitness had also been deteriorating for some time. She'd always been a bit off-kilter, ever since Leo had gone to live with them when she'd been nine years old. But now, nearly sixteen years later, Flora had reached a point where conversation was next to impossible and comprehension, even more obscure.

With Flora becoming increasingly erratic and emotional, the only people who were able to soothe her were Claude and Mrs. Shaw, the nurse that Claude's position at the city morgue allowed him to afford. In fact, it had been Mrs. Shaw who'd sent a message to the morgue earlier, saying Flora was in an especially bad way and that Claude was needed. He'd gone at once, leaving the John Doe in Leo's capable hands.

Now, however, a locked door stood between her and her task.

Had the lock been built into the door, she might have reached into the knot of hair at the nape of her neck and pulled out a few pins. She had no idea how to pick a lock, but it wouldn't hurt to try. However, as this was a padlock, she could do nothing but hope her uncle would notice her absence soon and come looking for her. Then again, he wouldn't want to leave Flora alone to walk the ten minutes to the morgue. Goodness, if he didn't come,

Leo might actually have to sleep inside this cramped closet reeking sharply of chemicals.

She turned her back to the door and sank down to the stone floor, bringing her knees up to her chest. *You're perfectly fine,* she told herself. *It's not ideal, but you are fine.* This wasn't the attic from her nightmarish memories. It was a perfectly safe closet. There was no one out there looking to harm her, and she wasn't hiding from anyone.

With her sweaty hands clasped together, she began to rub circles into the center of her right palm. It was something she'd done for many years to calm herself. Her thumb would go over the old, raised scars there again and again until her pulse began to even out. Still, she couldn't quite escape the panic that small, tight spaces had inspired ever since that night, all those years ago. She often wondered if that night was still so vivid because of her curious memory, or if the horror of it had been strong enough to leave an indelible impression on her brain. Perhaps one simply aided the other.

Claude would find her eventually. She could depend on him, and she had, ever since she'd been a little girl and newly alone in the world. While Flora was her blood relation, her mother's much older sister had left the parenting to her even older husband. In all probability, had Claude not insisted they take Leo in, Flora would have been content to leave her orphaned niece with Gregory Reid, then a detective inspector with Scotland Yard. The Inspector had been the one to find Leo in that attic, and she'd spent the next two months in his care while he'd hunted down her only remaining family, Flora and Claude Feldman.

Sounds of a commotion came from the front lobby.

Leo stiffened her back. She got to her feet, her heart beginning to pound when she heard the muffled voices of men.

The postmortem room door opened.

"Leo? Claude?"

She squeezed her eyes shut. Curse her bad luck!

"Leonora! Claude? Are either of you here?"

The resonant baritone of Detective Inspector Jasper Reid's voice shivered through her, and briefly, she contemplated staying quiet. It was tempting. Jasper might have been Gregory Reid's adopted son, but he'd never shared his father's indulgent sentiments regarding Leo. If anything, Jasper viewed her as an annoyance, a proverbial thorn in his side.

The trouble was, if she pretended not to be here, Jasper would only go to her home on Duke Street and report her as missing. Her uncle would worry needlessly, and then of course, Claude would need to explain the unfinished postmortem on the table.

With mounting embarrassment and great reluctance, Leo lifted her hand and rapped her knuckles against the door.

"In here." Humiliation weighted the words. No doubt the newly minted detective inspector heard it too.

Jasper's footfalls approached the door. "Leo? Are you in the bloody closet?"

"Only until you open the padlock and get me out." She crouched to slide the key through the small gap under the door.

He grumbled as he took it up. Leo stood, pushing back her shoulders and preparing herself. Jasper would have seen the John Doe by now. She needed an excuse to explain her uncle's absence. Belatedly remembering her canvas apron, she hurriedly untied the strings and tossed the apron onto the floor behind her just as the padlock clicked. The door swung wide on creaking hinges. Light from the hanging gasoliers flooded in, and she winced.

Jasper stood directly in front of her, his tawny eyebrows pinched together, and chin tucked. Ever since she'd known him, he'd worn some version of this scowl, though now it was amplified to a new degree. A full head taller than Leo, he'd long perfected looking down his nose at her with censure, as he did right then.

"Leonora Spencer, just what kind of trouble have you gotten yourself into now?"

Chapter Two

Jasper stood aside, and Leo darted out from the closet. Though she kept her chin high, he sensed her disgrace at having been found in such a helpless state. She'd always been proud and distinctly cold in her demeanor, so the unusual flush of her cheeks brought him a bit of pleasure. He smothered his grin, no longer worried as he'd been while running toward Spring Street.

"How did you know there was trouble here?" Leo asked as she took measured steps toward the autopsy table and the poor sod who occupied it.

"PC Warnock caught me on my way out of headquarters," Jasper answered as she swiftly brought up the sheet. To cover the half-closed sternum, no doubt. "Someone reported seeing a man with a knife running from the Spring Street Morgue. What happened?"

Warnock and another constable, PC Drake, each took discomfited glances toward the sheeted corpses. Morgues had bothered Jasper when he'd been new to the job, but now, he paid the bodies no mind. Neither did Leo, which struck many men at Scotland Yard as peculiar. Unnatural even. Most disapproved of her presence at the morgue, but no one said anything. To do so would have been going against the opinion of Chief Superintendent Gregory Reid, and no one on the force would do that. The old man was too beloved. Too respected. And if he was of the opinion that Leonora Spencer could work alongside her uncle in the morgue, well then, she could.

Leo crouched to pick up a bowler hat from the floor and put it back on the dead man's pile of clothing. "A man came in, demanding this gentleman's bag. He wasn't asking nicely."

Her cool composure was another thing that unnerved plenty of officers. That type of seriousness was better suited to men or wizened crones, not young ladies.

"You're unharmed?" he asked.

"Yes, thankfully."

Jasper nodded to the two constables in dismissal. They fled with more alacrity than necessary. The morgue wasn't all that unsettled them; it was Leo herself. Her family's murder, specifically. The story had dominated newspaper headlines throughout London sixteen years ago, and plenty of people still remembered the gruesome tale of Leonard and Andromeda Spencer and two of their young children. For those who didn't remember, gossip and speculation still lingered to enlighten them.

Leo smoothed the sheet over the body, tugging out a crease. She peered after the quickly departing constables. "You don't think they'll say anything, do you?"

Jasper sighed. "You admit to it then?" He'd noticed the shaking of Claude's hands over the last few months, and he'd suspected Leo was helping in some impermissible way. But they'd yet to speak of it frankly.

She gave a nonchalant shrug. "I admit to nothing. However, it might have appeared...questionable."

"I doubt either of them looked long enough to notice the incision wasn't fully closed." Jasper shook his head. "Where is Claude?"

"Aunt Flora needed him."

He wanted to be understanding, as he was aware Leo's aunt wasn't well. Still, there were rules. "He really ought to have stayed to finish this." Jasper gestured toward the sheeted body. "If anything, just so that you wouldn't have been found alone with it."

He was obligated to report the violation. Leo, as intelligent as she was, was not a trained surgeon or medical doctor. Should she ever be found out, any death inquest report that she'd participated in would be questioned. Even invalidated.

"You know that Claude is the only one who can soothe her," Leo said. "It's only sutures. Coroners employ their assistants in this way all the time."

"Male assistants," he reminded her, then ignored her unimpressed glower.

"Would you like a description of the man with the knife?" she asked, moving on. She was a master at evasion, after all. Secretive to a fault too, though he couldn't entirely blame her for it.

"Go on," he said.

"An inch shorter than you; high widow's peak hairline, graying blond hair; blue eyes, milky. Some sort of cataract disease, probably. Sounded like a Liverpool accent. If I had any artistic talent, I'd draw a likeness." She shrugged. "Sorry."

Knowing her steel trap of a brain, she'd have drawn the burglar down to the last wrinkle on his face.

"And all he wanted was the bag?"

"It was all he asked for."

"What was in it?"

"Nothing of value," she replied. "A tatty coin purse containing three shillings, six pence, and two Luden's throat lozenges. A few other normal things like yesterday's *Telegraph*, reading spectacles, a half-eaten hand pie wrapped in brown paper, and a case for business cards, though it was empty."

Jasper frowned. "So, no identification and nothing worth stealing."

She shook her head as her attention drifted toward the other two bodies draped with sheets.

A fluffy gray cat darted toward him, the little bell on its collar chiming. Jasper stepped back as Tibia affectionately rubbed up against Leo's skirt hem. The animal couldn't be trusted; it had scratched at his shins one too many times, though it was docile enough for Leo and Claude. She stooped to pick the thing up and scratched between its ears while walking toward the other bodies.

Jasper followed. "Is something wrong?"

"I'm not sure. After the man locked me in the closet, he didn't leave straightaway. It sounded as though he came over here." She stopped abruptly next to one of the bodies and cocked her head. "This sheet wasn't like this before."

"Like what?"

"Bunched up." She ran her palm over a rumpled edge

of the sheet near the head, and then, without warning, tossed it back.

Tibia yowled at the sudden motion and leaped from Leo's arms. Jasper couldn't blame the cat for its reaction. He grimaced at what was underneath; the woman, still clothed, looked fresh into the morgue. Before he could avert his eyes, he noted the damage to her skull. It had been crushed. Her dark brown hair was matted in blood and what he presumed to be brain matter.

He groaned, his stomach churning. "Christ, I didn't need to be put off my supper."

In little more than one hour, he was to collect Miss Constance Hayes at her boardinghouse and bring her to the Albion in Covent Garden. They dined at least once a week, though now his appetite was scuppered.

Leo ignored his complaint. "Why would the intruder look beneath this sheet? Wait." She touched the high collar of the woman's dress, her fingers running over black lace and jet buttons. "Her necklace is missing. She was wearing a locket when she was delivered here earlier this evening."

"Are you certain?" When she hiked a brow, Jasper conceded with a nod. He knew better than to ask her such a question.

Now that the shock of the woman's crushed skull had settled, he stepped closer to the table. Her dress was made of black crepe and lace. She'd been in mourning. His attention caught on a pair of amethyst and diamond cluster earrings in her earlobes.

"Why peel off with the necklace but leave these?" he mused, then looked over at the other morgue resident. The white sheet appeared smooth, not hastily drawn up as this one had been.

"And why ignore that body entirely?" Leo asked, having made the same observation.

"The intruder might have believed his time had run out," Jasper suggested. "Decided that to look wasn't worth the chance of being caught."

Leo tugged the sheet up again, covering the woman's ruined head. In a quiet show of respect, she took care to flatten out the wrinkles. "I suppose it's possible."

She didn't sound convinced. Neither was Jasper. But as the intruder was now gone, there was no way to know for certain. At least Leo hadn't been harmed during the incident.

Jasper opened the cover of his pocket watch. He was going to be late meeting Constance. "From now on you should lock the lobby door after hours."

"Yes, yes, I will," she said, but she wasn't listening. She was too busy stepping in front of him to block his way toward the exit, hands clasped behind her back. It was a position she struck when about to ask him for something. "Will you please not tell the Inspector about this? I don't want to worry him."

Although Gregory Reid had not ranked at the inspector level for several years, he would always be *the Inspector* to Leo.

Jasper snapped his watch shut and tucked it into his waistcoat pocket. "He's going to find out anyway."

His father might have left the force several months ago after his health began to fail, but he still had friends there. Over the course of the summer and autumn, he'd received several visitors a week, some of whom were inquiring about his recovery, back when they'd optimistically thought his illness was temporary. Others had come asking for advice or opinions on different cases. More recently, the visits had fallen off as it became clear he would not be getting better.

"I'd best tell him myself then, so none of the details become overly embellished," Leo sighed as she went into the closet and retrieved an apron from the floor, where she must have tossed it. She slipped it on again.

"You cannot finish this John Doe," Jasper said with an exasperated gesture toward the partially closed body on the table.

She tied the strings at her back then tucked a loose curl of her dark sable hair behind her ear. "You're right. I can't. Especially if you continue to stand there." Leo drew back the sheet and picked up the curved needle. She peered at him, waiting for him to leave.

The woman was impossible. Indulged and spoiled to a fault. Not just by Claude but by his father too.

"There is no need for you to go to Charles Street. I'll stop in on my way to dinner and tell him before he hears about it from anyone else. Just finish up here quickly and get home," he said. "But I warn you, Leo, you're playing with fire, and I won't let it pass again."

A flicker of apprehension lit her hazel eyes before Jasper turned and left the postmortem room. She knew exactly what could happen if she were caught. She probably also knew that he wouldn't follow through with his threat. Jasper wouldn't have been able to bear his father's disappointment if he did.

To Gregory Reid, Leo would always be the little girl he'd found tucked away in the attic inside a house full of horrors. The little girl who'd spent a few months at his home, as his ward, during which time her aunt and uncle had been sought on the Continent and informed of the dire situation. She would always be the little girl he'd have very much liked to continue raising, if only to fill the gaping void left behind after his own daughter's death.

But family was family, and when Claude and Flora Feldman arrived on the Inspector's front step, he'd had no choice but to send Leonora off with them. Shortly afterward, he'd made sure Claude, a surgeon, was given a nearby position as an assistant city coroner at the Spring Street Morgue. Jasper imagined that no matter what Claude's profession had been, his father would have lined up some employment to keep the Feldmans and their niece close at hand.

Charles Street wasn't far from the morgue. A five-minute walk at the most. A fine rain dampened the pavements and cut through the brume of the raw January night. It had been a mild winter. Rainy and dreary, without even a speck of snow. Shrugging down into his coat collar, Jasper picked up his pace. He'd been planning to call on his father the next afternoon; going tonight instead wouldn't be a burden. Even though his caseload had become a mountain on his desk at the Criminal Investigation Department at Scotland Yard, Jasper made certain to stop in at least two or three times a week. With his father's heart growing weaker by the day, he didn't like to wait too long between visits. He hadn't just taken Gregory Reid's name for convenience; the man was as much a father to him as anyone had ever been. Never had Jasper met a kinder, more generous man. He had no memories of his real father, and he wished like hell he could say the same about those he did have of his mother, and of his uncles, aunts, and cousins.

The other Met officers had often joked that Reid was in line for sainthood after taking in both Leo, for a time, and then Jasper, a thirteen-year-old guttersnipe arrested for thievery and who probably should have been sent away to a workhouse. But the Inspector had seen something in Jasper. Some promise. At least that's what he said to anyone who inquired. Although Jasper suspected there was another reason he'd taken him in. One that had to do with Leo Spencer.

He thought of her now in the morgue, finishing up the closure of the John Doe. It was the oddest thing, for a woman to be at ease working with the dead. He often wondered if her interest in Claude's vocation had grown out of genuine interest, or if she only felt indebted to the old man for giving her a home. Perhaps she'd seen Claude's infirmities sooner than anyone else and had decided the only way to help was to step in herself. Any other woman attempting to work in a morgue would have been turned out on the spot, but not Leonora Spencer. Exceptions were made for her, and all due to the Inspector's lasting affection.

Jasper climbed the few limestone steps to the front door of 23 Charles Street, a fine terrace home in an upscale part of London. No man on a Met inspector's salary, or even a chief superintendent's, would have ever been able to afford a home like this. However, when he'd been younger, Gregory Reid had the good fortune of falling in love with a viscount's daughter, the Honorable Emmaline Cowper. He'd had the even better fortune of winning her love in return. When they'd married, Emmaline brought with her a generous dowry, and her grandmother had gifted them the home in Mayfair.

Jasper brought down the knocker and waited. He had his own key, but ever since he'd moved into bachelor's rooms on Glasshouse Street, he hadn't felt comfortable just barging in as he once had. The shadow of Mrs. Zhao's slight figure grew large through the frosted glass, and then, he heard the lock being thrown back.

"Mr. Jasper," she said, her smile welcoming as it always was. She stepped aside, allowing him into the foyer. The carpet was faded, the wallpaper too, but despite some of the dated touches, the home was neat and refined. The Inspector had never been inclined to update the decor after his wife's death. His children's rooms on the second floor remained untouched too.

"I'm sorry for stopping in, Mrs. Zhao. I would have sent a note ahead, but it was a last-minute decision," he said as she took his hat and overcoat, both of which were damp.

"You never need apologize," the housekeeper said with a shake of her head. "This is your home, and I am happy to see you in it."

It wasn't at all common to have a Chinese housekeeper, but when Greg and Emmaline had married, it had been difficult for them to find anyone in service who would stoop to serving a common police officer. Surely the story was more complex, but all Jasper knew was that his father had met Mrs. Zhao during an investigation in which she was a witness. When he learned she was looking for employment, he and Emmaline had given her an offer. She'd been his housekeeper ever since.

"Is he awake?" Jasper asked. The downward quirk of Mrs. Zhao's lips was his answer.

"He's had a difficult day," she whispered. "Doctor Bishop left not long ago. He says Mr. Reid needs rest."

Jasper could well imagine what his father's response had been to the doctor's advice: that soon enough, he'd have all the rest in the world.

"Did you need to speak to him about something important?" Mrs. Zhao asked while also pointedly eyeing the cuffs of his tweed suit jacket.

A few threads were loose, and she'd been waiting patiently for Jasper to ask her to mend them. Not wanting to impose on his independence, she wouldn't offer outright. However, he'd not asked. Worn cuffs were commonplace among the other detectives at the Yard. He was already suspected of having risen in rank due to his last name and connection to Greg Reid. He didn't want to look overly polished too.

"No, it can wait." He was grateful he wouldn't have to inform his father about the break-in at the morgue or of Leo being locked in a closet. His heart and lungs were already failing, and considering the upcoming date— January 15—any stress might push him over the edge.

Gregory Reid never bore that day well. This January 15 would mark seventeen years since the ice on the pond in Regent's Park broke, plunging skaters into the frigid water underneath. They'd mostly been women and children, out for a pleasant and curiously sunny winter's day. Forty had perished, among them Emmaline and their two young children, Beatrice and Gregory Junior.

Now, it was only a matter of time before he would see them again.

"I'll stay here, tonight, Mrs. Zhao, if you don't mind."

He'd catch his father first thing in the morning, when he usually had more energy.

"Good," she said. "Your room is always prepared."

He thanked her, then stepped out again to whistle for a messenger boy. Plenty would be roaming the street this time of evening, hoping to be dispatched. Given the hour, Constance would be at her boardinghouse, pacing and glimpsing the clock on the mantel as she waited for Jasper to arrive—something he would not be doing after all.

Chapter Three

Leo set the rack of toast onto the table and the crock of butter beside it. The air inside their kitchen on Duke Street was filled with its usual odor of charred eggs and sausage, but at least she hardly ever burned the toast. Cooking wasn't an undertaking she'd ever perfected, and thankfully, neither Claude nor Flora berated her for it. Probably because they, too, were terrible cooks. It was a wonder the three of them had survived for this long.

Sunshine streamed in through the windows, highlighting floating dust motes. The terrace house was small and modest, but tidy, in large part thanks to Mrs. Shaw. Though she was officially Flora's nurse, she usually kept the house neatly swept too. However now, she had given her notice.

"Was there no talking her out of it?" Leo asked as she sat adjacent to Claude. He slathered butter on a slice of toast, which he then placed on Flora's plate.

"None," he answered with a sad sigh. "But she said

she'd stay on for a week to give us time to find someone new."

Leo dropped a cube of sugar into her tea, then a splash of milk while her aunt spun the buttered toast around and around on her plate. She'd been quiet this morning, however last night, Claude reported that he'd heard her shouts from down the street on his way home. When he'd walked into the house, Mrs. Shaw had been crying out of frustration—and perhaps a bit of fear. Flora had been chanting at the top of her lungs that Mrs. Shaw's family would "perish painfully of poisoned pie." Alliteration had become a quirk of hers, especially whenever she became upset. Part of Leo wondered if her aunt had selected this ominous chant with the express desire to drive Mrs. Shaw away. But how much of Flora's mind was still aware? Sometimes, she seemed perfectly fine. Then, in a blink, she'd be gone again.

On her walk home last night—after finishing the closure, feeding Tibia a skewer of offal meat she'd purchased from the butcher that afternoon, and locking up the morgue—Leo decided the story of the intruder could keep until morning when she and Claude would be refreshed. Besides, the danger the intruder had imposed wasn't her main concern any longer. It was the necklace missing from the omnibus accident victim, Miss Hannah Barrett.

The oval locket, roughly two inches long and an inch wide, had been tarnished gold, and the face engraved with a design of lilies. Why the intruder took it, but not the much more valuable amethyst and diamond earrings, continued to perplex her over the short distance to Duke Street.

Jasper's warning for her to stop assisting with closing sutures had also weighed on her. She didn't think he would tell the deputy coroner...but Jasper was strict about rules, and ever since he'd been promoted to Detective Inspector at the C.I.D., he'd been more austere than usual. Then again, she'd hardly seen him over the handful of years he'd been at the Tottenham Road Police Station, earning his stripes, so to speak. Maybe this somber and disapproving man was just who Jasper had turned out to be.

In all honesty, he'd been solemn even as a boy, right from their first meeting at Scotland Yard. Even if Leo's memory had not been photographic, as it was sometimes called, she would have recalled that moment perfectly.

For the first four days after losing her family, Leo had been kept under guard at the Yard. Not in a holding cell, but in a room that had once been a bedchamber in the old Palace of Whitehall. The former royal residence had been destroyed by fire, piece by piece, over the centuries, until all that remained was a collection of buildings that had eventually been turned into the headquarters for the Metropolitan Police. The bedchamber had been outfitted with a cot for her, and the Inspector had brought in pillows and a thick quilt from his own home, so that she'd be warm.

A constable's wife had been assigned to watch her. At the time, Leo hadn't known why, but now she understood the Inspector was being cautious. He believed her family had been targeted and that once whoever did it learned a child had been overlooked, they might try to finish the job. So, Leo had remained under police protection.

On her fourth day in custody, the constable's wife was

walking Leo back to her room after meeting with the police surgeon. Her palm was healing from the gashes she'd given herself that horrible night in the attic, from a shard of her broken porcelain doll, and the doctor had rebandaged her hand. Too busy wincing from the tight, itchy sensation of her stitches, she hadn't seen the unruly drunkard barreling toward her at first. He'd broken away from a constable bringing him in, and the chase had driven him straight toward Leo and the constable's wife. But then, a gangly, flaxen-haired boy darted into his path, intercepting him. The surprise collision took down both man and boy, and the pursuing constable was given a chance to catch up.

Once the boy was on his feet and dusted off, his bruises had been visible. Leo had stared, aghast. Some bruises were fresh, others were fading, and they riddled his face to a grotesque state. When another constable scolded the boy and grabbed him by the arm, it became clear that, though just a few years older than she, he'd been brought in under arrest. The boy had held Leo's stunned stare a few moments longer before the constable unceremoniously yanked him away.

Even then, Jasper's dark green eyes had been the gloomy color of the Thames on an overcast day.

"I'll place an advert in the *Telegraph* for Mrs. Shaw's replacement," Leo told her uncle as she sipped her tea. Now didn't seem like the right time to tell him about the intruder in the morgue, especially as she watched him scoop up a forkful of burnt eggs and feed them to Flora, his hand tremoring slightly. But she knew she must. Briefly and straightforwardly, she explained what had unfolded the evening before. Claude sat back in his chair and pushed his wire spectacles higher onto the bridge of his nose.

"My dear, you could have been harmed. I should have been there."

She shook her head. "I don't want you to feel sorry. I'm perfectly fine. But unfortunately, Inspector Reid now knows that I assist you at times."

Claude waved it off. "The boy won't say anything."

"Jasper hasn't been a boy for a while now, Uncle. Unfortunately, he's a detective inspector and terribly pedantic."

"Well, he does have quite the pair of shoes to fill, doesn't he?" Claude said, fixing his own plate now that he'd taken care of Flora's.

He made a good point. To no one's great surprise, Jasper had followed in the Inspector's footsteps. He must have felt immense pressure to uphold the well-respected reputation of the Reid name. Perhaps especially so, considering he'd not been born with the name, but had it given to him.

Across the table, Flora, her expression devoid of any emotion these last many minutes, brightened. The lines around her mouth creased as she grinned. "Such a sweet boy, that Jasper. Isn't he a sweet boy, Claude?"

He sat forward again, visibly pleased for her moment of lucidity. It would be brief, but it was a gift just the same. "Yes, my darling, a very sweet boy."

Flora's longstanding soft spot for Jasper was baffling. She wasn't motherly in the least. Not toward Leo anyway.

Three quick knocks on the front door alerted her to the time.

"I'll be at the morgue a little later than usual," she said

as she drained her teacup and plucked a slice of toast from the rack.

She could tell Claude wanted to ask where she was going, but he'd become adept at holding his tongue. Now nearly twenty-five, Leo no longer needed to answer to him. Still, he'd never been overly restrictive, and so she didn't feel the need to be secretive.

"I'm going to walk with Dita to the Yard and stop in to see Jasper," she told him as she pushed back her chair, stood, and stooped to kiss the top of his head.

Her friend, Nivedita Brooks, was a matron at Scotland Yard, and most mornings, she and Leo walked the quarter hour or so it took to reach No. 4 Whitehall Place together. Dita had been granted the position the previous year, the first in which the Met had started to employ women to watch over the children and ladies taken into police custody. Most matrons were relatives of police officers, and that was true for Dita as well. Her father, a sergeant in the Public Carriage Office, had been with the Met for nearly twenty years.

Leo opened the door for her friend while putting on her coat, gloves, and hat. Dita grimaced as she looked her over.

"Please, tell me you aren't wearing that tonight when we go to Striker's Wharf."

Leo shepherded her outside and shut the door. "I'm not wearing this to Striker's Wharf because I'm no longer going. I'm sorry," she said as they started for the Strand.

Dita might not have looked like a woman of style, dressed as she currently was in her crisp, blue wool skirt uniform, half cape, and hat, with a pair of tall black boots to cover her ankles. But outside the Yard, she wore only the most fashionable clothing, and she was eternally pleading with Leo to branch out from her favored utilitarian dresses. The morgue called for subdued colors like muted green, dark blue, and charcoal gray, and it wasn't practical for her to wear anything but tweeds, twills, and cottons. Besides, while bright silks and satins looked splendid against Dita's darker complexion, Leo's own pale skin turned jaundiced against them.

"Is it John?" Dita sighed. "You know I'll tell him he can't come if it bothers you to be the odd one out."

Dita had been courting John Lloyd, a police constable, for a few months, and now whenever they went across the river to the dance hall on Striker's Wharf, he usually accompanied them. There was nothing Dita enjoyed more than dancing, and while Leo liked the club, she much preferred sitting at a table, listening to the band, and watching the revelry of the crowd.

"It's not that," Leo said. "It's Aunt Flora. You see, Mrs. Shaw has quit."

Dita, aware of Flora's condition, put an arm around Leo's shoulders and gave her a bracing squeeze. "Is there anything I can do to help?"

"That's very kind, but there isn't much to do other than place an advert for a new nurse." *Again.* Mrs. Shaw had lasted six months. Miss Baxter before her had stayed but a fortnight.

Dita hooked Leo's arm through hers and pulled, slowing her pace. "Why are you walking so quickly? You can't be that eager to open the morgue this morning."

"I'm coming with you into the Yard," she explained. "And since you'll likely hear all about it today, I'll be the first to tell you."

She quickly went over the event of the morgue intruder, the missing locket, and, albeit reluctantly, the fact that she'd been locked in a closet for a short while. Dita knew her well enough to understand which part of the incident Leo was least willing to discuss, and as any good friend would, Dita refused to let her ignore it.

"That animal put you in a closet? Weren't you terrified?"

"It was just a closet," she replied.

"A confined space just the same."

Every enclosed space would transform in Leo's mind into the steamer trunk in the attic of her old Red Lion Street home. She'd huddled for hours in that trunk, all the while knowing her family had been hurt. And yet, she'd been too frightened to come out and see for herself.

"The closet was the least interesting part," she assured Dita. "It's the locket I am interested in speaking to Inspector Reid about."

Miss Hannah Barrett's body had been delivered to Spring Street close to five o'clock the evening before, and Leo had immediately catalogued the departed's personal effects. A letter in her handbag had pointed to her identity, and the constable had left with the task of contacting her family. When they arrived today, Miss Barrett would not be wearing the necklace she'd come in with. If it was a family piece, the loss of it would be noted, and that would reflect poorly on her uncle's morgue. While that had bothered her all night, so had something else about the necklace.

Within the locket had been two more items that she'd logged into the possessions register: a clipping of dark hair bound together with a thin blue ribbon, and a very small, folded piece of paper with some confounding writing upon it: *Strange Nun B17 R4.* The contents of the locket might not have any relevance to why it had been taken, but Leo would at least tell Jasper about them. The night before, she'd overlooked reporting those details to him.

She was also a bit curious as to how his conversation with the Inspector had gone.

"I must say, there are times I envy you," Dita said as they approached the courtyard behind police headquarters. It was the very name of this courtyard, Scotland Yard, that had given the connected buildings the same moniker.

Leo peered sideways at her friend as they passed the horse stables and approached the main entrance. "I can't understand how that could be. You won't even set foot inside the morgue."

"Oh, no, I refuse to be around corpses," Dita said with a shudder. "But you seem to take it all in stride. Whereas I could barely sleep last night thinking about the poor children I watched over yesterday. They were found inside a photographer's studio, barely dressed. It seems he'd been keeping them dosed with laudanum and using them to pose for lewd photographs."

Leo's stomach cramped. It was cruel what some people could do to others. Especially to children, the most vulnerable of them all. No corpse, no matter how mangled, could affect her as keenly as an innocent child harmed.

"Do they have homes to return to?"

Dita shook her head. As Leo had suspected, these children had likely been lured off the street with the promise of treats or money. From the Yard, they'd go to an orphanage or workhouse.

"But never mind all that," Dita said as they nodded hello to the officer in the lobby, Constable Woodhouse. He knew Leo and let her pass; all other visitors would be required to stop and state their business. "I don't intend to remain a matron for very long," Dita whispered, then grinned, her dark brown eyes glittering with mischief. "If John steps up to the mark."

She wanted to marry, of course, and start a family. And apparently, with Police Constable John Lloyd.

They parted ways at the stairs, Dita going up while Leo continued down a hall toward the detective department. She held her chin high, having learned long ago to pretend to have horse blinders on and pay no attention to those in uniform, or in plainclothes, like those in the C.I.D. She was eyed with everything from curiosity to displeasure whenever she would visit Dita on the matron's floor for tea or a chat. Lately, she'd had no reason to call on the detective department as often as she once had, what with Gregory Reid no longer being there. Only a handful of times since Jasper's promotion to detective inspector had she hand-delivered requested copies of death inquests or a victim's personal effects.

The hallways were narrow and busy with passing constables, sergeants, detectives, and clerks, some of whom tipped their hats and gave her a wide berth, and others who scowled and brushed a shoulder into hers in an attempt to intimidate her. Women usually only came here to file complaints, and all too often, they were turned away, accused of being silly or hysterical. Leo had witnessed one too many officers do this, even the affable every day; but it had been a long time since she'd dealt with grief.

"Was that why you pushed your way in here?" Jasper scrubbed a hand over his chin. The golden bristle on his usually clean-shaven cheeks and chin gave him a slightly rumpled look.

"No. I wanted to give you more detail on the locket that was stolen from the omnibus victim. I thought a description of it could be placed in the *Police Gazette*."

The daily paper printed descriptions and sketches of stolen property as well as the names of wanted criminals and people of interest. Copies were distributed to all division stations throughout the city.

"Perhaps a description of the bag he took and of the intruder himself could be included," she suggested.

Jasper frowned. "That isn't necessary." He reached behind him and took something from his chair. When he dropped it onto his desk, Leo's mouth popped open. It was the John Doe's leather bag.

"Where did you find it?" Then, with a surge of hope, "Has the intruder been arrested?"

"No. A constable on his beat off Carlton Terrace found it on the pavement. He'd heard about the commotion at the morgue and thought it might be connected."

Leo took the bag and opened it. "That's close to Spring Street," she murmured.

"If your recital of the contents last night was thorough, there is nothing missing," he said. With a knot of confusion in her stomach, she picked up the tatty coin purse and counted the money inside. She met Jasper's raised brow with one of her own.

"Nothing has been taken."

"As I just said," he muttered.

"Then what was the point of stealing the bag?"

"Maybe he didn't find what he wanted inside, so he tossed it," Jasper suggested, though he didn't sound as if he cared one way or another. He was no Constable Wiley, but sometimes, Leo thought he could be a little unimaginative.

"Any self-respecting thief would have at least taken the money," she said, rattling the coins in the purse before putting it back into the bag. "And I still can't understand why he'd take the necklace from the omnibus victim. Not only that, but he covered the woman's face afterward, as if to make it look like he hadn't done anything at all."

Jasper groaned and picked up the pasty. "The man is a thief. He was checking around to see if there was anything else worth stealing." He took a large bite, thumbing away a flake of crust from the corner of his mouth as he chewed. Leo tried not to be jealous of his meal.

"How do you explain the earrings being left behind, then?"

"I can't explain it, Leo, and it doesn't matter. The intruder has likely already fenced what he took," he said with marked impatience. "You said you wanted to give me more detail on the locket?"

She went to the coal brazier in the corner of his small office to warm her hands and quickly explained about the lock of hair and the writing on the piece of folded paper she'd found tucked inside. He stopped chewing and set the pasty back onto the butcher's paper.

"The woman was wearing mourning clothes," he said. "The lock of hair is likely a keepsake from whomever she buried."

"Yes, I figured that much too. But it's the writing that has my attention. *Strange Nun B17 R4.*"

"What about it?"

"Aren't you curious as to what it means? And it's an odd thing to keep in a locket, isn't it?"

Jasper rubbed his forehead. "My larger concern is finding the man who broke into the morgue and held you at knifepoint. Identifying the John Doe could help us find out who might have wanted his bag."

"Have you identified him?" Leo asked, though now she doubted the intruder had, in fact, been there for the leather bag. Why discard it moments after running away and even before investigating the contents?

"We have an idea as to who he is," Jasper replied, then sealed his lips.

"You aren't going to tell me?"

"No."

"Why not?"

"Because I'm following protocol. Something I suggest you do as well," he said with a pointed look. He was speaking of her assistance with the sutures on the John Doe. "I don't want to see anything happen to Claude. Or to you."

She parted her lips, speechless for a moment. His concern set her back onto her heels. But then, he returned to his usual prickly self.

"After everything my father did for you and for Claude and Flora, the strings he pulled and the favors he called in, imagine how he'd feel if you jeopardized it all."

She hardened, hitching her chin and narrowing her eyes. "I need no reminder of everything the Inspector has done for us."

She also needed no reminder of how much Jasper had always seemed to frown upon his father's affection for her. The most obvious reason for it would be jealousy, but Leo had never truly believed that. Jasper simply had too much confidence in himself to be the jealous sort.

"Is that all, then?" He picked up a stack of folders, then let them drop back onto the desk. "As you can see, my hands are full at the moment."

Disappointment filled her. She should have known he'd brush her off. He might have taken the Inspector's last name, but that didn't mean he'd adopted any of Gregory Reid's best traits. Jasper was still just as abrupt, serious, and unyielding as ever.

"That is all," she said as she went to the door. But then she stopped and turned back. "Oh, and please tell me you don't think the John Doe is *C.S. Longberger*?"

By the softening of his brow, she could see that he did indeed think it. She shook her head. "The inscription on the inside cover of the empty silver card case may say C.S. Longberger, but it is a craftsman's signature, not our John Doe's identity."

Jasper crossed his arms. "How can you be sure?"

"I've already checked the city directory. Christian Smith Longberger is a silversmith out of Lambeth. Silversmiths tend to have their fingertips stained black or green from the silver oxidizing as they work their craft. Our John Doe's fingers are calloused but not discolored in the least." Leo shrugged, then opened the door. "Good day then, Inspector Reid."

A twinge of pleasure shot through her as she shut the door on his scowl.

Chapter Four

Sitting in the chair behind his desk, Jasper flipped open the silver card case and then shut it again. C.S. Longberger might not be their John Doe, as Leo had so smugly revealed, but if Longberger made this card case, he might recall the person to whom he'd sold it.

That the bag had been found so near to Spring Street, with its most valuable contents still inside, certainly hinted the thief's interest hadn't been in the bag. Leo had been coming around to that theory earlier too, when she'd barged into his office, but agreeing with her would only have put more bees into her bonnet. Enough of them nested there already.

Jasper could easily envision the stubborn woman trying to involve herself in an investigation. He couldn't stop her from visiting with Miss Brooks, the young matron upstairs, in the canteen from time to time, but Leo didn't belong here in the C.I.D.'s central office, and he wouldn't encourage her presence. It was as much for her own good as it was for his. The last thing Jasper needed was for gossip to set in that he was going to be just as soft and accommodating toward Leo as Gregory Reid had been.

She didn't seem to realize that she was an object of fascination at the Yard—and not the good kind. With her family's infamous, unsolved murders, the Inspector's unswerving adoration and support, and her position as a morgue assistant, it was never long before new constables on the force learned about Leonora Spencer. Some found themselves sweet on her for a time. Her glossy dark hair, intense hazel eyes, and pretty looks were more than enough to hook a green constable's attention. But sweet on her or not, the men kept their distance for three reasons: First, she worked with the dead, which was hardly normal for a woman. Second, she was as good as the chief superintendent's daughter. Which then, thirdly, made her as good as Detective Inspector Jasper Reid's sister.

The coiling in his stomach was always there whenever that phrasing ran through his mind. Leo was *not* his sister, and he wasn't her brother, no matter how much the Inspector might have wished for it, once upon a time. He'd never voiced that wish, but then, he hadn't needed to.

A perfunctory rap of knuckles on Jasper's office door preceded Detective Sergeant Roy Lewis, recently promoted into the department and now working under Jasper's supervision. Lewis was several years older than Jasper, which made for a nice bit of tension.

"Guv, there's a man here who says his sister was run over by an omnibus yesterday. Wants to know if we're investigating."

Jasper scrubbed his bristled jaw. There were few coincidences in life, he had learned, and this man was almost certainly the brother of the woman in the Spring Street Morgue. The one whose necklace had been taken.

"His sister's name is Barrett?" Jasper asked.

"Aye." Lewis winced his surprise. "How'd you know?"

"Long story." Jasper got to his feet and tossed the silver card case toward Lewis. He caught it after an initial fumble. "Find C.S. Longberger, a silversmith in Lambeth, and ask him who he sold that case to. I'm trying to identify a John Doe."

The detective sergeant looked less than pleased with the order, but he held his tongue.

"And this bloke out here?" He hooked a thumb over his shoulder. "Should I send him over to the carriages department to file his complaint?"

"No, I'll take care of him."

Jasper ran his palm over his cheek again before taking up his coat and hat. The short bristle made him feel unkempt. While Mrs. Zhao kept his old room prepared, he hadn't had his shaving kit that morning.

He kept a kit in his office on a small, mirrored stand, but he'd been out straight since arriving at the office. Briefly, he considered letting it grow in. It was the fashion, after all. But a few years ago, when he'd grown a mustache and beard, Leo had teased him, scratching her fingers through it a few times and telling him how much he resembled a grumpy golden walrus. He'd lost patience and finally shaved the bloody thing off. Being likened to a walrus hadn't been flattering, but mostly, he'd done it to stop her from touching him.

She had no idea what it did to him, and he wasn't about to tell her.

"You are Miss Barrett's brother?" he asked the man waiting by the department's front desk. Constable Wiley looked pleased with himself that he'd at least managed to stop this fellow from barging in.

"I am," he answered. "Samuel Barrett."

Jasper held out his hand. "Detective Inspector Reid."

Mr. Barrett held up his right hand, which was bandaged. "If you don't mind, I won't shake. I injured my hand last night while preparing supper. Hannah, she…she always did the cooking."

His voice pulled low as emotion squeezed his throat. Jasper nodded. "My condolences, Mr. Barrett. Have you been to view her yet?"

The man shook his head and looked somewhat peaky.

"I'll walk with you then. The morgue's a short distance from here," he said, then led the man from the department.

"My sister was probably on her way home from the hospital," Mr. Barrett said on their way out of the building. "St. Thomas."

"What would she have been doing there?" Jasper asked.

"She's a nurse's assistant." The use of present tense was normal. He'd not yet become accustomed to thinking of his loved one as gone.

It seemed unlikely his sister would have been wearing a mourning dress while at work. Unless she was accustomed to changing out of her nurse's uniform before leaving for home.

"Was your sister in mourning, Mr. Barrett?"

The man, who looked to be in his early thirties, waited

until they'd crossed the street to answer. "Yes, quite recently. Her fiancé."

It would explain why the brother wore no black armband, as he might have done had the death been a member of his own family.

"Inspector, I really must ask if the driver will be arrested. I've seen the way they charge along their routes, without a care for any pedestrians. Why, just last year, I heard about a young boy getting trampled under the hooves of a driver's team. His mother was quoted as saying the driver had plenty of time to stop but simply didn't care to."

He breathed deeply after his heated comments and, despite the cold January air, took a moment to wipe the sweat from his brow, under his hat. He was upset, and rightfully so. His sister, who had apparently still lived with him, had died an awful, likely very painful death.

"I haven't yet had the chance to look over the constable's report from the accident, but I will do so before the end of the day. There were bound to be witnesses who can help shed light on what happened."

The man stopped in his tracks just outside the door to the morgue. "Now hear this, Inspector. I refuse to allow my sister's death to be swept under a rug and forgotten."

Jasper understood the man's frustration. With over five million people in London and fewer than three hundred detectives, too many deaths went unsolved every year. It wasn't a matter of care; it was a matter of manpower. Namely, the lack of it.

It also wasn't a secret that the police weren't held in high regard by those of the poorer classes, whose losses, it was felt, weren't valued as much as those of the wealthy or the influential. And after the dismissal and reorganization of the entire detective branch a decade ago due to criminal corruption, regaining the public's trust had been a long slog uphill.

"I am not the sort of man to sweep any death under a rug," he told Mr. Barrett. "If there is fault to be found with the driver, he will be held accountable."

Jasper opened the front door to the morgue, setting off the trilling of a brass bell. The lobby was small, with just a few chairs for those waiting to be summoned into the viewing room. Someone long ago, most likely Flora, had thought to hang a painting on each of the walls to cheer up the space, but it was unlikely the attempt ever worked.

Through the closed door leading to the postmortem room, Jasper heard whistling; a jovial sound that had no place within a morgue.

"Give me a moment, Mr. Barrett," he said, then quickly slipped inside.

The vast room had accumulated three more bodies since the previous night. Claude, with his nearly bald pate circled by neatly combed wisps of gray hair, was standing over one, the sheet drawn back to reveal the man's open torso. Bowls filled with organs and intestines were within Claude's reach, and under the autopsy table, a large bucket had amassed a sickening amount of liquid as it dripped through the opening at the base of the angled table.

Jasper averted his eyes. Bodies, he didn't mind. The innards, however, were a different matter.

In addition to the whistling, there was the steady striking of a typewriter's keys originating from the back office.

Claude glanced up, and his whistling fell off. His spectacles, thick as bottle glass, enlarged his eyes to an owlish state. "Oh, hello, Inspector. I didn't hear the bell. How may I be of service?"

The clacking of the typewriter stopped.

"I have Mr. Barrett here to view his sister, Miss Hannah Barrett."

Leo emerged from the back room, and Jasper couldn't help but stare—she had the gray tabby cat draped around her shoulders, its tail lolling languidly, and its crystalline green eyes half-closed in contentedness. Jasper shook his head, trying to picture Constance wearing a cat like a mink stole, and failing.

"He is here? May I accompany you in the viewing room, Uncle Claude?" Leo asked, with a touch too much eagerness.

"Not with Tibia on your shoulders," the assistant coroner replied as he shed his bloodied canvas coat and gloves. He removed his shin-high rubber boots and stepped into a pair of black Prince Alberts before going to a covered body on a wheeled table. Hannah Barrett, Jasper presumed, as Claude unlocked the wheels. He pushed it toward the viewing room, which connected to both the postmortem room and the lobby. To bring the grieving in here, where multiple bodies might be lain out, would be uncouth. In Paris, morgue surgeons might think nothing of laying out bodies in glass windows for passersby to view like carnival show specimens, but at least here in England, there was *some* respect for the dead.

Leo set her cat onto the floor and picked up a small, covered box, the kind that held personal possessions, to be returned to the deceased's family.

Jasper held up a hand to stay her. "The man is grieving. Mentioning anything about the missing necklace or the morgue intruder would only upset him more."

"Thank you for your advice, but I know how to handle family members," she said. "I'm not going to say a word about either of them."

She pushed past him and followed her uncle into the viewing room. Jasper gritted his teeth and joined them, opening the door to the lobby to summon Mr. Barrett.

Like most people in the brother's position, he hesitated before doffing his hat and coming in. His eyes went straight to the sheeted figure. Though Jasper couldn't read minds, he always saw what he thought might be a small flare of hope, that the one laid beneath the sheet would not be their loved one. That it had all been some terrible mistake. But as usual, when Claude drew back the sheet to reveal the face and neck, Mr. Barrett's hope scattered, and sorrow flooded in.

"It is Hannah," he whispered, his fingers gripping his hat's brim.

He removed his spectacles to press the heel of his palm to his eyes, clearing tears. It would have been better for him to leave the spectacles off. Though his sister's skull was still misshapen from the killing blows of either the horse's hooves or the omnibus wheels, the blood and gore had been cleansed away. Her hair had been arranged to help cover the indentations as well.

"I...I suppose I'll require a funeral service to collect her?"

"That is customary," Claude answered. "I can recommend a few respectable companies we often work with, if you like. Unless you'd prefer to have her removed to your own residence?"

"No, no. I know of a service, thank you." Mr. Barrett replaced his spectacles and blinked rapidly to clear away his welling tears.

"We are very sorry for your loss," Leo said, then presented the small, lidded box to him. "These are your sister's belongings. Would you be so kind as to confirm the contents for me?"

She removed the lid, and Jasper braced himself for whatever her plan might be. Claude's forehead wrinkled with curiosity. It wasn't standard practice to have the family member go through the deceased's personal possessions at the time of viewing.

With a furtive look at Jasper, she made an unspoken plea for him to stay silent on the matter. He rolled his eyes but said nothing as Mr. Barrett searched through the belongings, albeit distractedly. A gown and underclothes, a beaded purse, a pair of heeled boots, lace gloves, a ruined bonnet, and a woolen shawl, all black as a mark of her mourning, were within the box.

"Yes, these all look to be hers," he said after a moment.

"We just want to be certain you have all of her belongings," Leo said, her eyes drifting toward Miss Barrett's still uncovered face and neck. Trying, no doubt, to draw Mr. Barrett's attention to the fact that something was missing.

"We try to be as organized as possible here," Leo went on when the man continued to look helplessly between the contents of the box and his sister. "However, there are times when possessions are left behind or are accidentally misidentified as another person's property, and then there is nothing to do but to store them in the crypt."

Mr. Barrett blinked. "The crypt?"

"Yes, the crypt. The cellar here at the morgue, which was originally a church vestry, you see." Her rambling was wearing on Jasper and visibly concerning Claude. "We hardly ever go down into it—the crypt, I mean—and all the items there are collecting dust, so it would be a pity if any of your sister's possessions found their way there." Again, her attention drifted toward Miss Barrett's bare neck.

Jasper had endured enough. "Thank you, Mr. Barrett. As I said before, I will go through the report filed by the constable who attended the scene. I'll be in touch."

Claude gestured toward the exit into the lobby and then stepped out with him. He shut the door, and Jasper turned to Leo.

"What was that ridiculous charade?"

She pulled the sheet back up over Miss Barrett's face. "I wanted to see if he realized the necklace was missing, and if so, what his reaction would be."

"Anger, I imagine. Perhaps he would even accuse someone in this morgue of stealing it."

"But I keep thinking," she went on, returning to the postmortem room and ignoring his comment. "What if there is something important about it? The writing on the paper must be significant. What if the intruder broke in here, not for the bag but for the necklace?"

"Then why ask for the bag?"

"I'm not sure, maybe as a decoy. He clearly didn't want it," she replied as she walked to the back office. The door to the alley running behind the morgue was ajar, allowing in fresh, if chilled, air.

Jasper had already considered the same scenario, though he didn't plan to admit it to her.

"If Mr. Barrett asks about the necklace at a later point, you can direct him to me. Until then, kindly allow the man to bury his sister in peace. You're not involved in this case, Leo."

She yanked the paper in the typewriter free and slapped it onto the desk, scattering a few other papers in the process. "I think you are forgetting that I am the one who was put into a closet at the point of a knife."

"I think perhaps *you're* forgetting that I am the detective here, not you," he retorted, his temper sparking. He swallowed an order for her to stay out of it. Telling her that would only inspire more hostility. Instead, he exhaled. "I haven't forgotten you were in danger."

Her hard glare softened into one of mere annoyance. She collected the scattered papers, her temper cooling. "Very well, Inspector Reid."

He cocked his head. "Why do you sound teasing when you address me as Inspector?"

She balked. "I do not."

"You do." And it pricked just under his skin too.

Contrition wasn't one of Leo's common expressions, but as she clasped her hands in front of her, it spread across her face. "I'm sorry, I don't mean to sound mocking. I suppose I'm just not accustomed yet to calling you *Inspector*."

He nodded, his pulse evening out. "To be honest, I'm not entirely accustomed to it either."

There had never been any doubt in his mind that he wanted to join the Met and follow in Gregory Reid's footsteps. But it wasn't until he'd been promoted to detective inspector that he recognized the weight of having the same surname.

After an awkward beat of quiet, Leo said, "I'm going to pay the Inspector a visit tonight. Will you be there?"

Jasper grimaced. "No. I have a dinner with Miss Hayes." He'd sent a messenger first thing that morning to her boardinghouse with the invitation. He needed to make up for the previous evening.

"Oh, yes, of course." Leo pressed her lips into a thin line, the way she usually did whenever Constance's name was mentioned. The two had met just twice, and they were as different as night and day. Leo thought Constance too high in the instep, and Constance thought Leo peculiar and her work at the morgue disturbing.

"He might not be himself tonight," Jasper said. "You know what day is approaching."

"Yes, I am aware of the date," she said, again peeved. She crossed her arms at her waist and looked toward the open door to the alley.

Guilt flushed through Jasper's veins. This time of year was difficult for her too. In just a few weeks, her own dreaded anniversary would arrive. And for the first time, the Inspector might not be there for it.

Chapter Five

Leo went straight to Charles Street after leaving the morgue. As she took the walk at a fast clip in a sleeting rain, she thought of what Jasper had said earlier, about the possibility that the Inspector wouldn't be himself. It irritated her, even hours later, that Jasper had thought she might forget that January 15 was a black day for Gregory Reid and that the days surrounding it were equally gray and gloomy.

She might not have stayed on to live with the Inspector as Jasper had after those first two months when they were both there together or taken his name and become accustomed to calling him *Father*, but she'd remained close to him. Gregory Reid had been a family man who wasn't ready to no longer have a family, and so now, looking back, it made perfect sense that he'd offered up his home and his affection to two children who'd needed it.

Jasper had been a bit older, just starting on his way to becoming a young man, and no relative had been available to show up and claim him as Claude and Flora had done for her. There had been no reason for Leo to stay. And yet, the Inspector had never been able to mask his bittersweet regret that she could not have. At least Claude had benefited from the Inspector's care. He'd left his position as a surgeon in a tiny, ill-equipped hospital on the island of Crete to return to London, but with no home and no job, he'd been ready to go back, this time with Leo in tow. That was when the Inspector had stepped in.

The windows inside the house on Charles Street glowed with gaslight as she approached, her fingertips chilled. She sometimes imagined how things might have been had Claude and Flora not materialized. If instead, they'd elected to let her grow up here in this fine home, with a large bedroom and delicious food from Mrs. Zhao's kitchen to eat every night at the dinner table with the Inspector. And Jasper, of course. He might have become a sort of brother—though she wasn't at all certain she liked that idea. She'd had a brother. Jacob.

Given her perfect memory, it was odd that Leo could remember so little about him. Except, of course, for what happened on that night. A night that always loomed large and unwieldy in her memory. Three years older than Leo, Jacob had enjoyed teasing her about her favorite doll, Miss Cynthia. The porcelain doll had rosebud lips and glossy black curls, a flowered blue dress with lace and silk ribbons, and a pair of leather shoes able to be slipped on and off, along with white silk stockings.

That night, after dinner, Jacob had taken Miss Cynthia's shoes and hidden them. Leo had grown angry— so angry that she'd stomped on his foot. Shocked at her violence, he'd retaliated by grabbing Miss Cynthia and throwing her to the floor. The doll's porcelain leg had cracked into several pieces, and her cheek had broken off completely. Sobbing and furious, Leo had collected the shards and her doll and run upstairs, ignoring Jacob's claims that he hadn't meant to do it.

Leo hadn't gone to her room, which she'd shared with her younger sister, Agnes. She'd taken the stairs to the second level, then opened the door to the attic. There, she could be alone with her grief. There, no one would be able to find her.

The sleeting rain dripped down the back of Leo's neck as she stood outside the Inspector's home, and the chill of it brought her back to the present and her purpose. Leo brought down the knocker, and a few moments later, Mrs. Zhao was greeting her warmly and ushering her into the house. The air inside was filled with the savory scents of roasted meat and vegetables.

"Mr. Reid is having a good day," Mrs. Zhao said. "Will you stay for supper?"

Ever since watching Jasper eat his Cornish pasty earlier, Leo had been longing for some of Mrs. Zhao's cooking. "I will, thank you."

Before she could make her next request, the housekeeper anticipated it and said, "I always prepare too much for Mr. Reid. I'll send a basket with you for Mr. and Mrs. Feldman too. How is your aunt?"

"Much the same, I'm afraid." To say *worse than before* would be far too melancholy. There was enough of that in this house as it was.

Mrs. Zhao sent her toward the study before returning to her kitchen, and Leo took the stairs to the first floor. The Inspector vastly preferred the study to any other room in the house. It was nearly always where she found him, and tonight, like so many other nights before, he was seated in the quilted leather chair behind his desk with a newspaper spread out before him, a cigar smoldering in the ashtray at one elbow, and an empty crystal whisky glass at his other. If not for the sallow pallor of his skin, the frail hands holding the paper, and his soft chuff of a cough, Leo could have fooled herself into believing everything was normal.

He looked up, and the bright blue eyes that had always radiated kindness shone once more.

"My dear Leonora." His gravelly voice cracked with disuse. The Inspector pushed himself up, and Leo tried not to notice how thin he'd become. Thinner than the last time she'd visited two weeks ago. Her heart twisted.

"Oh, do sit down, sir, I've not come to put you out of your favorite chair," she said, injecting a falsely bright note into her tone.

"I've been sitting all day," he said, "and a gentleman stands when a lady enters the room."

"I admit, it is a pleasant change. None of the gentlemen I see on a regular basis are usually able to stand when I enter a room."

It was just the sort of humor he appreciated. *Morgue humor*, he'd once called it, and Leo thought it an apt term. He cracked a laugh, which quickly turned into a hacking cough.

She rushed forward, but he put up a hand. "I am fine." He then crinkled his forehead. "That is to say, these aren't my final breaths just yet."

Leo didn't chastise him for joking about his own death, even though it was on the tip of her tongue to do so. He wouldn't want her to coddle him, so instead, she snapped open the kiss lock on her tapestry handbag and reached inside.

"That is lucky for you then. It would be a shame not to have anyone to share this with," she said while pulling out a small bottle of his favorite cherry liqueur.

With a little bounce in his step, he rubbed his palms together as he rounded the desk and went straight to the sideboard. Leo joined him, and as soon as the bottle of Grants Morella was uncapped, he poured two glasses. Leo tapped her cordial glass against his, and they each sipped.

"You do spoil me," he said as he led them to the leather Chesterfield in front of the hearth, inset with a coal brazier. It was warm, though the burning coal left a haze in the air. Wood was too expensive for a policeman's purse, and for the last seventeen years, that was what he'd been running this household on. Following the deaths of his daughter and his only grandchildren, the Viscount Cowper had rescinded Emmaline's dowry. The house, however, had been a gift, and with or without Emmaline, it legally belonged to Gregory Reid.

"Now, tell me what happened with that burglar," he said.

Leo lowered her glass slowly. "How did you hear of it?"

"Nathaniel, of course," he answered, referring to his good friend, Sir Nathaniel Vickers, the Commissioner of Police. The two men had entered the Met as constables together; Sir Nathaniel, however, had joined the army for a time, and when he'd returned, he'd shifted his focus to prison reform and the penal service, eventually rising to

Commissioner of Prisons. From there it had been a short jump to Commissioner of Police.

The Inspector, however, had preferred to stay a detective. That was where his talent lay, and he'd been proud of it.

"I should have known," Leo said, resuming her sip. Sir Nathaniel called on a regular basis. He'd lost his wife in childbirth, not very long after Emmaline Reid had died. Neither widower had remarried, and the two had found much in common, standing together against the social expectation of taking second wives.

"I am perfectly fine," Leo insisted. "The intruder took a bag and a necklace and then ran off." She chose to omit any details that might worry him—or inspire him to want to sift through possible motives. Though ill, he was a detective at heart and loved a good muddle to sort out.

Peering at her with skepticism, he seemed to know that she was holding back. However, before he could press her, she changed the subject.

"Mrs. Zhao said it's been a good day. How are you feeling?"

He grumbled, endlessly annoyed by the topic of his own health. "Shipshape," he answered as he sipped his cherry liqueur. "I should be back at the Yard any day now."

Leo raised a brow, accustomed to his sarcasm. They both knew it was what he wanted but would not be able to achieve. Turning serious, the Inspector set down his glass on the end table beside the Chesterfield and got to his feet. "I have something to show you."

Her curiosity rose as he shuffled back to his desk. There, he opened one of the deep-bottomed side drawers.

He kept old case files there—the investigations that he'd been unable to solve but on which he'd never quite given up. A shiver ran up her spine as he took out a thick folder.

There was no need to inquire as to which case this was.

She set her cordial glass next to his and stood as he came back toward the sofa with the folder.

"I want you to have this, Leonora," he said. She didn't reach for it. Her hands hung unnaturally heavy at her sides.

He'd never stopped trying to solve the murders of the Spencer family. Seeing the file now, at least two inches thick, she marveled at the extent of his work. The backs of her eyes stung.

"You know what it is?" he asked when she continued to stare.

"Yes."

He ran his hand over the worn brown cover, the spine frayed from being opened and closed, time and again. "My case notes. Interviews and research. Some leads, though none of which ever gave answers. A few crime scene photographs you might not wish to see. Everything is in here."

Not everything.

There was one thing from that night Leo had kept to herself. She'd never spoken of it to anyone. It certainly wouldn't be in the file.

She'd been trying for so long to put the memories of that night behind her, but they persisted. They'd formed a fortress-like wall around other memories from before the murders, ones she wished she *could* remember. It was as if Leo's life *before* had been lost; there was only that one night and what came afterward. If she were to look through the Inspector's file, blurred memories might become sharper. And the ones that had remained sharp over the years could very well slice her open again. Already, her mind was a cluttered trap. Everything she saw became a photograph in her mind; a picture she could mentally draw up and look at, concentrating on different aspects and elements that most minds chose to forget.

"I'm not sure I wish to see any of it."

She clasped her hands together and rubbed her thumb along the two parallel scars on her right palm. The ridges were like a talisman. A reminder to keep breathing.

"If that is what you wish, I understand." He set the folder beside their cordial glasses. "Do with it what you will. I just needed to give it to you before I was gone."

Her eyes welled. "Don't speak like that."

"My dearest Leonora," he said, his hollowed cheeks creasing with an effusive grin. "Promise me something."

She frowned and blinked rapidly to clear away the hot tears. "That depends on what it is."

The Inspector laughed. "Wise lady." After another light chuckle, he became solemn again, then grasped her shoulder. "Don't open it until you are absolutely sure you're ready."

Leo nodded. She could promise him that.

The door to the study opened, but it wasn't Mrs. Zhao announcing supper, as Leo had expected. Jasper, dressed in a well-cut evening suit, stepped in.

"Father," he said, though his attention stuck on her an extra moment. He frowned. "What's happened?"

She turned away to dab the corners of her eyes.

"Nothing at all, my boy." The Inspector went to the

sideboard to pour cherry liqueur into another cordial glass. "Leonora has brought my favorite."

Jasper grimaced as he took the small crystal glass. "You know I can't stand the stuff."

"One sip," the Inspector said brightly. "I'll make you a lover of it yet."

"I sincerely doubt it," he replied, though he still tossed the drink back. Predictably, he hacked and stuck out his tongue.

The Inspector winked mischievously at Leo. "It seems Jasper is already sweet enough."

They both grinned at the absurdity of calling him such a thing. Jasper cut them a wry look before going to the sideboard and pouring himself some single malt.

"I thought you were having dinner with Miss Hayes tonight," Leo said, eyeing his black tails, white waistcoat, and crisp, black necktie. The elegant clothes fit him well, accentuating his handsome looks. They could not refine him, though. Not fully. There was an innate intensity to Jasper, one that lacked polish but inspired respect.

"I do." He contentedly sipped his scotch. "I thought I'd stop here first."

Leo held her tongue. She'd announced earlier that she would be visiting the Inspector; did Jasper truly think she would upset him over the morgue break-in? He must have raced here to be sure she hadn't.

"That was good of you," the Inspector said as he clapped Jasper on the shoulder. He seemed to lean on him a bit, and Jasper put an arm around his father's shoulder. "I wish I could stay awake to visit, but I'm afraid I've suddenly grown tired. I'm for bed, my son."

Jasper set down his scotch and tried to guide the Inspector to the study door, but he was waved off.

"I'm fine, I'm fine," the Inspector assured them, sending Leo a departing nod. "Goodnight, my dear." He lingered a moment, as if wanting to say something more, but then decided against it and left.

Jasper, observant as ever, slid his eyes to the worn folder on the table, then to Leo. He looked less than pleased.

"You know what it is?" she asked, echoing what the Inspector had asked her.

"Of course. He's been obsessed with it for as long as I've known him." Jasper took another sip and tugged at his collar.

Though it felt like reaching her hand over an open flame, Leo picked up the case file. "There are others in his desk drawer, not just this one."

"None he looks through as much as yours."

She didn't know if he was disapproving or simply stating a fact. Jasper was notoriously difficult to read. He hardly ever gave anything away in the tone of his voice or in his inscrutable expressions.

Leo took the file back to the desk and returned it to the drawer. "Have you ever looked through it?"

"No."

She frowned and slid the drawer shut. He'd never approved of the Inspector's *obsession*, as he'd described it. But sometimes she wondered if Jasper's disapproval was, in truth, only bitterness. Leo was the one with a tragic story and a mystery that had eluded the Inspector. Jasper, on the other hand, had been an orphaned street urchin who got into trouble with the law.

"Nothing worth talking about. I'm a dime a dozen," he'd said before on the few occasions when Leo had asked what his life had been like before being taken in by Gregory Reid. When she'd realized that he was never going to speak about his childhood, she'd quit asking.

She joined him by the hearth now, picking up her cordial glass on the way. "Where are you taking Miss Hayes for dinner?"

He checked his fob watch. "The Albion. I should probably go."

She sipped the last of her drink. "You don't sound very enthusiastic about the evening."

Jasper put away his watch, making a face. "I'm plenty enthusiastic."

Leo suppressed a grin. "Are you two becoming quite serious then?"

"Why do you ask?" From the shocked way he peered at her, one would have thought she'd just asked him to commit a murder.

Leo collected the other cordial glasses and set them on a tray to bring to the kitchen. "Can I not ask questions?"

Jasper finished his scotch in a single toss. "About the woman I'm courting?" he answered, pausing halfway through to consider. "No."

She narrowed her eyes as she brought over the tray. At times, he could be such a stick in the mud. "Very well. Then you can't ask questions about who is courting me."

Bristling, he set his empty glass on the tray. "You aren't even seeing anyone." Then, in doubt or perhaps disbelief, he asked, "Are you?"

Leo nearly laughed at the confusion pulling his dark

blond brows together. She wasn't seeing anyone at all, but it was amusing to tease him.

The study door opened again, and Mrs. Zhao entered. She wasn't alone. On her heels was Jasper's fellow officer, Detective Sergeant Lewis. He held his hat in his hands, a look of urgency in the taut press of his mouth.

"Sorry, guv, but I thought you might be here."

Jasper walked forward, alert. "What is it?"

"A body's been found." He cast an apologetic glance toward the housekeeper. He didn't spare Leo the same look, but she wasn't offended. He already knew her sensibilities did not require an apology.

Leo set the tray down, curious as to why he'd gone to the trouble of seeking out Jasper here at the Inspector's home rather than waiting until the following morning when he arrived at the Yard. But then Lewis explained: "The constables who reported it say he bears a striking resemblance to the man Miss Spencer described as the morgue intruder."

Chapter Six

The hired coach that Lewis had taken to Charles Street set out for Duck Island, a small promontory on the lake in St. James's Park. It would be a short drive, giving Jasper little time to regret agreeing to Leo's company. When she'd suggested it in his father's study, his first reaction had been to say no.

"But I can identify him on the spot, if it is indeed the intruder," she argued, and Jasper hadn't been able to refute her reasoning.

So, while Leo fetched her coat and hat, he'd asked Mrs. Zhao to signal a messenger boy. He would, once again, need to postpone his dinner with Constance. He tried not to think about what her reaction would be or Leo's comment that he didn't seem enthusiastic about his evening plans. He enjoyed Constance's company and looked forward to her cheery disposition. It was so different from his own. Whenever he was with her, he could usually set aside whatever case he was investigating. For a short while, at least.

Lewis took furtive glances at Leo, seated next to him on the bench, while he gave the details he knew so far. The body had been discovered by the resident bird keeper on Duck Island, which had long been a haven for birds and waterfowl, organized by the Ornithological Society. While taking his nightly stroll around the island, he'd come upon a man, lying face down in a patch of shrubs near the water's edge. As quickly as he could, he'd rushed toward nearby Downing Street and flagged the first constable he'd seen.

"Don't you think it odd that the morgue intruder would be found dead such a short distance from Spring Street?" Leo asked as the driver brought his horses to a stop on the promontory causeway.

"If it's even him," Jasper reminded her, though he did think it odd. The morgue was no more than a ten-minute walk from Duck Island.

Lewis opened the door of the cab and descended, and Jasper followed. He turned back around and held his hand out for Leo. She'd no more than put her foot on the step when he lowered his voice and said, "You are accustomed to dead bodies but not to crime scenes. So please, stay back and do as I tell you."

He heard his condescending tone even as he spoke but refused to apologize. The idea of bringing a woman to the scene of a murder—even if that woman wasn't likely to faint or have a fit of the vapors—set his teeth on edge. Leo ripped her hand from his as soon as the soles of her boots hit the ground. Other than a harsh glare, she made no reply as she followed Lewis toward the grove of trees on the promontory.

There were no gas lampposts beyond the bird keeper's

cottage, but a constable was waiting with a lantern by a pair of police wagons. After greeting them, the constable led the way across the man-made causeway onto the wooded island, the cool, earthy scent of trees and underbrush greeting them. St. James's Park and the large lake centering it had been carefully designed to give the impression of being in the countryside, instead of a few skips away from the Houses of Parliament. In the past, gentlemen would shoot game here or ride along the wooded acres of The Mall, and earlier in the century, before it became illegal, a great number of duels were held here for the privacy it afforded.

The bird keeper himself joined their party.

"I take a stroll around the island every night," he informed them as they followed a well-worn path, his walking stick stabbing the ground as they went. "I won't have no rough sleepers bedding down here, nor any indecent transactions, if you take my meaning. Once, I found two young lads sleeping in the hollow of a downed tree." He shook his head as if the discovery had disgusted him.

Homelessness was a blight on the city, but Jasper could understand the draw of a dark, quiet stretch of woods for someone wise to the dangers of their fellow drifters. When he'd been young and in that same position, he'd selected the boughs of a tree in Green Park, off Piccadilly. He'd climbed up into it past dark so that he might not be seen and used a length of rope to tie himself to the trunk, preventing him from tumbling to the ground as he slept. Jasper could easily recall the crick in his neck each morning and the bruises on his backside from the unforgiving tree limb. But at least he hadn't been set upon in the night as he might have been in some alleyway.

"Did you come through here during daylight hours today, Mister…?" Jasper asked.

"Gates. Billy Gates. And no, I was at my brother's in Hammersmith."

"And does the island receive many strollers during the day, Mr. Gates?" Leo asked. Jasper sent her a quelling glare, but she was pointedly not looking at him.

"Not this time of year. Maybe one or two come past the cottage each day, if that."

Ahead, four more constables were gathered. They'd placed their lanterns on the ground, just off the path. Together, the lanterns shed light over the prone figure of a man, face up, in the low-lying shrubs that were leafless due to the time of year. He would have been easy to spot during daylight hours.

"Inspector," they chorused as Jasper joined them. He saw then that one of them was Constable Wiley.

"What are you doing here, constable?" Jasper nearly barked. As a desk officer, his duties didn't include a patrol beat.

"I happened to be walking nearby when I heard the police rattle," he answered. Jasper nodded, though he was uncertain what Wiley might have been doing in Westminster. There wasn't much in the area for nighttime amusements, and any residences were strictly upper-class.

"The victim looks to have been dragged off the path after he was attacked," Wiley went on with an air of importance. "There's some blood just here." He pointed to another lantern on the path, lighting some dark spatter on the ground.

"I thought Detective Lewis said he'd been found face down," Leo said as she stepped into the lantern light.

Constable Wiley's expression darkened. "What is this woman doing here?"

"I've come to identify the body," she answered, then reiterated, "He isn't face down."

Jasper recalled Lewis's claim as well. If the constables had followed proper protocol, they would have stayed out of the shrubs, away from the body.

"Did you turn the body over, Mr. Gates?" Jasper asked. The bird keeper tucked his chin into his neck as if repulsed.

"You couldn't have paid me."

Jasper then caught Wiley's guilty expression. He merely stared at the constable until, finally discomfited, Wiley smoothed his mustache and shrugged.

"I didn't think it mattered."

The inept excuse was even more infuriating.

"It matters," was all he said in reply, even though he was tempted to upbraid him for the mistake.

Leo took a step into the shrubs, but Jasper caught her arm and held her back.

"Stay where you are for now. I don't want the scene disturbed any more than it already has been."

He alone took careful steps toward the circle of lantern light. A smattering of footprints on the ground had been made soft and muddy from the recent rain. Several smaller limbs on the shrubs and pricker bushes had been snapped and now hung broken. Dark smears, most likely blood, could be seen alongside two long ruts in the ground—made by the heels of the dead man's boots while he'd been dragged off the path. Those boots had been removed from his feet and left on the ground.

"Mr. Gates, other than the change to this face-up positioning, was he like this when you found him?" Jasper asked. "Did you move him at all? Remove his boots?"

"Move him? Not on me life."

It wouldn't have surprised Jasper to discover that Mr. Gates had gone through the man's pockets and boots before fetching the street patrols. But he did appear genuinely disturbed at the thought of touching a dead body. Jasper sank into a crouch and, picking up the closest lantern, held it to a defined boot print. He drew his fingertip around the outline. A man's shoe, size nine or ten. The toe was slim, and the heel print was deep, indicating a taller heel. Not the heavy workman's boots the victim had been wearing. A pair of Prince Alberts, perhaps.

"Have you found anything?" Leo asked.

Jasper stood with the lantern still in his grip. "No, but we might find more when the sun is up. I want two constables to stand guard here the rest of the night. No one is to enter this area."

"May I have a closer look?" she asked. Jasper waved an arm, gesturing her forward.

Leo gathered her skirt to step high over the prickers and shrubs. Coming into the light, she gave a decisive nod. "It's him. That's the intruder."

He again sank into a crouch and held the lantern over the body. "You're certain?"

"You know I am. He was wearing a kerchief over most of his face, but his eyes and receding hairline were distinguishable." Leo reached out toward his chest but didn't touch. "Look here. It looks like a gunshot wound."

The man's coat was unbuttoned and opened, exposing his shirt. In the upper center of his chest, there was a small hole in the blood-soaked fabric. Jasper removed one of his gloves and ran his fingers over the shirt. "The blood isn't fresh." It had dried and stiffened the material. "He's been here for some time."

"How long do you think, guv?" Lewis asked as he stepped gingerly through the shrubs.

"May I?" Leo asked, as she, too, removed a glove. Jasper clenched his jaw but nodded.

She pressed her fingers against the exposed skin around the dead man's neck. "I don't have a thermometer to be certain, but I'd estimate his body temperature to be well under sixty degrees." Leo lifted his arm and manipulated it, bending it at the elbow and wrist.

"You're letting *her* touch the victim, Inspector?" Wiley asked as he rustled through some prickers, swearing under his breath as they caught his trousers.

"Stand back, constable. I'd like to preserve what I can of the scene for when we have better light," Jasper said, irritated. Lewis had probably also questioned his decision to let Leo handle the body, but at least he was wise enough to keep his lips sealed.

"I am determining how long he's been deceased," Leo explained, as she continued to move the man's arm. "Rigor mortis has almost entirely passed, which, paired with his lowered body temperature, means he's been dead for at least twenty hours."

"Did Claude teach you that?" Jasper asked.

"He did. It was one of the first things, in fact."

With Leo holding the man's arm at a ninety-degree angle, the cuff of his sack coat slipped down, exposing his forearm. There was a dark marking on his wrist.

"What's this?" Jasper pushed the cuff lower, and Leo brought the lantern closer.

Black ink had been pricked into the man's skin in a design he'd seen before. An inverted triangle with a hand clenched into a fist in the center.

"He served time at Wandsworth." Jasper pointed to the poor depiction of the closed fist. "An organized gang inside the prison gives these tattoos to its members."

Leo lowered the limp arm to the ground again. "Considering it's been about twenty-four hours since this man broke into the morgue, it's reasonable to say he was killed shortly after leaving Spring Street."

Behind them, Wiley scoffed at her deduction. Jasper ignored him. "Lewis, you found nothing on him?"

"Nothing, guv. But his trouser pockets were turned out."

Moving the lantern, Jasper saw it was so.

"Coat pockets are empty too," Lewis added. "And the boots removed."

Leo stood from her crouch. "He had a slip joint pocketknife at the morgue."

Jasper flipped the man's coat panels open further, searching the waist of his trousers, then maneuvered him onto his side. When he didn't find anything, he picked up one of the boots; underneath it, a closed pocketknife lay on the ground. Jasper held it to the light and flicked the blade open. It was clean.

"The killer appears to have removed the boots and upended them after shooting his victim," he said. "He was looking for something."

"Not the knife, if it was left on the ground," Lewis

observed. "This bloke didn't even bother to have it out to defend himself."

"He was either taken by surprise, or he knew his killer." Jasper folded the knife and stored it inside the boot. It would be catalogued at the morgue, along with his other effects.

"So presumably, he stole the bag from the morgue, dumped it near Carlton Terrace, then continued on his way here to meet someone he knew," Leo said. "Perhaps that someone was waiting for him to arrive with something."

Jasper looked up from the body to find Leo prodding the ground with her pointer finger. "What have you found? You shouldn't touch evidence."

"I'm not. It's just a strange indentation." She shifted herself to the side and reached to another spot. "There are a handful of them, all around here."

Jasper joined her, keeping the lantern low. Leo pointed out the holes, all of which were perfectly round, about an inch in diameter, and pressed an inch deep into the ground. He closed his eyes and held back an oath.

"Mr. Gates." He got to his feet and stared down the bird keeper, who'd been waiting with Wiley and the other constables on the path. "Did you come over here and walk around the body? Turn out his pockets?"

"I've already told you I didn't get nowhere near the bloke," he answered, voice pitched high in self-defense.

"There are indentations on the ground here that look to have been formed by the point of a walking stick." Jasper gestured toward the one in Mr. Gates's hand.

The bird keeper goggled. "I'm telling you the God's honest truth. I didn't go near him!"

There was something shifty about the bird keeper, but for now, Jasper let it go. He directed the constables to bring the litter forward to load the body and then deliver it to the Spring Street Morgue.

"The night keeper isn't on duty until ten o'clock," Leo said. "But I can let them in."

As the constables moved toward the body, Jasper led Leo back to the path. She lowered her voice. "Do you believe Mr. Gates?"

He shook his head. "I don't know. He seems genuinely appalled at the idea of going near a corpse, but those indentations look like those of a cane."

"If the intruder still had Hannah Barrett's locket in his possession, it is gone now," Leo said. "What if Mr. Gates is only acting appalled and, in fact, took it?"

"Miss Barrett, the omnibus victim?" Lewis asked as he joined them. "What's this about her locket?"

Jasper groaned. The locket was becoming the bane of his existence. Quickly, he explained to his detective sergeant about the necklace going missing from Miss Barrett's body and that Leo suspected the intruder had taken it during the break-in.

"Not only that," she continued, "but I think this man came to the morgue for the necklace specifically. He took the bag as a decoy and put me in a closet where I couldn't see him take the necklace. He tried to cover up the fact that he took it at all."

"So you're saying he knew Miss Barrett's body was at the morgue and that she would have this necklace that he wanted?" Lewis asked, readily going along with the theory. Jasper wished he wouldn't, but Leo seemed pleased.

"Yes, he must have. But I don't understand how. She'd only been there a few hours."

"Not to mention it's a lot of trouble to go to for what Miss Spencer has described as a tarnished gold locket," Jasper added. "Items like that don't fetch more than a few guineas at a pawnbroker. No seasoned convict would risk it for such a slight reward."

The earrings on Miss Barrett's lobes would have fetched far more. Yet, he'd left them behind. Perhaps there had been something special about the locket, as Leo suggested. However, showing interest in her speculation would only spur her on.

"Well, he couldn't have fenced it between Spring Street and here," Lewis said. "There isn't a pawnshop along the way."

"Whoever killed him might have taken it," Leo suggested. Her eyes slid toward the bird keeper. Jasper didn't think Mr. Gates had anything to do with the murder, but he shared her skepticism that he hadn't leaned on his walking stick while checking the man's pockets.

"We still have no evidence he even had the necklace to begin with," Jasper said. "Considering it is nowhere to be found, there is nothing more we can do. For now, we concentrate on identifying the intruder. Lewis, go through the convict books for Wandsworth, starting from ten years ago. We're bound to find his photograph. Once we know his name, we question his known associates."

It was clearest path forward.

Lewis left to assist the constables in removing the body. A breeze swept through the wooded island, blowing some raindrops from branches and pine needles. Leo shivered as she breathed hot air into her steepled palms.

"I'll have a constable bring you ahead to the morgue," Jasper offered, but she shook her head.

"That isn't necessary. I'll be fine traveling with the body. Jasper..." She turned to him. "Did the officers attending Miss Barrett's accident interview witnesses?"

He stood back at the question. "That would be standard practice, yes. Why?"

"I'd like to look at the file."

He took her by the elbow and led her a few paces away from the others. "I can't give you a case file, even if I wanted to—which I don't. Leo, you are not a detective."

"What if our convict here was at Trafalgar Square at the time she was struck?" Leo went on, ignoring him as she was wont to do. "Let's say he saw her go down, and that's how he knew she would be at the morgue."

He scrubbed a hand over his jaw, suddenly exhausted.

"Consider that he deliberately led us down the wrong path by taking that bag," she continued. "He didn't want us following up on anything having to do with Miss Barrett's death because there is more to it than just an omnibus accident."

"That is pure conjecture," he argued. "And there is no *us*."

"If I could just see the case file—"

"*No.*"

Leo's eager expression crashed, and she stared balefully at him. With a twist of guilt that he stoutly shoved aside, Jasper set his shoulders and returned her stare. He would not roll over for her the way his father once might have done. She assisted Claude with his work, but Jasper would not allow her to assist him with his.

Without any more argument, she turned on her heel and started away.

"Lewis," Jasper called. The detective sergeant came over. "Go with the body and Miss Spencer to the morgue."

Lewis started away with his task, but Jasper called for him to wait. He spoke softly so Leo wouldn't overhear. "And fetch me the attending constable's report on Miss Barrett's accident."

Chapter Seven

St. Thomas Hospital sat like a stalwart fortress directly across the Thames from the Houses of Parliament. As Leo crossed the Westminster Bridge on foot and came about onto Lambeth Road, nervousness bubbled in the pit of her stomach. Then again, it might have just been the undercooked eggs she'd served for breakfast. Attempting not to char them this morning, she'd taken them from the hob too soon. All in all, she thought she might prefer them blackened. Mrs. Shaw had come to see out her final week with Flora, as promised, but she'd been later than usual, and quiet and distant when Leo and Claude had left for the day.

While arranging for their neighbor's son, Liam, who often ran messages and errands for Claude, to go to the *Telegraph* and place their advert for a new day nurse, Leo had a stroke of inspiration. The letter Miss Barrett had been carrying in her reticule that had helped to identify her, had, in fact, been a letter of character from the matron at St. Thomas Hospital. Leo reasoned that the hospital had been her place of employment—or at least her most recent employment. With Jasper refusing to give her the file on Miss Barrett's accident, she couldn't know what had occurred on Trafalgar Square, but there was still an opportunity to learn more about Miss Barrett in general—and why a convicted felon might have desired her locket. Someone at St. Thomas Hospital might be persuaded to gossip.

Presenting herself at the hospital truthfully, as a city coroner's assistant who had observed the postmortem on Miss Barrett, would only bring shocked stares and confusion. She'd be turned away, almost certainly. However, after sending Liam with their advert to the *Telegraph*, she realized a newspaper reporter would be expected to ask questions. Forgiven for it, even.

On her brisk walk across the Thames, she'd honed her false identity. Ignoring the toss of doubt in her stomach, Leo presented herself to the nurse at the front desk, her chin high.

"I'd like to speak to Matron Adams," she said, citing the name of the nurse who'd signed Hannah's letter.

"Is Matron expecting you?"

"No, I'm afraid not. My name is Miss Jane Smith from the *Daily Telegraph*, and I'm writing an article on the city's inadequate driving regulations, which lead to scores of deaths each year. I'd like to talk to the matron about one such victim, a nurse's assistant employed here, Miss Hannah Barrett, for my article."

While it was mostly all a complete fabrication, it *was* true that far too many traffic accidents each year led to death—Leo and Claude had seen eleven last year in the Spring Street Morgue alone.

The nurse's disapproving frown softened at Miss Barrett's name. Sorrow pinched the space between her brows.

"I learned of Hannah's death yesterday. I was shocked."

The use of her given name fed Leo some hope. "Were you and Miss Barrett well acquainted?"

This nurse was in her forties or thereabouts, with graying hair drawn back in a severe bun, which she wore under a starched white cap; a standard gray nurse's uniform with white pinafore completed her ensemble. Her chin wrinkled as she pressed her lips together.

"We'd take tea now and then. She was a sweet young lady." Her eyes glistened.

"I've spoken to Mr. Barrett, her brother," Leo said. "But I wanted to get a sense of her work and of the things that were important to her. Perhaps a profile on Miss Barrett will inspire regulatory changes for public carriage drivers."

The nurse nodded vigorously. "It's a wonderful idea. However, I'm afraid you'll need an appointment to speak with Matron Adams, as she is quite engaged."

"If you and Miss Barrett were known to each other, perhaps I could put my questions to you, Nurse…er…?"

The nurse straightened. "Oh. Nurse Wright. Yes, I suppose that couldn't hurt."

"Excellent. I understand Miss Barrett was in mourning. Can you tell me more about that?"

The nurse looked to Leo's empty hands. "Aren't you going to take notes?"

She hadn't thought to bring along a pad of paper as most other reporters would have done.

"I won't need it. I have an excellent memory," she answered.

The nurse accepted her explanation with a wrinkled brow but then shook her head sadly. "It is the most tragic thing. Hannah was to marry this spring, but then…" She shrugged. "He died."

Miss Barrett had been mourning her *fiancé*?

"When was this?" Leo asked.

"Just days ago. Can you believe it? Hannah was devastated." Then, lowering her voice, she added, "Some here are saying that she stepped in front of that omnibus on purpose, lost as she was in her grief. Mind you, I don't think that. I think it more likely she was distracted."

Leo considered that the fiancé had died only days ago. How very strange. "How did he come to pass?"

Nurse Wright lifted a shoulder. "I don't know. Hannah was quiet about him. I didn't even know his name. She wouldn't say."

That was certainly intriguing. Why would she be so secretive, not just about whom she was going to marry but also how he had died?

"When did you last see Miss Barrett?"

The nurse recalled easily. "Two days ago. The day of the accident." Her expression darkened. "She *was* upset, now that I think of it. But when I asked after her, she just said that she and her brother had argued again that morning."

Leo perked up. "Again?"

"They'd been at odds over Hannah's beau."

Now this was truly becoming intriguing.

"Do you recall a necklace Miss Barrett wore? A gold locket?" Leo asked.

The nurse frowned. "Yes, but how does the *Telegraph* know of it?"

A flare of panic threatened to stain her cheeks with a blush. She'd forgotten for a moment that she was supposed to be a reporter.

"It was mentioned in the morgue report. My editor read there was a clipping of hair inside the locket, and what with Miss Barrett's mourning clothes, he thought it a possible tragic angle to appeal to readers," Leo fibbed.

Nurse Wright continued to peer at her skeptically. "I see. Well, yes, she always wore it, as far as I know."

If that was the case, Mr. Barrett was sure to have noticed it missing by now. It wasn't so out of the ordinary that he hadn't realized it at the morgue, especially if he'd been in a state of shock.

There was one last thing that had been on Leo's mind. "Miss Barrett was carrying a letter of character from Matron Adams when she was struck down," she said. "Had she been let go from her position here?"

Nurse Wright's eyes widened. "Begging your pardon, Miss Smith, but I'm not sure why that should be in your article."

"I'm sure it won't be. I'm only trying to get a fuller picture of Miss Barrett at the time of her death." Again, it was a poor excuse. It seemed the nurse thought so too, and she had wearied of Miss Jane Smith's questions.

"She was a woman in mourning, and yes, Hannah had decided to leave St. Thomas. She wasn't told to go. But that has nothing to do with unsafe driving regulations, I'm sure."

Leo forced a grin. "Quite right. Thank you for your time, Nurse Wright."

She turned to leave, her bootheels clicking swiftly over the marble tiles. Everything about Miss Barrett's fiancé intrigued her. His mysterious identity, the manner and timing of his death, and that Mr. Barrett had been opposed to him as a match for his sister. And why had Hannah decided to leave the hospital?

At least one thing seemed obvious to Leo as she exited onto Lambeth Road: if Hannah had wanted a letter of character for a future position, she hadn't planned to step out into traffic to her own demise.

Leo rushed to a cab stand near Westminster Bridge where an omnibus was gathering passengers. She was too pressed for time to go to Spring Street on foot. Claude would be performing the autopsy on the morgue intruder, and Leo wanted to be there in case he needed assistance.

He'd been surprised to learn that the intruder was returning to the morgue, this time as a corpse. She'd told him all about it as soon as she'd arrived home the previous evening, after opening the morgue for Detective Sergeant Lewis and the constables transporting the body. Lewis said that they would collect the victim's belongings the next day after the coroner had prepared the body.

After seeing them out, Leo had removed the clothing on the corpse herself. She'd long since become immune to the naked flesh of the dead. One body looked much like another. She'd wanted to see if any hidden pockets held anything of importance—specifically, a gold locket. But a thorough search turned up nothing except for some additional ill-designed and crudely done tattoos on his chest and abdomen.

Leo got off at Trafalgar Square, the closest stop to Spring Street, and entered the morgue office through the back door. Immediately, she heard a commotion in the postmortem room. Removing her coat and hat along the way, she walked in to find Aunt Flora, pacing between examination tables. Although she was fully dressed, her long silver hair wasn't done up as it normally would have been whenever she left the house. Instead, it hung loose around her shoulders. She muttered to herself as she walked forward and back, her widened eyes distrustful. Claude stood watch nearby, hesitating with marked concern.

"Uncle Claude?" Leo approached them slowly. "Where is Mrs. Shaw?" The nurse was supposed to have been watching Flora at the house.

He appeared worn to the bone when he turned to Leo. "She brought your aunt here and left. Apologized, but said she couldn't stay the rest of the week after all. Apparently, Flora's treatment of Mrs. Shaw was worse this morning."

Leo deflated as she put back on her coat and hat. Without Mrs. Shaw, there would be no one to look after Flora. No one, except for Leo.

"Will you be able to handle things here today without me?" she asked.

"Of course, of course." He laughed softly. "I'll have to be, won't I?"

Leo peered at the sheeted body of the intruder, disappointed she'd miss the postmortem. Surely, the results would show that he was killed by the gunshot to his chest. But an examination could turn up much more about the man. Attending her uncle appealed to her far more than spending the day with Flora and managing her fluctuating moods.

"Very well. Come, Aunt Flora." Leo moved toward her,

extending a hand. "Let us walk home, and I'll fix you some tea."

Her aunt's eyes flared. She screamed and whirled away from Leo's hand. "No! You're trying to murder me!"

Leo froze to the spot. "Of course, I'm not. I only want to walk you home."

"Flora, dear." Claude advanced, but she shuttled backward, colliding with one of the tables.

"Murdered. All murdered!" Flora shouted, her voice bouncing off the high ceilings.

Leo stared, her eyes beginning to water. Somehow, she knew her aunt wasn't speaking about the bodies around them right then, but about Leo's family.

"Calm yourself, my dear. No one is murdered," Claude soothed, managing to successfully take his wife's arm. She yelped, but then clung to him. She peered out at Leo as if expecting her niece to harm her.

"Murdered, murdered, all but one," Flora whimpered. "All but her. What did she do? How did she escape?"

A boulder sank through Leo's stomach. Claude's spectacles enlarged his eyes as he gave her a pleading look.

"Leonora, I'm so sorry. Your aunt doesn't know what she is saying."

Flora whimpered again and buried her head in her husband's chest.

"I'll take her home," he said, patting his wife's back. "There's nothing to be done for it. I'll just have to stay with her until she calms."

Leo could only nod, her body thrumming with shock and deepening remorse.

"I'll let Jasper know the postmortem will be delayed," she said with a hitch in her voice.

As Claude and Flora shuffled from the room, Leo put a hand to her stomach and concentrated on breathing until a dizzying sensation passed. Her aunt couldn't possibly believe *she* was to blame for the murders of her family. She'd been a child, for heaven's sake! Flora had always been a bit distant and, as she'd deteriorated, wary of Leo. However, this outburst was unlike anything she'd expressed before. It took Leo's breath away that it might be a suspicion her aunt had harbored all this time.

If Flora questioned how her niece had survived, surely others did as well. It wasn't fair, was it, that Leo had lived while her parents, brother, and sister had not. What made her so special? So lucky? These thoughts had plagued her, and they were the reason Leo had never spoken to anyone about what really happened in the attic that night.

How did she escape? Flora had asked.

The answer had haunted Leo for sixteen years: Someone had helped her.

And she was absolutely certain it had been one of the murderers.

Chapter Eight

The photographs on the page turned blurry, and Jasper dug his knuckles into his eyes to clear them. He'd been looking through the pile of convict albums from Wandsworth Prison since coming into the office at dawn. The night before, Lewis had gone through just one of the thick prison albums from the early 1870s before Jasper found him asleep with his cheek propped in his hand. He'd sent him home, and Jasper had gone back to his own rooms on Glasshouse Street to read the file on Hannah Barrett's accident.

Afterward, frustration kept him from sleeping well. Constable Richard Carey had written the report, in which he'd interviewed the omnibus driver, who claimed the woman had jumped in front of his team of horses. He hadn't had time to pull them to a stop before she'd fallen under their hooves. However, a passenger seated high on the roof's knifeboard had been recorded as saying that the woman had come toward the street at a run and that a man seemed to be chasing her. The only description of this man had been "rough, uncouth, patched sack coat, no hat, balding." The morgue intruder had been found in a patched sack coat, though to be sure, thousands of other men in London owned the like. And the intruder had a widow's peak, which could have been confused with "balding" in the report.

Constable Carey cited carelessness on the victim's part as the reason for the accident, writing nothing more about the man whom the witness on the knifeboard had seen. It was lazy policework, and it would have to be remedied.

Leo's theory that the intruder had been there and witnessed Miss Barrett's death had kept Jasper restless into the early morning hours. The report noted that passengers helped pull the poor woman from underneath the chassis, but she'd already perished. With so many lookers-on, the intruder wouldn't have been able to go anywhere near her—until, perhaps, she was alone at the nearest city morgue.

The intruder might have hung about, waiting for his opportunity. Then, after seeing the coroner leave, decided to go in. He would not have expected to find a young lady there doing the work of a coroner.

A single knock on his office door preceded Lewis, who entered without waiting for Jasper to respond. "Got it, guv," he said triumphantly, holding up a photograph. "Our victim is one Clarence Stillman."

Jasper had started to stand from his seat, but at the name, his knees locked. "Stillman?"

Lewis handed him the photograph. "You've heard of him?"

Jasper stared at the man in the photograph, his oddly

cloudy eyes notable in the black and white image. It was indeed their gunshot victim from last night. Jasper hadn't recognized him then and still didn't.

"I might have, but I'm not sure in what capacity," he answered.

"He's connected to the East Rips."

Slowly, Jasper lowered the photograph to his desk. His ears began to chime. *Stillman.* He'd thought the name had been familiar.

"Spent three years in Wandsworth for accessory to murder," Lewis went on to say. "His file is what you'd expect it to be. Petty theft. Assault. Drunk and disorderly. Looks like he was some kind of East Rips underling, recruited out of Liverpool. Hired muscle. That sort of thing. No connection to the John Doe whose bag he stole. The silversmith, Longberger, remembered making that card case for a Mr. George Kendall. I ran the name down. He's been missing for a few days. Looks like Kendall is our John Doe after all."

Lewis handed him the thick file. Jasper held it without opening the cover.

"Good work."

The moment demanded more of a response, but his mind had muddled at the mention of the East Rips. He'd known a position in the C.I.D. might someday lead to an investigation dealing with the powerful gang run by the Carter family, whose territory encompassed the East End from the St. Katharine and London Docks to Whitechapel Road. He hadn't thought it would happen so quickly though.

"Stillman was released last month, given a ticket-of-leave," Lewis said, oblivious to the uptick in Jasper's pulse.

Any time the name Carter or the East Rips entered a conversation, it was an untamable reaction.

"And he was already back to thieving," Jasper said, getting on with it. He took a second look at the photograph. No. Stillman wasn't a familiar face. Then again, it had been many years since Jasper had come off the streets.

"He might have fallen back in with the East Rips," Lewis suggested. "Or maybe one of their enemy gangs. The Angels out of Spitalfields are recruiting hard."

It seemed the most likely conclusion. The East Rips had strengthened over the last five or so years, ever since their original leader, Patrick Carter, died. His oldest son, Sean, took his place. Since then, their operations had expanded. Rumor was that, in addition to the usual protection rackets and prostitution rings, the Carters were making political connections.

"So," Lewis said after Jasper had stayed uncharacteristically quiet. "Are we investigating?"

The detective sergeant's true question was clear: He wanted to know if they were going to waste police time and resources on investigating what would almost certainly amount to a gang murder. Along with the Spitalfields Angels, the Grims out of Stepney were the East Rips' known enemies. One of them would likely be tagged with the blame.

Jasper looked at the piles of papers on his desk; robberies, disappearances, and a suspicious death had started to languish as leads dried up. Investigating Clarence Stillman's murder would cause those cases to further wither on the vine. Besides, who cared if an East Rip had been wiped from the earth? Good riddance, most would say.

But then, there was the missing necklace. That and the inexplicable revelation that Miss Barrett had been running toward the street. Possibly being chased by Stillman. Most importantly, however, there was Gregory Reid. He would never approve of Jasper closing a case when he still had a shadow of doubt.

"Find a last known address for Stillman in his convict record," Jasper told Lewis. "We'll inform his next of kin and begin there."

If he had one, Lewis kept his opinion to himself and left. A bare second before the door closed behind him, Constable Wiley began to shout, "You need permission, Miss Spencer! You cannot push your way in!"

Jasper opened the door just in time for Leo to come sweeping inside, her pace hurried to outstrip Wiley, who was once again chasing after her, red-cheeked. Jasper held up his hand to stop him from crossing the threshold. "It's fine, constable, thank you." He shut the door before Wiley could complain.

Leo struggled to mask a small grin of victory as she took off her gloves. He shook his head on his way back to his desk. "You're a menace."

She seemed to take it as a compliment, a grin breaking freely over her lips. But then, it disappeared. "I've come to let you know the postmortem on the intruder will be delayed."

He straightened. "Why? What's happened?"

Leo fiddled with her gloves and kept her eyes from meeting his. "It's Aunt Flora. She needed my uncle today."

Jasper frowned. "I thought a nurse came to the house to care for her."

"Mrs. Shaw gave her notice, effective immediately." She was still avoiding his eyes.

"I see," he murmured. "Is there a reason you couldn't stay with her while Claude performed the postmortem?"

The coroner's report would surely declare that cause of death was a gunshot wound. But it would be nice to have the report to give to Chief Inspector Coughlan when he asked for it.

Leo's gaze finally shot to his, full of defiance. "You know she doesn't like me. And she was worse today. She was afraid of me, screaming nonsense when I tried to take her hand."

"*Afraid*? Why?" Leo might have been a little odd, but she wasn't frightening in the least.

Her eyes skated away from his again. "It doesn't matter. She's losing her mind and saying things that… well, things I hope she doesn't mean."

He was curious as to what had been said. Leo's aunt had always been kind to him, but he knew that warmness had not been extended toward her own niece. He suspected Flora resented having to take in a child—a sentiment Claude had not shared.

"Fine," Jasper said, nodding. "But I need that postmortem done first thing tomorrow."

"It will be."

He cocked his head. "And not by you."

She soured, her hands clenching around her gloves. "Claude may have taught me some things, but I don't have the skill to do a postmortem examination entirely on my own. Nor would I try."

He wasn't sure he believed her but let it rest. Standing

next to his desk, Leo caught sight of the photograph of Clarence Stillman. She snapped it up.

"You've found him."

Jasper came around the desk and took it from her. No sooner had he emptied her hand than she filled it again, this time with Stillman's convict file. Leo whirled away, behind the desk as she opened it.

"Clarence Stillman."

"That is police property," Jasper said, following her. She tried outstripping him as she had Wiley, but his office was only so big. He cornered her against the bookshelves and took the file from her. She'd already seen the top page, however, and so it would be imprinted onto her brain. All she needed to do was look at something for a few seconds, and she was able to picture it again in perfect detail with her circus-trick memory.

"He was an East Rip?" she said with visible awe, her back still against the shelves. Jasper loomed over her, irritated. He held the file up.

"This is not meant for your eyes. Or that bloody memory of yours."

"Why would an East Rip want to steal a worthless locket from Miss Barrett?" she asked.

Jasper tossed the file back onto his desk. "Before you try to take it again, I'll just tell you what is in there: He was released from a three-year stint at Wandsworth in December. He has a history of thievery and violence, and with his connection to the East Rips, it isn't surprising he ended up shot to death."

"But if he didn't have the locket on his person, and if he couldn't have fenced it on his way to Duck Island, then it stands to reason the person who killed him took it."

"For the last time, Leo, we have no proof he even stole the locket from Miss Barrett's corpse."

She threw up her hands, as exasperated with him as he was with her. "I know that he did, proof or no proof. Miss Barrett's death and Clarence Stillman's murder are connected. I can feel it."

Jasper bit his tongue against imploring her, once again, to leave the investigating to him. He'd have had better luck telling a goat to stop bleating.

"And you should also be aware that there is something suspicious about Miss Barrett's dead fiancé," Leo added.

He held still, his mind spinning back to his conversation with Mr. Barrett on the way to the morgue the previous day. The man had revealed his sister had been mourning her fiancé, but Jasper had not shared as much with Leo.

"How did you know about the fiancé?"

She narrowed her eyes. "You knew about him? Why didn't you say anything?"

"Because he had nothing to do with her accident." But then, he reconsidered. "How is he suspicious? And how did you learn of him to begin with?"

Digging around on her own could have been dangerous, not that it would have stopped her.

"On top of dying just a few days before Miss Barrett, it appears she was extremely secretive about who he was with her fellow nurses at St. Thomas. She didn't even reveal to them how he'd died."

"You went to the hospital?" Jasper recalled the letter of character listed among her possessions in the morgue register.

"I did, and I learned that Mr. Barrett and his sister had

been in some disagreement over her mysterious fiancé. They were at odds before her death, according to a nurse there."

The more Leo said, the more his muscles hardened with irritation. She'd investigated on her own. The untrained, bullheaded woman had followed a lead without his permission or knowledge—and instead of turning up something worthless, she'd brought him something that lit his interest like a lucifer match.

He didn't want to resent her, but she was making it damn difficult.

"Furthermore, she'd worn the locket for a long time," Leo went on, oblivious to his surly mood. "Which means Mr. Barrett should have noticed it missing."

Jasper held up a hand. "People who are in shock aren't always observant."

"But he should have noticed it missing by now," she pressed. "Clarence Stillman went to great lengths to take her necklace. You know it's true."

Christ. Yes, he did. Especially now that he'd read the constable's report and knew she'd been running toward the street, possibly because she was being chased.

He sighed. "You said her fiancé died just a few days before her accident?"

Asking Mr. Barrett at the time for more details on the fiancé's death hadn't crossed his mind. But now, after learning about the animosity between brother and sister, Jasper needed to find them out.

"Yes, isn't that a bit odd? And I keep thinking of the writing on the folded piece of paper inside the locket: *Strange Nun B17 R4*," Leo recounted. "What if it has some importance?"

"I can't think of how it would," Jasper replied, raking his hand through his already ruffled hair. But if Stillman was the one who chased Miss Barrett into the street, then came to the morgue to steal the locket, it stood to reason the paper *was* important. The lock of hair inside surely couldn't be, and the locket itself wasn't worth the risk.

"All right," he said, still inflamed. "I will pay Mr. Barrett a call."

"Right now?" Leo started for the door. "I'll come with you."

He caught her arm. "On what grounds?"

She cocked her head and pressed her lips thin. "On the grounds that you wouldn't have wanted to speak to him if not for what I learned at the hospital."

He shouldn't have been surprised by her tenacity. She was more like Gregory Reid than she knew.

"That's not necessarily true," he replied. "I told Mr. Barrett that I'd look at the accident report, and I have."

Interest brightened her eyes. "And?"

Jasper sighed and grabbed the photo of Clarence Stillman from his desk. "And there is a witness to Miss Barrett's death that I would very much like to speak to."

She bit her bottom lip and grinned hopefully. *The incessant gnat.*

"If I don't take you, you're just going to turn up at Mr. Barrett's on your own, aren't you?" he asked as he plucked down his coat and hat from the stand next to the door.

"Excellent foresight, inspector," she said with a prim smile.

Chapter Nine

To Leo's everlasting astonishment, Jasper had still not changed his mind when they'd reached the open yard behind police headquarters. She'd expected him to come up with some reason or another for her to return to the morgue, which she'd closed for the day, or to Duke Street, which was the last place she wanted to go. But all he'd done was instruct Constable Wiley to tell Lewis he'd return shortly. Then, he and Leo had left the detective department together, the eyes of the other officers burning holes into their backs. That was what it had felt like to her at any rate.

"Do you think Mr. Stillman was the man chasing Miss Barrett?" she asked once they were outside.

Jasper squinted against a sudden break of sunlight. "That is what I'd like to find out. I'll show Mr. Yardley the photograph."

The witness's name and place of work had been included in the report, Jasper had explained. Mr. Yardley would be found not far from Trafalgar Square at Kendall and James Furriers, where he was employed as a salesclerk.

"Reid!"

They slowed at a voice hailing Jasper, and crossing under the arch, into the courtyard behind headquarters, was the dashing figure of Viscount Hayes. Oliver Hayes was his good friend, though the connection did inspire raised brows from time to time. A detective inspector and a lord of the peerage weren't likely to have much in common, but the two had not yet quite caught on to that. When he'd been a police constable, Jasper had arrested Lord Hayes for public intoxication and unruly behavior, which included riding a horse bare-chested down Pall Mall. After resisting arrest and berating Jasper for daring to apprehend a viscount, Jasper had cuffed him across the mouth. Lord Hayes enjoyed telling the story of how the green Metropolitan police constable had followed up the thrashing by saying, *"That's how much I care about your bloody title."* Jasper had then left him in a cell until he'd sobered up.

"Miss Spencer." Lord Hayes tipped his hat. "It's been some time since we last met. I hope you're well."

The greeting was perfectly polite, and everything a lord should strive for, but Leo saw through it. It was true that they had not seen one another for a time; perhaps once or twice over the last several years, while Jasper had been serving at a few other stations in the city. During those years, Leo had seen Jasper only slightly more frequently. But the viscount had always been a bit stand-offish with her. He may have lowered himself enough to remain friendly with Jasper, but to be familiar with a woman who worked at a morgue was the proverbial line in the sand.

"Thank you, Lord Hayes, I am well," Leo replied, but his attention had already shifted back toward his acquaintance, and she had the distinct impression that her response hadn't been noted.

"Haven't seen you at the club lately, Reid."

The club? Leo peered at Jasper just as he glimpsed toward her. He rocked back on his heels, which he always did when uncomfortable, and replied, "I've been busy."

"So I hear," Lord Hayes said, his tone teasing. "My cousin is feeling rather neglected lately."

His cousin, Miss Constance Hayes, probably didn't have much experience with that feeling. Leo clasped her hands behind her back, impatient to be off.

Again, Jasper deflected. "What are you doing at the Yard?"

"The Home Secretary and I have a meeting with Superintendent Monroe and Commissioner Vickers," he answered with a wave of his hand, as if a meeting with a few of the most powerful men in London was something trivial. "Will I see you at the club soon? The others miss sparring with you."

Now Leo's interest was truly piqued. She stared at Jasper. "You belong to a boxing club?"

Before he or Lord Hayes could reply, their party was joined by two more: the police commissioner, Sir Nathaniel Vickers, and one of his deputy assistants. Tall, broad-shouldered, and lively for his fifty-odd years, Sir Nathaniel strode toward them with the intimidating bearing of a soldier. He'd seen many corners of the British Empire during his time in the army and had been knighted for his heroics in one particular conflict in Africa, the details of which Leo had heard numerous times at the Inspector's dinner table, whenever Sir Nathaniel joined them. The only indication of his advancing age was a slight limp. He'd been shot in that African skirmish, but rather than make him appear hobbled, the limp pointed toward a resolve of spirit.

"Miss Spencer," the commissioner said with a friendly smile and a short bow. He turned to his deputy assistant. "You are acquainted with Benjamin Munson, I believe."

The younger man nodded his head in greeting. Leo had met him a few times. Like Sir Nathaniel, Mr. Munson had served in the army. In Sir Nathaniel's regiment, in fact. However, with his wire pince-nez, trim mustache, and sedate expression, he reminded Leo more of a scholar than he did a soldier. Not only had he been present for the brief conflict in the Griqualand West Colony, when a territorial dispute with the Boer Republic had led to a bloody clash, but Mr. Munson had reportedly brought the commissioner to safety after he'd been shot. Ever since then, Sir Nathaniel had kept Benjamin Munson close, elevating him in society and in the political sphere.

"Commissioner, Mr. Munson, how do you do?" Leo replied.

It felt like ages since she'd seen Sir Nathaniel, when in truth he'd come to Charles Street for supper in December with his daughter, Elsie. The last many weeks had dragged on, it seemed, anchored down by the Inspector's rapidly declining health.

"Very well, now that I'm assured you are unharmed," the commissioner answered. "That was quite a commotion at the morgue that I heard about."

She smiled, though a bit uncomfortably. "It wasn't as exciting as it's been made out to be."

"That is good to hear. Though, if my Elsie heard tell of it, she'd think you even more fascinating than before," he said with a fond chuckle.

The commissioner's daughter, at just seventeen, had been endlessly curious about Leo's work at the morgue during a holiday supper in late December. The commissioner and Elsie didn't usually attend the Inspector's annual supper, but as Sir Nathaniel's elderly uncle, his only remaining family, had passed away the month before, he and Elsie had been invited to join them. Without ever having a mother figure to school her into minding her manners, Elsie asked a host of questions, some of which had been rather macabre. Constance Hayes, also present for this supper, had chastised both Leo and Elsie with pointed looks. Leo had ignored her censure, while Elsie had simply been unaware of it.

"You may assure her that I am not fascinating in the least," she replied, though the commissioner furrowed his brow playfully, as if to say he wasn't convinced.

"At any rate, I'm glad you weren't harmed." He turned to Jasper. "And now I hear the same morgue intruder has been murdered?"

"An East Rips gang member, Clarence Stillman," Jasper reported.

"You've identified him? Superb. Any leads?"

"Not yet, sir," Jasper answered while at the same time Leo said, "Perhaps."

Sir Nathaniel peered between them. "What's this?"

Leo pushed back at Jasper's chastising glare. "There *is* a

possibility that Mr. Stillman is connected to another incident."

"A very slight possibility," Jasper added, his voice restrained and teeth gnashing. He'd called her a menace earlier, and he appeared to be thinking it again.

Lord Hayes observed them with an amused grin. "Count me as intrigued."

"I believe Mr. Stillman also took an item from another body at the morgue," Leo explained.

The commissioner hitched his chin and waited for her to continue. Over the years and a number of dinners at Charles Street with Commissioner Vickers, she had learned his mannerisms. He clearly wanted to know more.

"A necklace belonging to Miss Hannah Barrett, who was struck and killed by an omnibus two days ago. It was a locket, and inside was a clipping of hair and a piece of paper with some writing on it."

"Writing?" Mr. Munson echoed, breaking from his silence so far. His eyes narrowed in confusion. "What sort of writing?"

"*Stran—*"

But Jasper cut her off by saying, "I'm following up on it." He punctuated his interruption with another pointed stare, as though he'd have rather smothered her mouth with his hand.

"Good. Keep me informed," the commissioner said. "Though, don't hang on to this one if it doesn't lead anywhere, Reid. There are plenty of cases involving our city's decent citizens that need seeing to."

Leo pressed her lips together to prevent herself from

objecting. Hannah Barrett had been a *decent* citizen. Her death shouldn't be dismissed.

The commissioner tipped his hat and started away. But then paused. "Tomorrow is the fifteenth of January," he said, his voice lowering. "I imagine you'll call on Gregory?"

Jasper nodded. He would, as would Leo. She always did on the anniversary of his family's deaths. Like always, she would accompany them to Kensal Green to lay flowers on their graves.

"Elsie and I may stop in early, but if we can't make it, give him my regards." Sir Nathaniel patted Jasper on the shoulder and tipped his hat to Leo again. Then, he and Mr. Munson continued toward headquarters.

"I should follow," Lord Hayes said, his amusement having dissipated after the serious turn in the conversation. "Good fortune with your investigating, Reid."

He glanced furtively at Leo, and by his tone, he might also have been wishing Jasper good luck with the exasperating woman at his side.

Grumbling low in his throat, Jasper set off toward the cabs lining the street, waiting to be hired by those leaving the Yard. Leo hurried to keep his pace.

"You're angry," she said.

"It isn't my job to bother the commissioner with the details of a case. Nor is it yours," he said, flagging an empty hansom cab.

"He was asking about leads."

"And I'd prefer to bring him evidence, not theories."

The driver, seated on a high bench behind the enclosed two-person cab, came along the pavement, and Jasper gave the address for the furrier shop. The ride was short, as it was just off Trafalgar Square, and Jasper asked the driver to wait as they went in.

"Are you Mr. Yardley?" he asked the clerk who greeted them. The man was short, with a slight paunch, and black hair silvering at the temples.

"You are correct, sir," he replied jovially, but when Jasper showed him his police warrant card, his expression turned grim. "You've come to ask about that wretched business with the omnibus."

Leo exchanged a glance with Jasper, who seemed equally taken aback by the man's assumption.

"Yes. I want to know more about the man you claim to have seen running after the victim," Jasper replied.

The salesclerk firmed his chin and nodded. "I told the constable that a man was chasing her. He ran off right after she was run down, so there wasn't much the constable could do. Awful business. Just awful." He shook his head as though gripped by what he'd seen. For his sake, Leo hoped his memories of it would fade someday.

Jasper reached into his coat pocket and withdrew the photograph of Clarence Stillman. In it, he was positioned as all those arrested and booked by the Met were—holding a chalkboard showing his name and arrest date.

"Is this the man you saw?" He handed the photograph to Mr. Yardley, who took one look at it before flicking the edge of the photo with his fingers.

"That's the fellow."

"You're certain?" Leo asked, her pulse rising. The salesclerk nodded confidently as he returned the photograph to Jasper.

"Absolutely. The hairline's right."

They thanked him and returned to the waiting cab.

"That settles it then," Leo said after Jasper handed her up into the carriage. "The locket was the item Mr. Stillman intended to steal all along."

Jasper wrinkled his nose. The cab smelled musty, and straw had been strewn on the floor to absorb the passengers' wet soles. But she didn't think Jasper was offended by those things. Leo groaned. "Come now, Jasper, you cannot still doubt it!"

"I don't doubt that he wanted the locket," he said as their driver turned toward SoHo, where Mr. Barrett lived on Great Chapel Street. "I simply wonder what an East Rip just out of prison would want with it."

Leo thought the answer was all too clear: the paper inside. It had to be some sort of coded message. As they rode on in silence, Jasper glared out the front window at the pair of horses pulling them, as though they'd insulted him. That scowl would certainly frighten his sparring opponents at the club Oliver Hayes had mentioned earlier.

"When did you begin boxing with the viscount and his peers?" Leo asked.

Seated next to her on the single bench, Jasper speared her with a warning look to not start in. He knew perfectly well that it was unusual for a man of his social standing to associate with the aristocracy. But then, the Inspector had also kept one foot inside the elite classes, while his wife had been alive, and afterward too, with Sir Nathaniel. Not for the first time, Leo wondered if Jasper had intentionally mirrored the Inspector by courting Miss Hayes.

"I don't go often," he finally answered. But he didn't want to stay on the subject. "What will you do about Flora?"

"I've placed a listing in the paper."

"*The Times?*"

She suppressed a roll of her eyes. Of course, he would think of that particular newspaper. It was where Miss Hayes was employed as a typist. As the daughter of a viscount's second son, Constance Hayes wasn't titled, but she was still a lady, and as such, polite society had expectations of her. She'd turned her back on them, however, by obtaining a job, and more scandalously still, living at a ladies' boardinghouse. It was marvelously independent and modern of her, and Leo vastly approved.

If only she could bring herself to like Constance, she might wish to be friends with her.

"The *Telegraph*," she answered. "We must hire another nurse, and with any hope, Aunt Flora won't drive this one away."

Jasper remained quiet, though she guessed what he was thinking. He'd asked her before: *Why can't you stay home and watch her?* Leo was ready to defend the fact that her aunt wouldn't have allowed Leo to assist her, but Jasper surprised her.

"You said she was saying things you hoped she didn't mean. What sort of things?"

His intent stare gave her the impression that he was questioning her as he would a crime suspect.

"I'd rather not discuss it."

It wasn't the right thing to say to a detective inspector. Jasper crossed his arms and sat back in a stubborn posture. "Why not?"

It was no use avoiding him. And she supposed, other than Claude, the Inspector, and her friend, Dita, Jasper was the only other person with whom she could speak openly about her past.

"She's suspicious of me. This morning, she wouldn't let me touch her and screamed about the murders. She asked why I made it out of that house when no one else did."

It was a question Leo was sure many people had asked at the time. Though she'd been young, she recalled the public's fascination with the story. When she'd stayed with the Inspector for those two months, he and Mrs. Zhao would hide the daily papers. But once, she'd managed to sneak one out of the burn basket. And regretted it. The article had detailed the killings, and as she'd read, a drowning guilt had consumed her. The reporter had drawn a vivid picture of the event, making Leo feel as if she were right there, with her mother and father, Jacob and Agnes as their lives ended violently.

Why had the murderer who'd come into the attic that night spared her?

Jasper shifted forward on the bench, his elbows coming to rest upon his thighs. "She can't think you had anything to do with it. You were nine years old, for Christ's sake."

"She isn't well," Leo said, repeating what she and Claude had been saying for over a year now, ever since Flora started deteriorating noticeably. "But I do wonder sometimes…"

The hansom slowed in a snarl of traffic.

"What do you wonder?" Jasper asked.

She looked up from her clasped hands. "Why I didn't die."

He was a master at protecting his thoughts with a

fixed stare, but at her question, Jasper pressed one brow low. She thought it might be an expression of sympathy.

"You weren't meant to. Not that day. That is all."

Leo had never liked that answer, and she'd heard it plenty.

"I wasn't meant to, but my parents were?" she challenged. "My brother? My little sister? Agnes was four. A four-year-old cannot be meant to die."

Jasper cast his eyes to the straw on the floor. "No child should. But we live in a world where that doesn't matter."

It was a bleak outlook, but it was reality. He'd seen plenty in his years at the Met to know it to be true, and so had Leo during her time as Claude's assistant, unofficial as she was. The bodies of children on his tables never failed to send pangs of sorrow and futility through her, though she tried to erect a wall around herself on those occasions.

The traffic cleared, and their hansom began moving again, picking up speed.

"You've never spoken about that night." Jasper's voice softened. "Not even to the Inspector."

"There isn't much to say," she replied. "I don't remember anything until he found me in the steamer trunk."

There was a tightness in her chest at the lie, but it was what she'd always claimed, and she wouldn't change her story now.

Jasper stared, unblinking. "It seems to be the only thing you can't remember."

She bristled. "That isn't true. I can't recall anything before that night, at least not with any clarity."

One of his brows popped up, as if in disbelief.

"What? Are you accusing me of lying?" she asked, incredulous.

"Are you?" The softness of his manner had abruptly changed, and now she felt like a fool for confiding in him. She imagined plenty of suspects he'd successfully cracked felt much the same. "If you remembered something about that night, you should have shared it with the Inspector."

Her eyes burned. "I don't understand your sudden concern. You've been telling him to give up on the investigation for years."

"Only because he was twisting himself into knots, trying to solve what happened to your family and why. He wanted to give that to you, but if you've been holding back all this time, keeping secrets—"

Fury, hot and unhinged, fired up her spine. "How dare you speak to me about keeping secrets, as if you haven't kept a lion's share of your own. But have I ever needled you for answers? Can't you understand that there are some things I just want to forget?"

Out of breath and suddenly stripped of her fury, Leo sat back against the bench cushion. Her heart raced, and her eyes continued to sting. But she wouldn't let a single tear fall in front of him.

"I understand wanting to forget," he said, after a few moments of strained quiet. "You're not alone in that."

She gave no response, uninterested in engaging in any more conversation. It would only lead to more tension. Jasper had his life before the Inspector too, and just as she'd said, he never spoke of it. In fact, his life before was even more of a mystery than Leo's.

Perhaps that was what had drawn the Inspector's interest in him initially. He'd always loved a good tangle.

After Jasper's heroic efforts to stop the runaway drunkard from plowing into Leo that day at the Yard, paired with his stubborn silence afterward when the Inspector treated him to a hand pie from a costermonger, how could he have resisted? At the time, Leo, too, had been slightly enchanted by the skinny teenage boy with bruises riddling his face. He'd refused to speak, not even to say his name.

He still didn't say much, only speaking when it was required or when something important needed to be said. But now that Jasper had become a man—a tall, broad-shouldered, muscular man—his restraint had a brooding, slightly intimidating nature that hadn't been present when he'd been a boy.

The cab driver called to his horses, and the hansom slowed. They'd reached Great Chapel Street. Jasper handed her down to the pavement, where several modest, working-class homes were within view. On No. 53, a wreath of black ribbon hung above the door knocker, marking the house as one in mourning.

"I will lead the interview," he said, the warning clear. Leo raised her eyes to the heavens but didn't argue. She would speak if she so chose, and truly, Jasper ought to have known that.

After knocking, they waited on the front step long enough for Leo to think Mr. Barrett wasn't at home. Or that perhaps he was and was choosing not to acknowledge them. Jasper brought down the knocker again, and soon after, the door opened an inch. Mr. Barrett peeked out.

Jasper held up his warrant card. "Detective Inspector Reid. We met yesterday."

The door opened further. "Yes. I recall." He looked at Leo and blinked. "You were at the morgue."

A blush stained her cheeks as she recalled rambling on about personal possessions getting stored and then forgotten in the crypt. She'd been trying to extend the moment, to give Hannah's brother time to recognize the locket was missing. To no avail, however.

"Miss Spencer and I have something to discuss with you, if we could come inside?" Jasper said.

Mr. Barrett's slender figure appeared even more drawn as he saw them in. The house reminded her of her own on Duke Street—a narrow terrace house with outdated furnishings and decor, the carpets worn but well kept. Despite the economical décor, a show of expense was further down the front hall—a telephone had been installed and mounted on the wall.

Bowls of dried flowers and herbs in the small sitting room into which they were led couldn't completely mask a sharp smell. Something akin to metal. Leo sniffed, and unfortunately, Mr. Barrett noticed.

"I am a locksmith and keep my workroom here in the house," he explained as he gestured for them to sit.

Leo nodded understandingly as her eyes drifted toward the hearth mantel and some framed photographs there. In the most prominently displayed frame was a portrait of Hannah and her brother. She was seated, while Mr. Barrett stood behind her, his hands resting on the back of the chair. He'd not had a mustache when the portrait was taken, though he did now, the thin tips of which he'd pomaded with wax.

Jasper remained standing while Leo lowered herself into a dainty chair.

"We're sorry to disturb you, but there is some question surrounding a necklace your sister was wearing at the time of her death," Jasper began.

Hannah's brother had taken a seat as well. He kept his back straight, his hands resting stiffly on his knees. A linen bandage covered most of his right hand, and a silvery-gray tinge discolored his fingertips. From his work as a locksmith, Leo deduced.

"Her locket? Yes, I've noticed it is missing. I thought perhaps it was taken when she was...in the street after..." He didn't finish.

"There was a robbery at the morgue the evening your sister's body arrived. Miss Spencer was present at the time," Jasper explained. "She believes the thief took your sister's necklace."

Mr. Barrett's eyes pierced Leo's with instant suspicion. "Why was I not made aware of this earlier?"

Before Jasper could try to answer for her, Leo said, "I was afraid you'd bring a complaint against the morgue. There are already so many, as no one wants a deadhouse in their neighborhood or near their place of business. But I am certain Miss Barrett arrived with the necklace. After the thief placed me in a supply closet, I heard him moving about the room. Then, when I was freed, I saw that the locket was gone."

He stood up from his chair, his back still rigid. "This thief knew she was at the morgue and came to steal it?"

Leo sat back. He'd concluded that it wasn't a crime of opportunity, but one that had been premeditated, rather quickly.

"Is there something special about the locket?" Jasper asked.

Mr. Barrett rubbed his bandaged hand as he turned toward the mantel of photographs. "It held sentimental value. It was our mother's, and when she died, Hannah took to wearing it as a reminder of her."

That would account for the tarnished, old-fashioned design.

"There was a lock of hair kept inside." Leo ignored a glance from Jasper, no doubt to remind her that he wanted to do the talking. "Was the hair a memento of your mother?"

"No," Mr. Barrett's voice suddenly turned terse. "It belonged to the man Hannah was to marry. As I've told the inspector, he died recently."

"You sound as if you didn't approve of him," Leo said.

The lines around Mr. Barrett's mouth deepened. "He was a criminal."

Leo jerked her chin, and she and Jasper shared a glance of interest.

"He'd been in prison?" Jasper asked, likely thinking what Leo was—that Clarence Stillman had been an ex-convict. Could this be the connection?

"No, he was too slippery for that. He and his family are well-trained in eluding the law," he said with a disapproving sniff.

A thrum of excitement beat through Leo. With her fiancé's criminal connection, it now made sense why Hannah had been secretive with the other nursing staff at St. Thomas about his identity.

"What was the man's name?" Jasper asked.

Mr. Barrett frowned. "Carter. William Carter."

Chapter Ten

"I didn't like him," Mr. Barrett said, carrying on after he'd revealed the name. "He was too charismatic, too good at saying the right thing all the time. My sister was enamored."

Jasper had managed to maintain a placid expression, though just barely. William *Carter*? Miss Barrett's fiancé had been an East Rip. Just as Clarence Stillman had been. His mind whirled forward with questions—most importantly: "How did Carter die?"

Mr. Barrett returned to his chair. "A housebreak. He was shot."

Leo made a small sound of surprise. "Like Mr. Stillman."

"Who?" Mr. Barrett asked.

Jasper retrieved the photograph from his pocket and showed it to him. "Do you know this man?"

It was only a blink and the tensing of his brow, but Hannah's brother couldn't mask his recognition. He'd seen Stillman before. Jasper would have wagered money on it.

However, he shook his head. "No. No, I don't, but I'd like to know what he has to do with my sister."

Jasper left the lie unchallenged for the moment.

"He was the morgue intruder. He was found dead. Also shot." Predictably, Leo's blunt explanation only stoked more confusion in Mr. Barrett.

"And he took my sister's locket? Where is it now?"

"That is unknown," Jasper answered. He was more interested in what William Carter had to do with all of this. And why Mr. Barrett was lying about knowing Clarence Stillman.

News of Carter's death hadn't made a big splash in the newspapers, and that was probably because he hadn't been one of the more active and notorious members of the Carter family. Jasper paid attention to anything in the papers regarding the East Rips and recalled that William and his father, the late Patrick Carter, had a public falling out years ago. Ever since, he'd been a fringe member. Not in, but also, not out.

"How did your sister meet Carter?" Jasper asked.

Mr. Barrett gazed upon the framed photographs on the fireplace mantel and sighed. "Our father died when we were both very young, but our mother only passed eight months ago. We used Hogarth and Tipson for the funeral."

Leo nodded. "They're reputable."

"Yes, so we were told," he replied bitterly, massaging his temple with his bandaged hand. "I've no complaints with their services, but that is where Hannah met William. He is—*was*—employed there."

"In what capacity?" Jasper asked.

Mr. Barrett fiddled with a loose end of the bandage. "Among other things, he was a photographer. He... immortalized the dead."

Death photography was no new thing; the practice of arranging the recently deceased for a final portrait before their burial, oftentimes in such a way that it appeared as though they were still alive, was quite common. It had always struck Jasper as unnecessary though. Not to mention macabre.

Leo rose restlessly from her chair and paced to the window, then back. "Was Mr. Carter's murder investigated?"

"I'm not sure." He cast an uneasy glance toward Jasper. "Hannah said she was turned away when she went to the police station to inquire what was happening with the case."

"Where did Carter live?" Jasper asked, curious about which division might be responsible.

"Off Russell Square. Bernard Street," Mr. Barrett answered, then fiddled again with his bandage.

He eyed the wrapped hand. People generally only fiddled when they were nervous. Leo, he had observed in the past, rubbed the scars on her right palm whenever she was uneasy or flustered. But already Mr. Barrett had lied about not recognizing Clarence Stillman. What more was he lying about?

"Back to the locket," he said, no longer doubtful that it had been taken from Miss Barrett's body purposefully. Stillman had been an East Rip. Hannah Barrett had been engaged to one. "Why might an East Rip gang member have wanted it?"

Mr. Barrett's already wan cheeks paled more. "How should I know what he wanted with it?"

"Perhaps there was something inside the locket?" Leo cut in.

"You already said there was a lock of hair," he pointed out.

Most people were wretched liars, and Mr. Barrett was one of them.

"It's important that you be forthcoming with us," Jasper said. "In addition to the lock of hair, there was a piece of paper tucked inside your sister's locket. What do you know about that?"

Mr. Barrett looked stunned and offended as he got to his feet. "Nothing. Nothing at all. I—"

"Stop lying, Mr. Barrett. You recognized the man in the photograph just now."

"No! No, I didn't. I swear." He paused. Then, his attention shifted toward the entrance to the sitting room.

"What is it?" Leo asked, following his gaze.

"All right. I do have some idea about the paper William gave Hannah."

Jasper asked him to explain, and he obliged, however haltingly. "I came down the stairs one night and saw William and Hannah in here, standing right where you are, Miss Spencer."

Leo was by the window, a spot that would have been easily visible from the bottom of the staircase.

"He was agitated. Hannah kept hushing him to lower his voice, but I did hear him say something odd." Mr. Barrett peered between his two callers with hesitancy.

"Go on," Jasper said impatiently.

"He said if anything were to happen to him to 'dig it up.'"

Jasper stared at Mr. Barrett, his pulse picking up speed. "Dig what up?"

"I don't know. I didn't want to intrude, so I went back upstairs. But William had been handing her something. Something small. I couldn't see what it was."

Jasper turned to Leo. "How large was the piece of paper?"

"An inch long. Two inches wide. It was folded into quarters," she answered. "It easily fit inside the locket."

It was possible William Carter had been giving his fiancée the paper; but with instructions to dig it up? How could whatever *Strange Nun B17 R4* meant be worth digging up? It made no sense.

"When was this specifically?" Jasper asked. "How long before Mr. Carter's death?"

"It was last Thursday," he answered with a grim furrow of his brow. "William was killed the following night."

Leo practically skipped toward Jasper in her enthusiasm. "Mr. Carter knew someone was coming after him. He knew he was in danger. It wasn't a housebreaking at all."

Jasper held up a hand. It was always easiest to jump to conclusions, but most often, it was folly. He fought the urge to do so now.

"Your sister said nothing to you about Carter's visit that night?"

Mr. Barrett shook his head. "It was better if we did not discuss her beau. He was the sort of man you knew, in your heart, was bad, but when he engaged you in conversation, he…well, he could change your mind. If only briefly, before you came to your senses again."

Jasper withdrew the convict portrait of Stillman from his pocket again. "You've seen this man before."

He wouldn't let Samuel Barrett wiggle away from the truth.

"He…" Mr. Barrett stammered, his pale coloring becoming even more pallid. "He came looking for my sister."

"When?" Leo asked, sounding astonished.

"It was…Monday." His chin quivered, and he let his face fall into his hands in distress. Monday was the day Miss Barrett had died.

"He injured your hand," Jasper said. "And you told him where to find Hannah."

Mr. Barrett's shoulders shook, and he sniveled into his palms. "Yes, but that can't have anything to do with her accident. An omnibus struck her."

"Did Mr. Stillman mention the locket to you?" Leo asked.

"No. No, he never said anything about it. He just wanted to know where to find her."

"And you didn't think this was important to tell the police?" Jasper asked, his temper flaring.

"I didn't think it mattered! I figured the man was some thug connected to William, and I know I shouldn't have told him where to find Hannah. I know I was a coward… But in the end, he never found her, did he? Hannah's death was an accident." He looked from Leo to Jasper. "Wasn't it?"

Pity for the man dampened Jasper's exasperation. He'd likely lied about his hand to conceal his cowardice. His sister, after all, had been struck down in the street with numerous witnesses, not shot as her fiancé had been.

"It looks to be an accident, yes," Jasper replied. To give Samuel Barrett any reason to doubt what the police and the coroner's report had determined would bring only trouble. The C.I.D. did not need more bad publicity, and if it came, Chief Inspector Coughlan would hold Jasper personally accountable. "However, I am not convinced Mr. Carter was the victim of a random housebreak. He told your sister to dig something up should something happen to him, and the next day, he was shot and killed."

"Might she have done as he asked?" Leo said. "Could she have dug up whatever he was referring to?"

"She said nothing to me about it," Mr. Barrett replied.

"Have you been through Hannah's room since her death?" Jasper asked. If she had dug something up, surely, she might have kept it there.

He shook his head. "I haven't had the heart."

"Would you allow us to have a look?" Leo asked, and at Mr. Barrett's surprise, she added, "To be sure there isn't some piece of evidence connected to Mr. Carter's death lying about in there."

It wasn't much of an excuse to snoop around Miss Barrett's room, but Jasper did want a look. And he didn't want to take the time and trouble to obtain a warrant to do so. Mr. Barrett hesitated and appeared to be on the verge of saying no.

"It's no trouble if you'd like the detective chief inspector present with a warrant. In fact, it might be faster for a team of constables to come through here and have a thorough look through all the rooms. We should also report that our most recent murder victim came to your home, asking after your sister."

"No, please, that isn't necessary, inspector. You may search her room, of course," Mr. Barrett said, reacting just as Jasper had hoped.

"I also need to know where you were the evening of your sister's accident," he said. He didn't truly think Mr. Barrett had anything to do with Stillman's death—he was far too meek and fidgety to be a killer—but there was no doubt he had motive.

"Here, of course. I'd just learned my sister was dead," he replied.

"Were you alone?"

He pressed his fingers against his temple. "No, though I would have liked to have been. My neighbor was outside when the police constables came to inform me. She spread the news among our other neighbors, and after that, I wasn't allowed to grieve alone until near to midnight."

It would be simple enough to corroborate. They followed Mr. Barrett upstairs to a narrow landing. On the left was a closed door, and to the right were two more. He opened one of the doors to the right. Inside, Jasper traced the lingering scent of rose water. A reminder of how recently the room's occupant had died. Floral paper covered the walls as did a few samplers and paintings. At a mirrored vanity, a collection of brushes, combs, and glass bottles had been left in a state of disarray, though not in any concerning way; it looked as if Miss Barrett hadn't tidied up before leaving the house on the day of her accident. And why should she have? She'd believed she would be coming home, not that the next person to enter her room would be the detective investigating her death.

On the nightstand next to her slim bed was a stained-glass lamp, a book marked off with a ribbon, a teacup and saucer, and a small, framed *carte de visite* of William Carter. Jasper hadn't laid eyes on him since he'd been a boy, but William hadn't changed much. Earlier in the hansom cab, Leo had accused him of keeping secrets, and she'd been right. He'd kept his life before the Inspector to himself, so it wasn't fair for him to become frustrated that she did the same.

Mr. Barrett picked up the teacup. Inside, cold tea had stained a ring around the white ceramic. His hands trembled. "I'll bring this to the kitchen." He left in haste. It was evident he didn't wish to be inside the room.

"Poor man," Leo said once he'd gone. "He seems unmoored without his sister."

"He gave up his sister's location to a thug without a second thought," Jasper said, feeling little pity for him. "He had to have known Stillman intended to harm her, and yet he didn't go to the police."

Leo opened the top drawer in a tall bureau and peered inside. "Now he must live with that guilt." She shut the drawer as Jasper stepped away from the nightstand.

"Might Mr. Stillman have already known about the locket when he arrived here, searching for Hannah? Mr. Carter could have given up the information before he was killed," Leo said as she opened the bottommost drawer, then shut it again.

Jasper crouched to peer under the bed. He was met with several pairs of footwear and nothing else. There was nothing here of interest. "It makes the most sense. Maybe Carter thought it would save his life."

"Come look at this," Leo said. He straightened to find her touching the edge of a framed picture on the wall. In the hazy, pastel-hued oil painting of a reedy pond on a summer's day, a man and woman were in a small rowboat, the lady with a parasol and the man at the oars.

Jasper grimaced. "I'm not fond of Impressionism."

"I wasn't asking your opinion on art," she replied with a small grin. She pushed the corner of the frame, which hung slightly askew on the wall. It moved an inch, and Leo pointed to the scraped wallpaper beneath. The spot was worn. So was the wallpaper under the opposite lower corner of the frame. This painting had been moved often.

Jasper removed the frame from its hook and set it on the floor. A small, oval-shaped hole had been cut into the wall behind it. A few inches in diameter and at least a few inches deep, the cut into the plaster had been smoothed. Leo ran her fingertip around the circumference.

"How strange. Why would—" She stopped speaking and retracted her finger. Then quickly stuck it back in. "Curious. There is a small lever in here." As she pressed it, Leo put her eye to the cutout. And gasped. "What in the world?"

Jasper suspected what she was seeing. Sure enough, when she stepped aside and allowed him a look, he was peering into the neighboring room. It appeared to be a bedroom.

"Why would Miss Barrett have wanted this peephole?" Leo asked.

Jasper stood back and rehung the framed painting. The corners rubbed the wallpaper again, and he determined Miss Barrett had done this same thing many, many times.

"And what or who was she watching?" he asked.

Finished with his search of Hannah's room, he went to the door and listened for any sound from downstairs. With a flick of his hand, he gestured for Leo to follow. Stepping quietly, he went to the neighboring door and tried the knob. It gave, and he and Leo entered the other bedroom. There was a four-poster bed, a privacy screen, a chaise longue, and a nightstand. Typical bedroom furnishings, and yet they were also spare and impersonal.

"It's a guest room," he said.

Jasper went to the wall that abutted Miss Barrett's room. The busy wallpaper pattern made it difficult to find the peephole, and he succeeded only because he knew where to look for it. It was a wafer-thin, papered-over oval, and when he pushed it aside, the peephole was revealed. When in place again, the lines of the pattern matched up perfectly.

"Why would Miss Barrett wish to spy on this room's occupants?" Leo whispered.

A noise sounded from downstairs. Jasper took Leo's arm, and they hurried out. It wouldn't do to be found snooping inside a room they had not requested to see. He closed the door quietly and met Mr. Barrett at the landing before he could ascend the stairs fully.

"Did you find anything?" he asked.

"No." Jasper's fingers tensed around Leo's elbow in a silent bid for her to say nothing about the peephole. It would be wiser to keep the discovery of it to themselves until they could determine if it held any importance.

"Have you some family or friends to keep you

company as you mourn, Mr. Barrett?" Leo asked as they descended to the ground floor, her elbow having wiggled from Jasper's hold. "Anyone to stay on with you here?"

It was a clever way to inquire about guests who might have stayed in the room Miss Barrett had spied on. Though, it bore no fruit.

"I'm afraid not," he answered, walking them to the front door. "Hannah and I don't have family, and we mostly kept to ourselves. I suppose, now…well, I won't burden you with my lonely circumstances."

Not knowing what to say to that, Jasper thanked Mr. Barrett for his time and promised to keep him informed on any lines of inquiry related to his sister. Then, he and Leo took their leave.

"What do you make of that?" she asked as they walked along the pavement, and Jasper searched for a hansom.

"Miss Barrett was watching someone in that guest room," he replied. "And by the marks on her wall from the picture frame, it was often."

"Someone she was cautious of?"

"Or infatuated with." But it was all theory. There was no way to link it to the missing locket, her death, or even her fiancé's.

"Will you look into the police report about William Carter's death?" Leo asked as they came upon a hansom at a nearby cab stand. Jasper directed the driver back to Scotland Yard before handing her into the carriage.

Once he'd taken the bench across from hers, he answered, "I don't think I have a choice. There is a connection between Carter and Stillman now—the East Rips. And if Carter gave Miss Barrett something that she then kept in her locket, Stillman was clearly after it."

"What can I do?" Leo asked. She looked so eager that Jasper almost felt guilty for shaking his head.

"Nothing. I'll take it from here."

She pressed her palms flat on the bench at her sides. Drumming her fingers, she merely held his stare. Her lips formed a little tuck in the corner of her mouth. She didn't argue, but she also didn't agree to leave off. By the time they arrived at the Yard, Leo still hadn't said anything. The silence had grown thick, their staring battle a drawn-out challenge. It gave Jasper plenty of opportunity to observe her face and not be reprimanded for it.

She'd always been pretty, in a dark and serious sense. But since his transfer to the C.I.D. a few months ago, he'd noticed a new intensity to her beauty. It had left him somewhat unsettled. The several years he'd spent in the Clapham and Highgate Divisions, he'd hardly seen her except for holidays and of course, each January 15. Now, they crossed paths more often, and she was no longer a remote, shy girl. She was direct and confident, though a layer of vulnerability still broke through every now and again. At nearly twenty-five, Leo could be considered a spinster. An unusual thing for a woman even half as attractive as she was. Her appearance couldn't have had anything to do with her unmarried state; it was her choice of work, no doubt, and her peculiar manner.

"When you change your mind, you know where to find me," she said, after they'd arrived at Whitehall Place and Jasper paid the driver.

"I won't. Leo, if the Carters are a part of this, you're to be nowhere near any of these cases."

"But Jasper—"

"*Stop.*" The order cracked through the air, loud enough

for a few constables walking across the open courtyard to glance over in curiosity. Jasper lowered his voice. "Don't make the mistake of thinking that our acquaintance gives you free rein to walk in on any of my investigations. There are rules and procedures in place for a reason, and I'm not going to break them. Not for you, not for anyone. Is that clear?"

At her stricken expression, swiftly followed by one of anger, Jasper knew he'd spoken too harshly. He'd allowed his irritation with her needling stubbornness to touch a nerve.

"Exceptionally clear," she replied, then spun away, leaving the Yard at a fast clip.

Jasper bit his tongue against calling her back and apologizing. It was better for her to leave. Better for her to be angry with him. Maybe then she'd keep her distance. What he'd said was true: if a criminal gang was involved, he wanted Leo out of it. It was the safest option—for them both.

Chapter Eleven

"Gracious, I started to wonder if I'd ever set eyes on you again."

Constance Hayes closed the door to her boarding-house and came down the steps to meet Jasper on the pavement. He extended his elbow, and she hooked her arm through it, leaning against him with familiar ease. He liked the weight of her against him and the delicately scented cloud of jasmine she brought with her.

"I'm sorry. These last few nights have been eventful," he replied.

He might have had to postpone with Constance yet again, had Mary Stillman, Clarence's widow, still lived at the address in Stillman's convict file. But after Jasper telegraphed Thames Division and requested that a constable from a local station bring Mrs. Stillman to the central office for an interview and to show her the body of her husband, he received the news that she no longer let the rooms there and couldn't be found. Lewis had turned to looking through the most recent city directory, searching for her there, when Jasper had left for the evening.

He walked Constance to the waiting carriage, but she pulled back.

"Where have you instructed the driver to take us?"

"The Albion, if you still wish to dine there."

She smiled brightly, the bridge of her nose crinkling with mischief. "I have a better idea. Driver, take the Waterloo to Belvedere Road. Stop at Striker's Wharf."

Jasper followed her into the carriage, and the driver started for the nearest bridge over the river.

"What is at Striker's Wharf?" he asked, wary of the location. The docks and wharves weren't suitable places come nightfall. They were usually overrun with punters and prostitutes as well as the upper classes looking to lower themselves for an evening.

"A fun little establishment I've heard about for ages," she answered, still holding onto his arm and leaning against him. She'd only started to do that recently. "Some of the girls at work said there's a band and dancing—"

Jasper sighed, his curiosity dulling. "Dancing?" He didn't like to dance. He wasn't any good at it, and he didn't have the inclination to better himself.

Constance nudged him with her elbow. "Yes, dancing. And I read in the *Illustrated London News* about a cocktail there that the bartender sets on fire! The flames are gone as soon as he serves it."

Jasper usually didn't mind being carried along on one of her bubbles of enthusiasm. Constance enjoyed having fun, much like her cousin Oliver, Lord Hayes. The two were alike in many ways, and in their company, Jasper always felt like a singular rain cloud in an otherwise blue sky. Their sunny dispositions balanced him out. Without their encouragement, he'd probably stay in every night at his bachelor's rooms with a bottle of single malt and a stack of case files.

For the last two months, he'd been taking Constance to dinner, to the theatre, to dinner parties thrown by Oliver, and on Sunday afternoons, they would go for strolls in the park—that was, whenever his work did not interfere. Somewhere along the way, they'd officially begun courting, and though neither of them had broached the subject of the natural next step, Jasper could feel it closing in.

He shifted on the seat as the driver took them across the bridge.

"You're distracted." She gave his arm a squeeze.

He turned to meet her gaze. She was beautiful, radiantly so, with cornsilk blonde hair, deep blue eyes, flawless, creamy white skin, and a full mouth that Jasper had kissed chastely a few times. She'd granted him no additional favors; she was a lady after all, even if she lived as a modern woman. However, there was no question in his mind that her favors would be abundantly pleasurable if he ever got the chance to know them.

"An investigation," he responded. "It has me preoccupied."

"Heavens, not another ghastly murder?" She sounded galled by the idea.

"With millions of people in this city, and the majority of them living in poverty, murder should come as no great surprise to anyone."

She pouted. "I'll never understand why some people are inclined toward violence."

"I don't suppose society page typists see a lot of it."

It was the only section of the paper that would not scandalize a woman of her good breeding—or so Oliver had explained to him when he'd first introduced Constance at a dinner party.

She loosened her arm around his. Belatedly, Jasper realized he'd spoken too harshly—again. He'd been doing that a lot of lately, since finding Leo locked inside the morgue closet.

"Yes, they are short on murders," she replied tartly.

"Is that why they're so dull?" he said, winking and trying to make her smile again. It wasn't a hardship. Constance preferred being merry to upset.

She laughed, and the tense moment passed. Things were easy with Constance. That was one of the things he liked about her. That, and she did most of the talking.

"It must be horrible, seeing those things all the time," she said. Then, sitting up straight as if struck by an idea, "I know—you should get a promotion!"

"I just did," he reminded her.

"Maybe you could get another one. A position where you don't have to investigate murders but stay at the office as a manager of some sort."

He cringed. "That sounds awful." Not to mention, he'd rather leave the force entirely than be relegated to a desk job.

"Why? Isn't that what your father did before he became ill?"

"Yes, but that took many years for him to achieve," Jasper answered. "Besides, I like my work. It's difficult, but I'm good at it."

"Yes, you are." She reached up to kiss his cheek. He

wasn't sure how she would know; she didn't make it a habit of asking about his cases. The few times she had, she'd been discomfited by the stories. Most young ladies did not wish to discuss crimes of the desperate and the poor, let alone investigate them.

Leo Spencer was a conundrum, to be sure.

Their biting words in the carriage on the way to Mr. Barrett's home had agitated him. For a long time, he'd suspected she remembered more about the night of her family's murders than she'd ever revealed. With her oddly perfect memory, she simply *had* to remember. And yet, she'd avoided his question by clapping back about his own reluctance to share anything about his life before he'd met Gregory Reid. She'd been right, of course.

"They're coming in June."

Jasper looked up from the floor of the carriage and peered at Constance. "Pardon, who is coming in June?"

"You weren't listening, were you?" she said, though she wasn't truly vexed. "My parents, Jasper. They're traveling from Hampshire in June. I'd like for you to meet them, and they would very much like to meet you."

If the carriage roof had suddenly fallen in, he wouldn't have been more stunned. Her parents? *Hell.* Mr. Stanley Hayes was Oliver's late father's brother. His wife was the daughter of a knight. The pair of them hadn't been supportive of Constance's decision to work for a living, but she'd done so, nonetheless. The only reason they hadn't dragged her back to Hampshire, Oliver had confided, was because they believed she at least had the protection of her cousin by living at Hayes House—a complete falsehood.

And now, Jasper was to meet them. June was still a

handful of months away, so he resolved not to panic prematurely.

"Perhaps by then, another position at the Met will open up," she said. "Something more civilized."

With a twist in his gut, he pulled back from her. "You don't believe they'll approve of my job."

Her pale brows pressed together. "I don't care what they think. You know that. But they're old fashioned and want me to be on the arm of a man of our set."

"A peer, you mean."

"Or landed gentry," she said with a shrug. "But that doesn't matter to me. I just thought if they were to see that you were rising in the force to, say, a superintendent or assistant commissioner—"

"Commissioner?" He couldn't help but laugh. "Constance, that is an appointed position through the Home Office, and it is only given to military men."

Men like Sir Nathaniel Vickers.

She gave another little pout, displaying her full bottom lip. "It was just a thought. It doesn't matter."

But Jasper couldn't get the suspicion that it *did* matter out of his head as they finished their drive to Striker's Wharf.

"Are you sure about this place?" he asked as the driver slowed alongside a rambling, well-lit building located at the end of a pier.

"Not at all," Constance replied with a giggle. "That's what makes it fun."

He bit his tongue and paid the driver, then started toward the club entrance with Constance on his arm. Lively piano music could be heard, and after paying the entrance fee at the door, the music hall tune wrapped around them as they stepped inside. It was an assembly room of sorts, with an open dance floor surrounded by a perimeter of tables. They were all occupied, as was the main floor, where couples danced arm in arm. This was no stiff waltz. The couples moved quickly, twirling and spinning, all of them looking like drunken miscreants.

Jasper's feet turned to lead as Constance wended her way toward a long, glossy bar. Patrons swarmed here too, but at least they weren't dancing.

"Isn't it marvelous?" she said after he'd ordered a whisky and one of the flaming drinks she'd mentioned. Jasper rested an elbow on the bar, his eyes peeled on the crowd. Men and women mingled freely, most of them young, and from their styles of dress, they looked to be from a range of classes.

"It's certainly spirited," he said, sipping his drink. No amount of liquor, however, would tempt him onto the dance floor.

Constance bumped his arm with her shoulder. "Try not to look so much like a policeman."

He grunted. It wasn't exactly something he could refrain from. After becoming a plainclothes detective and no longer needing to wear the standard blue uniform and custodian helmet, his father had joked that he now looked even more like a copper. *"That's because you have the heart of a policeman, my boy,"* he'd added with a proud nod.

The bartender lit Constance's drink aflame, and she and a few others around them squealed and laughed at the bit of theatre. As the blue flash receded, Jasper's eyes landed on a familiar face.

Across the dance floor, Miss Nivedita Brooks sat at a table, smiling and conversing. A couple on the dance floor twirled out of his range of vision and revealed Leo sitting beside Miss Brooks. Jasper lowered his whisky glass. The two women were close friends, so he wasn't surprised to see them together. But he hadn't expected to find them in a place like this.

They weren't alone. A curious friction scrambled through Jasper's veins as he recognized two men in their presence. PC Lloyd and PC Drake were out of uniform, but they still had the squared shoulders, straight spines, and clean-cut look of police constables.

"Did you know she would be here?" Constance asked. She'd followed his stare as she sipped her drink, the flames now fully extinguished.

"You chose this club, not I," he reminded her. She pursed her lips, her merriment tempered.

For the next few minutes, Jasper sipped his drink and endeavored not to drag his eyes in Leo's direction. The few times that he failed, however, he noted the differences in her appearance. Her dress, for one, was not a somber gray or blue, as she typically wore to the morgue. She wore a bustled gown of vivid emerald silk, trimmed with black lace. Her dark hair, usually in a low, plain knot, had been braided and swept up into a soft twist, leaving a few sable tendrils loose to frame her face. What wasn't different was her serious mien. While Miss Brooks and the two constables smiled and laughed, Leo sipped a glass of wine with a pensive expression, appearing distant from their animated conversation.

By all accounts, it looked as if she wanted to be at the club less than Jasper did.

The piano softened and slowed its pace, while a few violins joined in to play a waltz. Miss Brooks accepted the hand of PC Lloyd, and they moved onto the dance floor. Leo and PC Drake sat in silence, with Drake angling himself toward her as if to make conversation.

"Would you at least consent to a waltz?" Constance asked, breaking Jasper's concentration.

"If I knew how to waltz, I would," he answered.

"No, you wouldn't," she replied, and he grinned. She was right; he wouldn't. It was true, though, that he didn't know how to dance. It wasn't something his father had ever thought to teach him.

"I suppose you want to say hello to Miss Spencer," Constance said just as the constable placed his hand atop Leo's on the table. He leaned closer to speak into her ear. Leo fixed her attention on his hand, her posture stiffening.

"It would only be polite," Jasper said and, with his arm at Constance's back, led her in the direction of Leo's table. They skirted the dancers and some others milling about in the crowd.

Jasper had no idea what he was going to say beyond hello, but his feet wouldn't stop moving. He was several paces away from the table when Leo's eyes clapped onto him. Her hand was no longer on the table or covered by Drake's, and she'd moved her chair away from him. Now, her eyes rounded, and her lips popped open in surprise. They sealed again when she saw Constance.

"Detective Inspector," the constable exclaimed, standing to attention. Jasper acknowledged him with a nod, pleased by his alarmed reaction.

"This is the last place I imagined I'd see you," Leo said in greeting. She aimed a tense smile toward Constance. "Miss Hayes, how do you do?"

"I'd be much better if Jasper knew the waltz," she replied, hooking his arm again.

"Witnessing him dance the waltz would certainly be worth the price of admission," Leo said, then seemed to realize the constable was still with them. "Oh, I should introduce Constable Marcus Drake. Constable, this is Miss Constance Hayes."

After an awkward moment in which Constance smiled thinly but avoided looking at Drake directly, Jasper raised his voice above the music. "Why did you imagine I wouldn't be in a place like this?"

"Because of the person who owns it," she answered.

He clenched his teeth. "And who might that be?"

Miss Brooks and the other constable joined them then. PC Lloyd also jumped to attention, and both men now stood rigidly, their expressions masks of fright, as if awaiting orders—or a reprimand. Jasper suppressed a smug grin.

"Inspector Reid! Goodness, it's odd to see you here," Miss Brooks said, breathless from her dance.

"As I've been told." He shifted his attention back to Leo. "Just who owns this club?"

"Ladies, gents." A man stepped into their circle, his welcoming smile as smooth as his voice. "I see too many frowns at this table. What seems to be the problem?"

"Mr. Bloom, how good of you to join us." Miss Brooks pasted on a sparkling, if ingenuine, smile.

Bloom. *Eddie* Bloom. Jasper gave the middle-aged man standing with them all his focus. He was a few inches shorter than Jasper, but he was scrappy and streetwise. For good reason: Bloom headed a small syndicate on the riverfront, his dealings mostly in cargo, shipping, and prostitution. He was small beer compared to the East Rips, but he was trouble just the same.

And apparently, he operated this assembly hall.

"Bobbies always bring the mood down," Bloom said, giving Jasper a top-to-bottom gander and a disappointed shake of his head. A man like Bloom knew a policeman when he saw one. "Want me to get rid of him, ladies?"

Jasper shifted his footing, facing Bloom squarely with a clear challenge to try his luck.

"Oh, no, please, we're having a lovely time," Miss Brooks said with a nervous laugh. She glared at Leo. "Aren't we?"

"Yes, lovely."

At her placid tone, Bloom quizzed her with an assessing look. Then, furrowing his brow, he turned his inspection back onto Jasper. "It seems you've been exonerated, constable."

"Detective Inspector."

At this, Bloom laughed. "Detective Inspector. My, my. Are you on official business then? Or—," he took Constance's hand and bowed over it, his dark eyes never leaving hers, "—are you a copper of good taste, taking his lady out for a pleasant evening?"

Constance simpered and allowed Bloom to bow over her hand another moment before retracting it.

Jasper hardened his expression. To frequent an establishment owned by a criminal was to send the message that he was open to giving and accepting favors. Plenty of men on the force did so, supplementing their income by forming friendships and alliances with the less-than-savory citizens they were meant to police. But Jasper was not inclined, and he never would be. Bloom hadn't offered to toss out the two constables, and so Jasper had to wonder if they were already in his pocket.

After leaving Bloom dangling for a few moments, he replied, "We came for a drink, and now, we're leaving." Constance huffed and began to argue, but Jasper spoke over her. "These two were just telling me that they were about to bring Miss Spencer and Miss Brooks home too. Isn't that right, constables?"

Drake's pupils sharpened, and his facial muscles twitched with alarm, while Lloyd stammered out, "Yes, sir. That's right, sir." Leo and Miss Brooks exchanged vexed glances. They knew exactly what he was doing and that he had no remorse for it. There wasn't a chance in hell he was going to leave Striker's Wharf without Leo directly behind him, especially now that he knew the assembly hall was operated by Eddie Bloom.

At Jasper's side, Constance released his arm but said nothing as Bloom tipped his hat and bid them a good evening. As soon as he'd sauntered off, she whirled away, in the direction of the exit. Jasper cut the constables a firm glare.

"Get them out of here," he said.

"We can remove ourselves perfectly well, inspector," Leo said. "After we finish our drinks."

She took a slow sip of her wine, daring him to argue. He would have, had Constance not been about to walk out on her own. He had to go after her—the wharves weren't any place for a lady. Hell, what had she been thinking to even bring him here?

He gave Leo one last glare and then turned on his heel.

Chapter Twelve

Leo was grateful when, not five minutes after Jasper and Miss Hayes departed, Constable Drake and Dita's beau, Constable Lloyd, suggested rather strongly that they leave Bloom's club. It was one of Dita's favorite places for a night out, but as much as Leo enjoyed listening to the music and watching the dancers on the floor—whom she never joined—she hadn't been overly thrilled when John had shown up with his fellow officer in tow.

"I thought you might like the company for once," Dita had explained earlier when the two men had gone to fetch them drinks. "I'm always dancing with John and leaving you here at the table, alone."

"I like being alone," had been Leo's ill-mannered response, and though Dita didn't believe her, it was true. She'd have much rather sat alone while everyone else danced and laughed than endure Constable Drake's discomfiting comments and glances. He'd asked too many questions about the morgue and her duties there, and his attention had drifted from her hair to her bosom to her obscured ankles.

She'd had the sinking feeling all evening that Drake was the sort of officer who found her pretty, but strange. Leo wasn't blind to the looks of interest she received from some of the men at Scotland Yard, most of them new to the uniform. However, once they learned who she was and where she spent her days, most of them inevitably stopped paying her attention. Others continued their interest, though mostly, they were interested in her eccentricity, in her not being like the other women of their acquaintance. It had taken one overly forward sergeant the previous spring for her to see the truth clearly: because they did not think her conventional, they might also believe she would allow liberties when other, more ladylike women would never dream of it. She had set that sergeant right, crushing the bridge of his foot under her bootheel, and ever since, he'd given her a wide berth.

Constable Drake had pulled his chair too closely, and after he'd dared settle his hand upon hers, she'd quickly peeled it out from underneath his sweaty palm. Had he attempted it again, Leo would have employed the tines of her fork to deter him. She'd almost been relieved to see Jasper and Miss Hayes approaching their table—even with Jasper looking as if he'd swallowed a brazier full of glowing coals.

Now, after Lloyd and Drake had seen Dita and Leo off in a hansom outside Mr. Bloom's club, Dita threw up her hands. "Why would that silly woman bring a detective to a criminal's club?"

Though Leo didn't care much for Constance, she

defended her. "She probably had no idea who Mr. Bloom was or that he owned it."

Most likely, she'd read about the flaming blue drinks that had been featured in one of the issues of the *Illustrated London News*. After a woodcut print depicting the bartender making the drink ran in the popular weekly paper, Striker's Wharf had been overrun with ladies and men from more affluent parts of London.

"At least we can be at ease knowing Inspector Reid won't ever return," Dita said. Then, with a crinkle of her pert nose, she apologized for arranging for Constable Drake to come.

"The next time John wants to bring a friend, I'll ask you first," she added. "You might get on better with someone who *isn't* a police officer."

Leo murmured her agreement but wished her friend would let it rest. Dita, two years younger than her, was eager to marry and start a family. Her civilian position as a matron at the Yard was only temporary, until she wed. Though she was patient with Leo's lack of interest in romance and marriage, she refused to give up trying to find a suitor for her. But Leo was too busy to think about romance, what with Claude's tremors, Flora's addled mind, and the Inspector's illness.

Leo called for the hansom driver to stop at Trafalgar Square and, after saying goodnight to her friend, walked to the morgue. There was no pressing reason for her to be there at this time of night, but after their call on Mr. Barrett earlier in the day, she'd been unable to stop stewing over the many complicated pieces of a puzzle that may, or may not, fit together. Jasper didn't want her involved, but her brain wouldn't allow the confounding case to rest.

All afternoon, she'd alternated between typing notes and staring at Clarence Stillman's dead body, impatient for Claude to return so they could perform the postmortem. Her uncle managed a brief stop near the end of the day, while Flora took a nap and a neighbor, Mrs. Gareth, agreed to keep an eye out for her. But there hadn't been time for the postmortem.

Leo's mind was still humming and restless. If she returned home to Duke Street now, she wouldn't be able to sleep for hours yet. It would be a better use of her time to finish typing some reports, organize the files on her desk, or do some cleaning...anything to tire herself.

The back door to the morgue faced the gardens and burial ground behind St. Matthew's Church, and Leo fetched her key from her handbag as she approached. It was still a bit early for Mr. Sampson, the night attendant, to have arrived for his shift. He usually spent it sleeping at the desk, his boots propped up on the blotter—Leo had never caught him doing so, but the dirt and debris left behind were evidence. It would be a terribly dull job; if any corpses were delivered overnight, all Mr. Sampson needed to do was admit the body and leave it for the coroner. Then, he could return to his slumber.

However, as she reached for the handle, she saw a gap between the door and the frame. It was already open by an inch.

"Mr. Sampson?"

Leo stepped inside. But the back room was dark. Mr. Sampson would have at least turned on one of the gas wall brackets had he been there. With a knot of doubt in her stomach, she walked into the raw cold of the post-mortem room next. Stained-glass windows, relics from when the morgue had been a church vestry, let in some moonlight. Leo had never been frightened of the morgue or the prospect of dead bodies, but in the low light, the sheeted bodies lain out on tables were a bit eerie.

She'd most certainly closed and locked the doors when she'd left. She'd had to have done. It was habit now, routine. But then again, the day had been an odd one. From Claude being unable to perform the postmortem on Mr. Stillman, to her argument with Jasper in the carriage, to the unsettling discovery of the peephole in Miss Barrett's bedroom, Leo had to admit, her mind had been preoccupied.

She crossed the room to the turn on the gasoliers overhead. The hiss of the gas was loud in the quiet, but not loud enough to muffle the familiar groan of a rusty hinge on the back door. Leo twisted toward the office. She had shut the door behind her, of that she was absolutely certain. Swallowing a knob in her throat, she returned to the office. The back door was again open to the moonlight. She hurried outside to the dirt lane that ran between the morgue and the small burial ground out back. In a break of clouds, the clear moonlight—a rare thing on a London winter's night when coal chimneys pumped smoke into the air—showed a figure running through the grounds, between ancient headstones. It disappeared when the clouds knitted back together again. Her heart pounded. Someone had been inside the morgue when she'd arrived, hidden in the office. They'd waited until she was in the other room to make their escape.

Movement in her side vision spiked her pulse again. At

the head of the dirt lane, another figure was walking toward her. But this one, she recognized.

"Jasper?"

"I saw the lamps on," he said. "Why are you out here at this late hour?"

She jumped as Tibia raced from the burial ground, through the open back door, and into the office. The tabby must have snuck out earlier, when the door had been left ajar.

"Leo?" Jasper touched her elbow, calling her attention when she still hadn't answered.

"I…" She didn't want to tell him. Knew he would only overreact. But she also couldn't keep it a secret. "There was someone in the morgue when I arrived. He must have broken in by picking the lock. I didn't see who it was, but he took off running, that way." She waved a hand toward the church's burial ground.

As expected, Jasper started forward into the graveyard, as if he planned to rush after the intruder.

"He's gone," she said to stop him. "And if he wanted to harm me, he could have. If it even was a man. I only saw a black outline."

Jasper relented and ushered her back into the office. She turned on the wall brackets this time.

"Is anything missing?" he asked, sounding just as furious as he'd been at the club.

"No." Things looked the same as she'd left them earlier. "But don't you think it a bit coincidental that the night Mr. Stillman's body is lying in repose in this morgue, there is another break-in?"

Jasper, still dressed in his evening clothes, tugged at his ascot to loosen it. "Damn it, Leo."

"Don't be angry with me. I didn't invite him in!"

"I'm not angry with you." He rolled his shoulders, attempting to calm himself. "I would just like to know what in hell is going on."

He stormed into the postmortem room, and after closing and locking the back door this time, Leo followed.

"Mr. Stillman is just as I left him," she said. The sheet covering him was still perfectly smooth.

"All of his belongings are at the Yard, so there is nothing the intruder could have taken from him," Jasper noted. "Though, it's possible someone believed his possessions would still be here."

He circled the table, crossing his arms over the breadth of his chest and glaring at the covered body, as if hoping he could determine something more from it. Underneath his open frock coat, he wore a fine black wool suit, complete with a silk waistcoat, a high collar shirt, and an ascot. She'd noticed the suit at Striker's Wharf. It was different from the one he'd worn the previous evening, and Leo wondered how many he owned.

"Where is Miss Hayes?"

"I brought her home." He shifted his glare onto her. "And no, she had no clue that club was owned by a crime lord. You, on the other hand, cannot claim such ignorance."

Leo shrugged. "The music is superb, and Dita loves to dance. There's never been any trouble at Mr. Bloom's club while I was there."

"There is always a first time for everything," he retorted with a shake of his head as he kept circling the body. "The Inspector would have a lot to say about it if he knew."

It was petty and annoying for him to bring his father up. "And you're going to snitch and tell him?"

"No, of course not. He's better off thinking the most illicit thing you've ever done is sip cherry cordial before dinner. So am I, for that matter."

She laughed. "Going to a club is hardly illicit. Besides, coming over when you did was good timing, even if you were sour."

He stopped circling the table and faced her, brow taut. "Was Constable Drake giving you any trouble?"

"No, not really. He was only being…" She stopped herself from saying *too forward*, as she wasn't sure how Jasper would react. "Tedious."

He grunted and then turned back toward the sheeted corpse.

"What did you find on William Carter's housebreak?" she asked, hoping to move away from their run-in at the club.

"The rooms had all been turned over, as if the thieves had been looking for something," he answered gamely. It surprised her. She'd been certain he would continue to tell her to mind her own business.

"Housebreakers? There was more than one?"

"A witness saw two men hurrying away from the home in a suspicious manner. She couldn't see them well enough to describe them, but they gave her a bad feeling, and when she checked on Carter's welfare…" He shrugged. "Found him dead among the wreckage."

"So, there is no evidence they robbed Mr. Carter," she said. "Just that they were furiously looking for something."

Jasper nodded. "As there have been a few home

burglaries in that area over the last few months, the police presumed it was a standard housebreaking."

Leo sighed. "And I imagine the fact that the victim was a Carter weighed against their decision to investigate further."

Just as Commissioner Vickers had advised be done with Mr. Stillman's case. Why waste resources on the death of a criminal when there were innocent victims more deserving of police time and effort?

"That is my guess." Jasper stepped away from the table, wandering toward the stained-glass windows. Images on the leaded panes depicted a battle scene from the Bible. Some book and verse that Leo had never studied. As Claude was Jewish, she'd not gone to church after coming to living with him and Flora, and he wasn't active at synagogue either.

"According to the death report, Carter was shot in the chest," Jasper said, glancing back at her over his shoulder.

Leo stood at attention. It was where Mr. Stillman had been shot. "The same killer?"

"Possibly. I'd like to look at the bullet collected by the coroner who worked on Carter and compare it to the one in Stillman. I need the postmortem completed. Will Claude be here tomorrow?"

Leo bit her bottom lip and nodded. She would have to stay with Flora and endure her accusing glares and screams of terror, but it couldn't be helped. Her uncle needed to work. She only hoped he would be able to control the tremors in his hands for the procedure. As usual, frustration gripped her. If only she could perform postmortems herself. She'd observed them countless times and had read the texts her uncle had given her more than once. But she couldn't, and she wouldn't put her uncle's position at risk to prove a point.

"Have you found anyone to claim Mr. Stillman's body?" she asked.

"Not yet. Lewis is working on it. When we do, we'll have a better idea of who Stillman might have been associating with after his release from Wandsworth."

Jasper took his fob from his waistcoat pocket and checked the time. It had to be nearing ten o'clock, and the night attendant would be arriving soon. "Are you certain nothing is missing?"

"Nothing obvious at least. Why?"

"I can't help but think this new intruder was here for something having to do with Stillman. The man hunts down Hannah Barrett, possibly chasing her into the street where she is struck and killed. Then, he steals the locket from her body and makes his way to Duck Island, where he is killed. But there's no trace of the locket anywhere. A locket that had inside it a mysterious message that Mr. Carter gave to Hannah for safekeeping the night before he died."

Leo was gratified, and relieved, to hear Jasper finally accepting that there was something complicated at play among the three separate deaths.

"Do you think Mr. Stillman was hired to steal the locket?" she asked.

"He was no mastermind, if his file was correct about him. So yes, I think he must have been." Jasper came back toward the table. "He took the locket and brought it to Duck Island, where he'd arranged to meet someone."

"The person who hired him?"

Jasper nodded. "Precisely."

"A person with a walking stick," Leo added, thinking of the many impressions in the ground around the body. But Jasper grimaced his doubt.

"Not necessarily. Mr. Gates, the bird keeper, had a cane. I think he went through Stillman's pockets before summoning the police."

"So maybe he has the locket? We should go to his cottage," Leo said, eager to be off. It was late, but perhaps that was the best time to catch someone out in a lie. Startling him from his bed at a late hour could be to their benefit.

Jasper held up his palm. "No, I don't think Gates does. Whoever killed Stillman would have taken the locket, if it was on his person. And we don't need the locket anyhow. We know what was in it."

That did make more sense. Leo sighed out of frustration. "If Mr. Stillman did as he was hired to do, then why was he killed?"

An answer came to her as soon as she'd posed the question. Jasper, too, for they both spoke at the same time.

"He didn't hand it over," he said, just as Leo said, "He tried asking for more money."

They both smiled, though the expression was a strange feeling on her lips. Jasper, too, rarely grinned, and she noted the inward turn of one of his top incisors. They both became serious again.

"What if he kept the piece of paper, which must have been what the killer was after?" Leo mused.

Jasper continued with her theory. "Stillman knows he has something valuable and asks for more money. The killer decides he's not worth it. Shoots him, then searches the body for the paper, but when he doesn't find it—"

"He comes to the morgue tonight, thinking Mr. Stillman's possessions are still here, and maybe he'll have another, more thorough look?"

If that were true, then she'd been in close quarters with a killer. He could have easily attacked her the moment she walked into the dark office. But he hadn't. Instead, he'd run away.

"If any part of our harebrained theory is correct, and it likely isn't," Jasper said, "then the question remains: Where is the paper? If it wasn't in Stillman's pockets or in the locket, where did he put it?"

If his demands for more money had been met, he'd have needed to produce it quickly—*if* that was the scenario.

Leo viewed the sheeted body again. Underneath, Mr. Stillman was as naked as the day he was born. In a postmortem, he would have been thoroughly examined, but that had not yet happened. An idea spiraled into her mind, one that was too simple, too obvious to be correct, surely. But Leo still reached for the sheet and drew it back. The man's ashen face seemed to exacerbate the lines of age on his skin. He'd led a rough, likely thankless life. But he'd been crafty. He'd needed to be to survive.

"There is a place I might hide something at the last minute," she said. "Especially if I thought my pockets might be turned out."

She stepped away from the table and went to the shelves along the wall that held Claude's tools. Leo took up a clean pair of vulcanized rubber gloves.

"What are you doing?" Jasper asked, sounding wary.

"Nothing illegal, I assure you."

Carefully, she inserted a gloved finger into Mr. Stillman's mouth and pressed down on his bottom teeth to unhinge his jaw. She took shallow breaths through her mouth rather than her nose, as the corpse's unwashed body had already been fragrant and had now turned more so as necrosis advanced.

As she glanced up at Jasper, his twisted grimace caught her off her guard. They'd been so freely discussing theories that she'd imagined he'd still be intrigued. Instead, he seemed appalled to see her handling a dead body. Leo clamped down on a sudden surge of hurt and focused on what she was doing. She lifted the tongue—and the muscles along her shoulders and spine tingled with victory.

The small, folded piece of paper rested underneath.

Chapter Thirteen

January 15 arrived the next morning with a tactless amount of sunlight. The middle of January tended to be bleak and cold, and sometimes rainy, which would have better suited the mood at 23 Charles Street. Jasper's mood, too. He'd stayed up half the night trying to determine what the wording on the scrap of paper might mean in conjunction with William Carter's instruction to Hannah Barrett to 'dig it up'.

The writing itself on the paper had hardly been legible after being underneath Stillman's tongue for so long. Just so Jasper wouldn't forget, Leo wrote it down for him again: *Strange Nun B17 R4.*

"Why are you looking at me like that?" she'd asked as she handed him the new paper. He hadn't realized he was looking at her in any way at all.

"Your mind fascinates me." He'd been slightly embarrassed by his honesty when she'd blushed.

"It is two words and a short number and letter combination. Easy enough for anyone to recall," she'd replied.

Leo never flaunted her perfect memory. At least, not since the time he'd been home from boarding school at Cheltenham for the holidays, and Leo had recited an entire scene, word-for-word, from Charles Dickens's *A Christmas Carol* for the Inspector after supper one evening.

"I just gave you that book this morning!" his father had exclaimed, laughing.

That Jasper had brought home gloriously terrible marks in every subject that quarter, her display had only rubbed salt in his wounded pride.

As Jasper dressed at Broadview Place, a former private home on Glasshouse Street that had been turned into bachelor's rooms, a knot grew in the pit of his stomach. He'd have to find time that day to speak to Constance and smooth things over. They'd parted badly the evening before, after a tense drive back to her rooms. Her annoyance with him, however, had only spurred his anger.

"You were incredibly rude to that man," she'd said.

"*That man* is Eddie Bloom."

"I don't know who that is."

"You work at *The Times*, Constance. How do you not know Bloom's name?"

"I type the society pages!"

"You're telling me you never read the rest of the paper?"

She'd looked at him the same way she had the few times he'd discussed details of cases with her—appalled. "Why would I want to read the rest of the paper?"

He'd been lost for words after that. If he sought Constance out later that day, she'd likely expect an apology. The trouble was, he didn't agree she was owed one.

Jasper pushed the muddle aside when he arrived at the Inspector's home. As he reached for the brass knocker, the knowledge that this would be Gregory Reid's final January 15 gripped him with clarity. Profound sadness brimmed inside his chest, but for months now, Jasper had chosen not to acknowledge it. He wouldn't acknowledge it today either. Today belonged to the Inspector.

He greeted Mrs. Zhao, who took his coat and hat with a sad smile. "Mr. Reid is with Sir Nathaniel and Miss Vickers in the dining room. They're expecting you."

It had slipped Jasper's mind that the commissioner mentioned the possibility of a visit this morning. Elsie Vickers was bright, lively, and often candid, and she never failed to charm the Inspector. Jasper was glad they'd come, but when he reached the dining room, he saw they were already on their way out. And Elsie wasn't bright or lively at all.

As he met Sir Nathaniel and his daughter just outside the dining room door, he noticed Elsie's red-rimmed eyes and her mouth set in a dejected pout.

"Ah, Jasper, I'm glad to catch you." The commissioner clapped him on the shoulder with a warm familiarity that he never displayed at Scotland Yard. It was only in this house where he addressed him by his given name. Favoritism wasn't smiled upon inside the Met, and Jasper was grateful Sir Nathaniel was of the same mind.

"How is that strange case of the morgue intruder and the missing necklace coming along?" he asked.

Jasper wished Leo hadn't said anything about it. With more questions than he had answers, he didn't feel ready to present anything just yet. And when he did, he would take the information to Chief Inspector Coughlan, not the commissioner.

"Nothing illuminating," Jasper answered. "Detective Sergeant Lewis sent a message this morning saying he's found Stillman's wife, so we'll at least inform her of his death. She might know something more about his movements the night he died."

"Very good, keep me informed."

Jasper nodded, casting another glance toward Elsie. She stared at the carpet.

"Miss Vickers, is something wrong?" he asked, concerned by her sullen silence. This wasn't like her in the least.

She looked up but only briefly met his eyes. "Wrong? Oh. No, I… I'm sorry, I…"

"Elsie is upset. She didn't expect Gregory's decline to be so pronounced," her father cut in when she stumbled to find words. She nodded and again stared at the floor.

"Jasper." Sir Nathaniel lowered his voice. "If there is anything you require in the coming days or weeks, I am at your service. I've just been through all this with my uncle, so call on me. I'm here."

A sudden tightness around his Adam's apple surprised Jasper. Sir Nathaniel gave his shoulder a firm press. The commissioner's robust health only highlighted his father's ill health. They were just a year apart, with the commissioner being the elder. The several doctors that had come to evaluate the Inspector since last spring all agreed that his lungs were afflicted with a cancer and that it had weakened the functioning of his heart. They'd also agreed there was nothing to be done for it.

"You've been a good friend to him." Jasper cleared the

rasping of his words with a cough. He tried to regain Elsie's attention. "Both of you have been."

It didn't work. She still wouldn't look at him.

Sir Nathaniel smiled sadly. "And you've been a good son."

As the commissioner and his daughter left for the front hall, Jasper felt the same roiling of his gut whenever someone referred to him as Gregory's son. An uneasy guilt.

When Jasper had been fourteen, just one year after accepting the invitation to be his ward, the Inspector had decided that it would be in Jasper's best interest to attend a boy's school. Though Viscount Cowper had rescinded the dowry that his daughter, Emmaline, had brought to her marriage—a legal, if bitter, act—the Inspector had insisted that he had enough set by and could afford it. Jasper hadn't wanted to go. The local school would do just fine, he'd insisted. But the Inspector had flatly refused, saying he'd planned to send his late son, Gregory Junior, and there was no reason Jasper deserved any less of an education.

"Things would be easier for you at Cheltenham if you possessed a surname," he'd told Jasper one evening at dinner.

He hadn't wanted to attend any starchy school, where he'd be surrounded by milksops who hadn't known a moment of struggle their whole pampered lives. He'd have nothing in common with them, that was certain. Yet, at the same time, he'd recognized an opportunity.

"I don't know it, even if I do have one," Jasper had said. He'd stuck with that fib since day one, and he hadn't wavered.

"Then may I suggest Reid?"

The weight of the offer, the consequence of it, had settled keenly on his shoulders even then. He'd said no, at first, immediately thinking of little Gregory Junior, who held proper claim to the Reid name. Had he and his sister and mother not gone skating on the sunny day of the ice disaster, the Inspector wouldn't have been offering to give Jasper his name. He wouldn't have been in his life at all.

But Gregory Junior was dead. So was the person that Jasper had been before going to live with the Inspector. He'd hoped that by taking the Reid name, he would feel more like a son to him. Instead, he'd felt even more like a fraud. At twenty-nine, he still did at times.

Jasper entered the dining room to find his father at his usual spot at the head of the table. Two additional settings had been laid to his left and his right. One for Jasper, the other for Leo.

"I thought I heard you and Nathaniel conspiring out there," he said, his fork and knife in hand as he ate his kippers and toast. "I offered, but they wouldn't stay for breakfast."

"Good morning, Father," he said as he went to the sideboard.

"It is a good morning, indeed."

Jasper halted briefly as he started to fill a plate. "I don't think I've ever heard you say that on this day before."

He chuckled. "I like to think I have a few surprises left in me."

Jasper took his usual seat to his father's left and spread a napkin over his lap, eyeing the Inspector. "It seems you do."

He poured himself some coffee from a carafe, then refilled his father's cup.

"Thank you." He then puckered his brow. "Nathaniel just announced the most surprising thing. Elsie is to be betrothed."

Jasper lowered his cup. He'd presumed the young lady's miserable state had been from seeing the Inspector and realizing he would soon be leaving them. However, that didn't make much sense now. His father was in unusually high spirits, after all.

"Betrothed to whom?" Jasper asked.

His father arched a stern brow. "Benjamin Munson, if you can believe it."

The idea of it threatened to sunder Jasper's appetite. Sir Nathaniel's deputy assistant was at least twenty years Elsie's senior.

"I'm not sure what to make of that," Jasper said honestly. Munson was quiet, respectful, and by all accounts, an effective assistant to Sir Nathaniel. But as a match for Elsie?

"She's quite young to be betrothed," his father said, sipping his coffee. "But I suppose Emmaline wasn't much older than she is when we fell in love and decided to marry."

A gentle grin touched his lips as he lowered his cup. He sat back and set aside the soft memory. "Anyhow, Nathaniel says the man who broke into the morgue is dead?"

"I don't want to talk about work," Jasper replied. "I'd rather know why you're so cheery."

"I'd hardly say I'm that." He grimaced, and Jasper regretted his comment.

"That was insensitive. I'm sorry."

His father waved it off. "No, you've only noticed a change in me. And I must admit, I do feel differently today than I have in the past. I woke up this morning and realized something." He laid down his fork and knife. "I'm not afraid."

The statement lingered in the ensuing silence. Jasper wasn't sure how to respond. That he was glad his father wasn't afraid of that final breath? That knowing so put him at ease, at least a little bit?

"I had another revelation this morning upon waking," his father continued. "It had to do with you."

"With me?"

"There is something I need to tell you before Leonora arrives." He turned in his chair to face Jasper more fully. "Something I need to confess."

Jasper's appetite shriveled in earnest now. "That sounds serious."

His father hesitated. Then, after a long exhalation, he said, "I know that you lied."

Jasper didn't move. He didn't breathe. He just stared, unblinking, as his pulse began to knock in his neck.

"I'm not angry," the Inspector added quickly. "I know why you did it."

"Father—"

He raised a hand to silence him, and Jasper obeyed.

"A few weeks after you were brought to the Yard, and I offered you work as an errand boy," he began to explain, "a woman came to the detective department. Her nephew was missing, and she wanted us to find him."

Numbness stole up Jasper's spine, rendering the rest of his body immobile.

"There'd been a row between her husband and the boy, and after a serious beating, the boy had done a runner. They'd let him be for a week, to cool off, or so she said. Once her husband calmed, they'd looked for the boy, though without luck. Her husband refused to go to the police. So, defying him, she'd made the trip and was asking for our help."

Shallow breaths were all Jasper's lungs could accommodate. His father sat back in his chair and drummed the table with his fingers.

"You were shrewd to conceal your name," he said with a hint of pride. "But you couldn't conceal your face, could you?"

Jasper closed his eyes. "She brought a photograph."

The Inspector nodded. "She did."

Jasper knew the one it would have been. A tintype of him at age ten that his mother had kept on the night table next to her bed. When she'd died, his aunt Myra had placed it among the portraits already lining her own hearth mantel, shuffled in amongst his cousins. Just as he had been. Aunt Myra hadn't been awful; she'd just been married to a brute—a man she'd always defend.

"Why didn't you hand me over?" Jasper could hardly look the Inspector in the eye.

His father stopped drumming the table and laid his fingers flat. With an oddly serene tone, he answered, "Because I knew who her husband was."

Unblinking, Jasper stared at the man adjacent to him. He nearly seemed a stranger. He'd known. All this time, all these years Jasper had buried his secrets, had kept his story straight and consistent, and the Inspector had *known*. Weightless in his chair, he thought he might be hallucinating. Dreaming. He half-hoped he was.

"What…" His voice cut off, but he tried again. "What did you tell her?"

Before, the Inspector had looked almost impish. Now, a frown turned his lips downward, accentuating the lines bracketing his mouth.

"Do you remember when I took you to the tailor for your new clothing?"

How could Jasper forget? He'd been measured and maneuvered and dressed like a doll while he stood on a small stool, the whole time so certain he was going to hate wearing the clothes of a toff. But he couldn't be an errand boy for an inspector while wearing his own rags, the hems two inches too short after he'd so recently shot up like a stalk. In the end, the new clothes had fit like a glove. They had been the finest things he'd ever felt against his skin.

"You asked where your old clothes had gone," his father said.

Jasper recalled, especially the spate of panic when he realized he'd left his grandmother's rosary in one of his pockets. Losing it had been a blow. It had been one of the last times that he'd felt the sting of tears. "You told me you burned them."

"I didn't burn them," his father whispered. "I took them to the Yard, and I assigned them to a cadaver. A boy with dark blond hair, about your weight and height, had been pulled from the Thames. He'd bloated badly over the week he'd been in the water, so when your aunt came to view the body, she couldn't recognize you. It was the clothing and the rosary, which she knew to be yours, that convinced her."

Jasper melted into the chair as shock loosened every muscle. The cunning didn't stun him; the Inspector was one of the smartest, sharpest men he'd ever met. It was the deception that bowled him over. It wasn't like Gregory Reid at all, or so he'd thought.

"Why did you never say anything?" Jasper asked.

He lifted a knobby shoulder, decimated by ill health. "I was ashamed. I betrayed my conscience and went against the law. I lied to your aunt and dashed her hopes of finding you. All because..." His guilt practically radiated from him as his spine bowed, as if all his years were stacking on, quick and heavy. "I thought you'd leave if you knew she was looking for you. I am sorry, Jasper. I was selfish—"

"You were trying to protect me."

"I told myself that."

Jasper sat forward, no longer stunned numb. "I ran away for a reason. I wasn't going back. Even if you hadn't done what you did, I wasn't going back."

The Inspector had to have known that, especially if he'd known who Aunt Myra's husband was.

"Can you forgive me?" he asked. Jasper shook his head.

"There is nothing to forgive."

The Inspector's eyes glistened. "I'm a proud father." He sniffled but blinked back the tears. "I hope you know that."

For the first time, Jasper knew, unswervingly, that he wasn't thinking of Gregory Junior.

The clicking of footfalls on the parquet floor sounded outside the dining room entrance. Jasper and the

Inspector had just a few moments to sit straight and clear the emotion from their expressions before Leo entered.

She seemed to sense that she'd walked in on a serious conversation, and she held still. "I'm interrupting."

The Inspector rose from his chair as rapidly as his frail body would allow. "Not at all. We were starting to wonder where you were. Coffee?"

She came forward. "No, thank you, I've already breakfasted."

Passing on Mrs. Zhao's cooking was slightly concerning, and Jasper wondered if the morning had been a trying one with her aunt.

"Would you like some company to Kensal Green?" she asked, as if she did not come with them every year as it was.

Jasper set the napkin back onto the table, his breakfast untouched. She was right; it would be best to get underway before the day took its inevitable toll on his father.

"Indeed, I would," he said, draining the last of his coffee. "Let us be off then, shall we?"

Chapter Fourteen

They arrived at the cemetery just under an hour later. The ride in the hired coach had been mostly quiet, with the Inspector's attention distracted as he gazed through the window. Leo could understand his silence, though she wasn't certain he was only thinking about his late wife and children. She'd interrupted something in the dining room when she'd entered; there had been a shine in both the Inspector's and Jasper's eyes that she was accustomed to seeing in those who came to the morgue to view their loved ones. They'd been having an important conversation, and she wished she hadn't trodden upon it.

As they'd wended the roads north of Hyde Park, the Inspector attempted to pull himself from his reverie by asking about the dead morgue intruder. After a fleeting glimpse toward Jasper, Leo decided not to mention anything about the paper found underneath Mr. Stillman's tongue. Today was not the day to introduce a fine mystery. There was an intensity to this visit to Kensal Green. This time last year, the Inspector had not been ill.

He'd been a man in his early fifties who still believed he had a few decades to endure before meeting with his beloved family again. Now, that had changed. He was closer to them than he'd been before.

The parklike cemetery was one of the Magnificent Seven, a fashionable place to be interred, and as the daughter of a viscount, Emmaline and her children had been buried in a section where they were surrounded by relatives. The Inspector used a cane as they walked over the wide dirt lanes cutting through the plots, with headstones, mausoleums, and statues, all spread out around them in blocks bordered by trees and hedgerows. Leo and Jasper stayed a few steps behind him. The Inspector wanted their company, but he also enjoyed his solitude when visiting the graves.

"Claude will perform the postmortem this morning," she said softly to Jasper. "Our neighbor, Mrs. Gareth, offered to sit with Flora."

"That's kind of her."

"It is, especially since the whole street has heard her screaming blue murder lately."

She half-wondered if they suspected her and Claude of abuse. Or worse, if they would grow weary of Flora's screams and call for a police officer to investigate the situation. A medical officer could force her admittance to an asylum, if he saw fit.

"Is everything all right?" she asked. Jasper was usually reserved, but like the Inspector, he seemed distracted.

He snapped to attention and nodded. "Everything is fine," he said. But then, he slowed his pace and touched her elbow to hold her back. "Have you heard about Elsie?"

"What about her?"

"She and Mr. Munson are to be betrothed soon."

Leo's first reaction was to cringe. "Elsie is far too young to marry. And to Sir Nathaniel's assistant? He's so much older than her."

Jasper agreed with a discontented crinkle of his brow. "She didn't appear happy when I saw her this morning. They were leaving the Inspector when I was arriving."

"I'll see if I can speak to her. Perhaps she didn't know how to turn down the offer."

"All she had to say was *no*," Jasper said with a soft laugh.

Leo bit back a retort that he was being simplistic. Instead, she explained her meaning. "Mr. Munson is her father's close friend and assistant. She may have feared rejecting his offer would cause trouble between the two men."

"So, she felt obligated to accept," Jasper worked out.

"I'll speak to her," Leo said again. "I don't have any experience rejecting unwanted offers of marriage, but I am quite adept at doing what others wish I wouldn't."

Jasper laughed lightly again. "I won't argue with that."

They'd arrived at the peaceful, secluded end of the path, where a small mausoleum stood between a pair of oaks. After the accident, the viscount had spared no expense on its construction. Leo had only met the viscount once. Jasper had been away at Cheltenham, so on that particular January 15, Leo and the Inspector had marked the day with a visit to Kensal Green on their own. When they'd arrived at the granite monument, a tall man in an expensive suit had been standing there, gazing at the edifice. He'd been older with snow-white hair and a pair of incisive eyes that attempted to flay skin from bone when he turned them upon the Inspector. Without a word in greeting, he'd walked away.

The loss of his daughter and two grandchildren had been an enormous blow to Viscount Cowper, the Inspector had explained to Leo afterward. *He thinks I should have been there with them,* he'd said. *To rescue them.* Instead, he'd been at work—something true gentlemen of quality did not do.

Leo had investigated the Regent's Park ice disaster after that, furious on the Inspector's behalf that the viscount would hold him responsible. Saving his wife and children would have been next to impossible, she'd determined. The ice had given way, and nearly one hundred skaters had plunged into the deep water. It had been pure chaos afterward, with those who hadn't gone in trying to either escape the ice or rush toward those who'd fallen in, to help. With heavy skates attached to their feet, people sank rapidly, and by the end of it, forty people had died.

The Inspector climbed the mossy, Portland stone steps to the mausoleum door and placed his palm to the oxidized bronze. Winged angels with bowed heads flanked the sealed door, and above it, the names of his wife and children had been chiseled into the granite mantelpiece. There was a blank, smooth surface just above his daughter Beatrice's name, waiting for another to make the family mausoleum complete. Leo's throat cinched tight.

After taking a moment alone at the door, he retreated to a bench underneath the boughs of one of the oaks. Leo and Jasper joined him there.

"There is some comfort that I feel," he said after a few

moments, a small grin bowing his lips, "knowing that I will see them again much sooner than I expected."

Leo settled her hand on his shoulder as an ache expanded deep in her chest. He longed for them, just as Leo had once longed for her own family. The years had dulled that longing, and she felt a touch guilty for it. Especially since the Inspector's longing had only seemed to increase with time.

He covered Leo's hand with his and gave it a squeeze. "I'm going to sit here for a short while, if you don't mind."

"Not at all."

It was his way of saying he wanted a little time alone, so she and Jasper stepped out from under the oak and continued along the path. Most of the headstones and statuary were familiar to her. The passing seasons had dulled the engravings and allowed moss to accumulate. Other stones, however, were polished and new. An onyx marble angel, the carved details incredibly lifelike, hadn't been there last year.

"Some of these are quite beautiful," she said.

"And expensive. I wouldn't be surprised if the cost of that one matched a full year of my wages," Jasper said, nodding toward another plot that had been fully encircled by alabaster Corinthian columns, each one topped by a different animal carving—a hare, a stag, a swan, and so on.

Leo shrugged. "Funeral services can be lucrative businesses." She thought of William Carter and his position at Hogarth and Tipson.

Awareness fired through her, and her feet dragged to a halt along the gravel. *"Dig it up."*

Jasper stopped. "Pardon?"

She met his perplexed stare, a notion unfurling. "He worked for a funeral service."

His brow smoothed. "You mean Carter."

"Hogarth and Tipson arrange for everything from embalming to interment. If Mr. Carter organized burials—"

"He could have put something into a casket that was then interred," Jasper finished.

She felt giddy as a second notion spiraled through her, lifting the small hairs on her arms. "Jasper! Not 'Nun'. It was an abbreviation. For *Nunhead*!"

Why hadn't she thought of it earlier? All Saints Cemetery in Nunhead, located a short drive south of the River Thames, was where her family had been buried, after all. "But what could *Strange,* and the letters and numbers mean?"

He shook his head. "I'll go to Hogarth and Tipson and see what they might know about Carter's burials shortly before he died. But first, Lewis and I are calling on Stillman's wife."

"I can go to Hogarth and Tipson while you question Mrs. Stillman," she said, but to no great surprise, he was shaking his head before she'd finished speaking.

"There's no call for that. I will get the information without you."

Frustration brimmed. Leave it to Jasper to take the revelation she had made and dismiss her with all haste.

"As my uncle and I have worked with Mr. Tipson and Mrs. Hogarth numerous times, they will be much happier to speak to me than they might be to you, inspector. I can give you a full accounting when I'm done, and it will be more thorough than any police report you've likely seen."

He exhaled, his breath clouding the air. She practically shuffled her feet with excitement at his expression of resignation. "Fine. Go," he said, grinding out the words. "But I'm warning you, Leo—don't become accustomed to this."

Her gratification dimmed somewhat with that high-handed counsel; however, she wouldn't let him see the effect his words had on her. She turned back toward the mausoleum. "Whatever you say, Inspector Reid."

On the drive back to Charles Street, the sun disappeared behind a solid banking of clouds. Rain began to spit as Leo and Jasper walked the Inspector to his front door. Mrs. Zhao had prepared for their somber return, offering tea or something stronger, in the study. But the Inspector's vigor had faded on the ride home, and he needed rest. He kissed Leo on the cheek and said his goodbyes before slowly climbing the stairs.

"I'll come by tomorrow," Jasper said softly to Mrs. Zhao as Leo returned to the pavement. Rain pattered the top of her velvet-lined bonnet and darkened the shoulders of her cloak. She signaled an approaching hansom with a lift of her hand, torn between going to Spring Street first to check in on Claude, or directly to Hogarth and Tipson off Cambridge Circus. But she knew if she went to the morgue, she would likely find a reason to stay and help her uncle. So, she decided on the funeral business.

"You'll tread carefully?" Jasper asked as he joined her on the pavement. It was less of a question as it was an order.

"I won't cause a commotion, if that is what worries you."

"That's not what worries me. If Carter's home was turned over, his killer was looking for something. Probably the item he had already buried. I don't want anyone knowing that you're looking for it too."

Leo hadn't considered that angle before now. If the killer was still searching for the buried object, it wouldn't do to be obvious about their own search. The killer wouldn't want the competition, to be sure.

She nodded. "I'll be discreet."

He gave her a doubtful look but didn't comment. Instead, he opened the door to the cab that had pulled along the pavement and handed her in. Leo called out the address for Hogarth and Tipson, and the driver set off. After the long ride to and from the cemetery, her tailbone felt bruised and her spine out of joint by the time the driver delivered her to the funeral service.

The corner entrance to the shop was a melancholy affair with black painted steps, a black door, and a bow window dressed in somber crepe and black, white, and purple silk flowers. An ornate coffin was open, to display what looked to be a comfortably cushioned final resting place.

Inside, the scent of lilies permeated the air. She couldn't understand why people chose them for funerals. The sickly sweetness of the beautiful flowers reminded Leo of death and rot. A single whiff would instantly transport her back to her family's funeral. Most of the time, she was able to put the vivid memories from her mind, but there was something about lilies that wrenched them out of the dark corner where she kept them.

After Leo's family had been killed, and Claude and Flora had not yet been located as her next of kin, the Inspector had worked with her father's solicitor to help arrange for the service. Four plots inside All Saints Cemetery had been selected, as had four coffins: two standard coffins and two shorter ones, for Jacob and Agnes. Mrs. Zhao had dressed Leo all in black for the day, even giving her a black lace veil to bring down over her face. Mostly, it was to protect her from the hordes of newspaper reporters and gawkers who turned out to view the funeral procession. The Inspector and some of his Met friends helped keep them away from the cemetery for the interment. She'd paid no attention to the priest speaking over the open graves; the breeze was lifting the scent from the lily bouquets placed on each coffin and hurling it up her nostrils, making her feel ill.

Leo clasped her hands now, rubbing the scars on her palm through the glove she wore. It didn't eliminate the sweet, cloying scent, but it did lower her skipping heart rate.

"Why, Miss Spencer, what a delightful surprise it is to see you." The pudgy-cheeked Mr. Tipson joined her, grinning, but then drew back with an expression of alarm. "Or have you come on some grave personal matter?"

He was likely thinking of Claude, whom he'd met numerous times when he'd come to the morgue for a collection.

"No, all is well, Mr. Tipson, I assure you." His grin slid back into place. "I've come to inquire about one of your former employees."

To this, the middle-aged man wrinkled his brow in

interest. "I hope none of them have put a toe out of line at your uncle's morgue."

"Not at all. Everyone I've met from Hogarth and Tipson have been nothing but professional and courteous." Pleased by the praise, he gave a nod of acknowledgment. She continued, "I'm only curious about Mr. William Carter. I've learned of his murder."

He put a hand to his heart, his silver and gray three-piece suit appropriately bleak for his role. "Mrs. Hogarth and I are devastated," he said, mentioning his widowed sister, with whom he partnered. She was a short woman, stout and hard-nosed, and was much better left to the sundry details of a funeral than to dealing with a grieving family. Mr. Tipson had a softer, warmer nature about him, which suited him well to that task.

"Were you acquainted with William?" he asked.

"Only through an acquaintance of my own," Leo said, the fib slipping out with ease. "Miss Hannah Barrett."

The funeral director smiled warmly. "A lovely young woman. We were very sorry for her loss."

Unsurprisingly, it didn't sound as if he knew of Hannah's death. Leo dealt the blow, and Mr. Tipson braced himself against a table display of silk-flower coffin sprays. "No! Miss Barrett? That cannot be."

"I'm afraid it is."

Only then did Leo realize that Mr. Barrett had not secured Hogarth and Tipson for the funeral as he had for their mother. Mr. Tipson seemed to come to that point much faster.

"I wonder why her brother didn't call on us." He looked bewildered rather than affronted. "We arranged for his mother's service, you see."

Leo took in a long breath. The moment had arrived for her to play her hand.

"Mr. Tipson, I'm afraid there was some concern over a family heirloom belonging to Miss Barrett. Mr. Carter had taken her mother's gold locket to have it polished, but unfortunately, he misplaced it. There was quite a row between him and Mr. Barrett over it, as you can imagine."

Mr. Tipson blanched. "You don't suggest William stole it?"

"I don't want to suggest anything. I'm only here on Mr. Barrett's behalf, as he's far too distraught to come himself. I thought I'd see if I might find the locket among Mr. Carter's things here. I understand he kept a photography studio on the premises?"

It was all a rather muddled explanation, and Leo was grateful Mrs. Hogarth was not present. She would have sniffed out the lie in a trice. Mr. Tipson, however, was not as discerning.

"Yes, though without William, we've had to pause that service." He gestured for Leo to follow him toward the back of the room. "My sister and I haven't gone through his things yet. We're rather hoping another photographer might make use of them as soon as we advertise for the position."

"What other services did Mr. Carter provide?" Leo asked. "Just the photography?"

"Oh, no, he worked closely with Mrs. Hogarth on planning the burials. Plot purchases, casket and headstone selection, the arranging of ephemera. He didn't have the stomach for the embalming process, so he left that to us, but he was a pair of strong arms for any heavy lifting."

He would have certainly had ready access to a casket if

he wanted to slip something inside. Leo entered the back room behind Mr. Tipson. Heavy velvet curtains blocked the bleak winter light from entering, cloaking the small room in shadows, but as he turned up the gas jets, destruction came into view.

A damask settee with gold braid had been overturned, the fabric slit open, and the stuffing pulled free in tufts. A black tapestry arranged behind the settee as a backdrop had been knocked over, and a large urn had been tipped onto its side; the silk flowers that had been arranged within, were strewn on the floor nearby. The photographer's set, where Mr. Carter had carefully arranged the deceased to appear lifelike, had been tossed about, and so too had been the various footstools, bolsters, boards, ropes, and even a paint set that he would have used to paint pupils, irises, and eyelashes on closed lids.

"My goodness!" Mr. Tipson stared around at the mess with a grimace. "It wasn't in this ransacked state the last I saw it."

"When was that?" Leo asked as she walked deeper into the room, stepping around a pile of blank mounting cards spilled across the rug. She crouched to pick one up. Developed photographs would have been mounted to these cards, which were pressed with a gold-foiled scrollwork frame.

"It had to have been the day after William's death. Yes, my sister and I heard the news from a police inspector, who'd come here to ask questions. It was a housebreaking and murder, after all. I showed the inspector into the studio and haven't been in since."

She dropped the mounting card and stood. "Do you recall the inspector's name?"

"I'm afraid I don't," he answered. "I was much too shocked to think straight. But I do know the room was just as William had left it. Not like this."

Mr. Carter's home had also been turned inside out, its belongings tossed about as the housebreakers searched for something. Leo resolved to ask Jasper what the police file said about the investigating officer, but for now, it was obvious someone had broken into the studio and searched madly for something: Whatever Mr. Carter had wanted Hannah to dig up, she suspected. For all she knew, Mr. Stillman had made this mess. It would have had to have been Saturday or Sunday night, as Mr. Carter was slain Friday, and Hannah, the following Monday.

She crouched again to pick up a hand camera that had been left on the floor. The contraption was much smaller and lightweight than a larger bellows camera. One of those had been knocked to the floor too and looked to have split apart. Made of wood and brass fittings, the hand camera had one main lens flush to the box, and next to it, a smaller lens. Leo peered at it and thought of the strange peephole in Miss Barrett's bedroom wall. The side-by-side lenses looked as if they could have lined up well with the hidden oval-shaped opening. Miss Barrett had been spying on someone inside the guest room. Had she also been taking *photographs*?

Whether she had been or not, Leo still needed information on Mr. Carter's last burial at All Saints. Quickly, she changed course.

"Mr. Tipson, do you think this could have been done by someone upset with the services they received here?"

The notion utterly shocked him. "No, never! Our customers are only ever satisfied."

It was an odd thing to consider, that one would find satisfaction in the funeral of a loved one.

"Are you quite certain?" Leo asked. "Perhaps Mr. Carter's last client had some grievance you're unaware of. Who might that have been?"

It was not smoothly done, but she'd instilled enough doubt in the undertaker to give him pause.

"No, I know for certain Mrs. Strange was quite content with the services we provided for her husband. I just received a letter of thanks, in fact. Kind, really. Most don't think of that."

The small hairs along Leo's arms stood on end. Strange. It was a *name*. "When was Mr. Strange's burial?"

He blinked. "Early last week. Why? Is it of interest?"

"Mr. Tipson, I know this is going to sound like a very odd question, but can you tell me what plot Mrs. Strange purchased for her husband at All Saints Cemetery?"

He frowned and pulled in his chin. "How did you know he'd been buried there?"

"A lucky guess," she said, impatient to know if her theory was correct.

He goggled at her irreverent answer but left the destruction of the photography studio to return to his desk at the front of the shop. Murmuring that he couldn't begin to know why she would wish to know such information, he flipped through a ledger.

"Yes, here it is. Barnabas Strange. Block 17, row 4, plot 8."

A strike of victory lit the ends of Leo's nerves, and she nearly hopped with excitement.

B17. R4. She couldn't wait to tell Jasper what she'd discovered.

Chapter Fifteen

Jasper and Lewis eyed the narrow lane ahead. The driver of their cab had gone as far as Hanbury Street before bringing his horses to a stop. He wouldn't be going any further. *Too bloody dangerous*, he'd said. Then, with a shake of his head, as if the two coppers were fools, he left them to go the rest of the way on foot.

This was a part of London Jasper had been all too happy to forget existed. The squeeze of the tenement buildings, the center gutters high with refuse from horses and humans alike, the laundry strung on lines overhead that even after washing still appeared stained and soiled. Beggars, children, and prostitutes all mixed in with costermongers, newspaper hawkers, and open-air butchers. The warrens were rife with criminals, and Jasper and Lewis were sorely out of place here.

They received suspicious looks as they walked toward Great Pearl Street. Lewis's search through the city directory for Mary Stillman had turned up the address, and Jasper could only hope she would be at home. Now, as they reached their destination, vagrants skulked about the tapered backstreet, staring with unmasked menace.

"You sure about this, guv?" Lewis murmured as they entered, trying to appear confident.

"No," Jasper answered. "We have our sidearms. Be vigilant, detective."

Metropolitan officers weren't routinely issued firearms; the truncheon was generally effective enough. But detectives could elect to carry a weapon, and Jasper knew too well the realities of the East End to have declined the offer.

A layer of grime nearly blackened the wooden shingle hanging above No. 10. The door was propped open, and he and Lewis entered to find a musty, dark space. Bareboard steps led to another upstairs hall. The floor groaned under Jasper's boots, the wood soft. A pram had been left outside a closed door, and with mounting concern and disgust, Jasper saw a fussing baby within it. The poorly swaddled child thrashed its skinny arms and legs, its red face pinched in distress. With startling care, Lewis reached for the blanket the child had kicked off and covered him again.

"My missus would froth at the bit if she saw this," he said.

The detective sergeant rarely mentioned his wife and young sons. Lewis had only married after joining the force as a constable, as married men with more than two children were not accepted as recruits. Some officers married after spending a few years on the force, but many more didn't. Jasper had never given marriage much thought...until Constance. He still avoided thinking of it, mostly. The announcement of her parents' upcoming visit to London, however, had put a rock in his gut.

The pram had been parked outside the room they wanted, and inside, a pair of voices were raised in a quarrel. Jasper brought down his fist on the door. The shouting ceased. The door swung open, revealing a glaring man equal to Jasper's height though double his weight.

"Wot d'yer want?" He was a surly-looking bloke. Several of his teeth were missing from among the other rotten ones, and his head was shaved nearly clean. He had a faded bruise under one eye from a recent fistfight.

Jasper flashed his warrant card. "Detective Inspector Reid and Detective Sergeant Lewis from Scotland Yard. Is this Mary Stillman's residence?"

If possible, the man's countenance grew even more ominous. "Wot d'yer want wiv 'er?"

Jasper kept his expression flat. "I'd like to inform her that her husband is dead."

A high squeal came from behind the burly man, and a second later, a woman pushed her way forward. Face sallow, eyes sunken, she had a haunted, nearly starved look about her.

"Clarence is dead?"

Jasper couldn't tell if her tone was one of hope or dread. If the baby in the pram belonged to her, it couldn't be Stillman's, not if he'd been in prison for the last three years.

"He is," he answered, "and I'd like to know the last time you saw him."

The bruiser shoved Mrs. Stillman from the doorway. "She's got nuffink to say to yer mutton shunters."

Jasper paid no attention to the insult but instead noticed that when the man had pushed her back from the door, his rolled sleeve lifted, exposing more of his wrist. A prison tattoo much like Clarence Stillman's flashed into view.

"Mrs. Stillman," Jasper said, addressing her even though she was hidden behind the man. "Your husband was murdered. Shot."

She barged in front again, her coloring even starker. "Shot? When? 'Oo did it?"

"I'm willing to share what I know, but I'll need some answers from you as well." Jasper lifted his eyes to the man. "And possibly from you. I see you've spent some time inside Wandsworth."

He tugged down his sleeve. "Wot of it?"

"What is your name?" Jasper asked.

When he hesitated, Lewis said, "You might as well tell us. You're in the prisoner directory anyhow."

"And I'm willing to bet you and Clarence did your time together," Jasper said. "But you were released first and made sure to check in on his wife."

"Considerate," Lewis said, with a wry nod.

"Angelic," Jasper added.

"His name's Tommy Welch," Mrs. Stillman said with a huff. "Now tell me 'oo did in Clarence."

From Welch's glare directed toward her, Jasper knew it was his real name. It wasn't familiar, but he'd be sure to check through his convict record.

"This your baby?" Lewis gestured to the child kicking up a wild fuss again. It grated on Jasper's ears and his patience. Mrs. Stillman huffed in vexation and scooped up the baby. She bounced the sad thing roughly on her hip as she waited for Jasper to answer her question. They remained in the hall; it was clear they weren't to be invited in. From what he could see of the room from the doorway, it was a small mercy.

"We're looking for his killer, Mrs. Stillman, but we're curious about the people he'd been associating with since his release from prison."

"People from his past, maybe," Lewis said. "We know he was an East Rip."

"*Were*," she said, emphasizing the past tense. "He broke wiv 'em when they left 'im ter be caught by the bloomin' bobbies. It weren't 'im 'oo killed that lady."

"No, he only stood by and watched it happen," Lewis scoffed.

According to the arrest record, Clarence Stillman and another East Rip had been at a German bakery, collecting for one of the gang's protection rackets when the bakery owner—who was most certainly accepting this *protection* against his will—came up short with his monthly payment. When they started beating him, the baker's wife stepped in to stop it, and she ended up bludgeoned to death. Witnesses outside the shop saw it all and named the other man as the killer, but Stillman had been there.

"Did you see him after he was released from prison?" Jasper asked.

She shrugged. "Once. But when 'e seen wee Robbie," she indicated the baby, "Clarence made 'imself scarce."

Welch stood with his arms crossed, his grimace fixed. Jasper peered at the baby again. There was no question of paternity there. Robbie had been cursed with Welch's curiously short forehead and heavy brow.

"And you, Welch, did you see Stillman?"

"Sure."

"I imagine he was none too pleased to see you'd taken up with his wife," Lewis commented, the statement purposely leading.

Welch only shrugged. He seemed to take pleasure in answering vaguely.

"We believe someone hired your husband for a house-breaking and after seeing the job through, he was killed. I want to know who hired him." Jasper's statement was met with a blank stare from Mrs. Stillman and an unchanged grimace from Welch.

"I don't know a 'fink about that," she said. "When 'e found Tommy and me, right, 'e went off 'is top. Them two were too busy murdering each uvver ter say a word about a job."

"You didn't see him after that?" Lewis asked.

Mrs. Stillman insisted she hadn't, and her expression was too open to be lying. Welch's attempt to sever eye contact with them, however, was a clear tell.

"When did you see him again, Welch?"

He snapped his eyes back to Jasper. "'Oo says I did?"

"You did, without so many words. So, when was it, and what was said? I'll remind you that impeding a criminal investigation is cause for arrest. I'm sure the chief warder at Wandsworth would welcome you back."

"Ye can't nick me for not talkin'."

"Try your luck. I promise, you won't like the result."

He bared his sparse teeth, but Jasper wasn't intimidated. His threat was working, so he stood patiently.

"Arright, I seen 'im," he began. "He were at the Jugger a week or so after our scrap."

Jasper peered at Lewis, who met the revelation with a

twitch of his eye. The tavern near the St. Katharine Docks was a known hot spot for East Rip activity. The Jugger was owned and operated by a woman named Bridget O'Mara, who also happened to be one of the C.I.D's informants. She'd gotten herself into a tight spot a few years back, after a brawl with her menace of a husband ended with him at the bottom of a flight of stairs, his neck broken. In addition to feeling somewhat sorry for her, and being a touch sweet on her too, Chief Coughlan had seen an opportunity with Bridget. In exchange for her release from custody and all charges dropped, she would provide information on gang dealings when requested by the Yard. She'd agreed.

"When was this?" Jasper asked.

He shrugged. "Last week. Friday."

"And what happened with Clarence when you saw him?"

"Tried ter talk ter him, right, but 'e told me ter leave off. He were waitin' for some bloke. Had 'imself a job."

"What job?" Jasper asked, becoming more intrigued. "Who hired him?"

"Didn't ask. I told 'im ter piss off and found m'self anuvver table."

"Did his companion arrive?"

Welch nodded.

"What can you remember about him?" Jasper asked when he didn't provide anything more.

He shrugged. "Some rum cove wiv specs and a mustache."

The description wasn't very distinctive. Almost everyone Jasper knew had spectacles and a mustache.

Welch licked his lips as if considering some new inspiration. "When they left, I might've followed. Might've seen sumfink."

For the right price, he'd tell them too, Jasper imagined. He wasn't averse to a bit of bartering.

"Tell us what you saw, and the next time you're arrested—and there will be a next time—I'll let the magistrate know you assisted us in an investigation. It might lessen your sentence."

Mrs. Stillman glared. "He's finished wiv that life and don't need no promises."

But Welch appeared to be a little more circumspect. He nodded to accept the deal. "Clarence followed the cove ter a fine carriage outside the tavern and got in."

It wasn't a lot to go on, and certainly nothing revealing.

"Did you see any markings on this carriage? The driver?" Jasper asked.

"All I know is when the carriage pulled away, I seen three men inside. Clarence, the rum cove, and some uvver bloke."

"Can you recall anything about this third person?" Lewis asked.

Welch shook his head. "He were dressed fine. Top 'at and all. They rode off," Welch finished. "After that, I ain't seen Clarence again."

Detective Chief Inspector Dermot Coughlan dug his knuckles into his desktop and leaned forward, locking Jasper into a dead stare. "You want permission to exhume a *casket?*"

The conversation with the chief was going just as badly as Jasper expected it would, but after returning to the Yard with Lewis and finding Leo in his office, giddy with what she'd learned at Hogarth and Tipson, he'd known it couldn't be avoided.

"Barnabas Strange was the last person William Carter interred at All Saints in Nunhead," he explained to the chief. "And the piece of paper he gave Miss Barrett for safekeeping and which she put in the locket—"

"The locket that may or may not have been stolen by Clarence Stillman," Coughlan interjected, reminding him that there was still a lack of proof.

"Yes, sir. The paper read *Strange Nun* and the plot number where Strange was buried. According to Mr. Barrett, Carter told his sister to 'dig it up', should anything happen to him."

"And then he was killed by housebreakers," Coughlan said. Though he'd recalled the order of events from Jasper's first accounting, he wasn't pleased. Neither was Detective Inspector Tomlin, who'd been the lead investigator on Carter's murder.

"There is no evidence to suggest it was anything but a house break-in," the other detective said, his arms crossed over his puffed-up chest. Tomlin was part of the Special Irish Branch, organized the previous year to focus on Fenian crimes and activity. Carter, being Irish and related to the East Rips, had qualified as a potential suspicious murder, and so Tomlin had been assigned to the case.

"What was stolen?" Jasper asked, though he was just goading the man. He'd read the report himself. Simple thieves wouldn't have left behind the kitchen's silver or the money in Carter's billfold.

"The housebreakers were interrupted in the act," Tomlin insisted. "They panicked. Carter was shot. That's all there is to it."

"Tomlin is still following leads on the identities of the housebreakers," Coughlan said to quell the tension.

"That may be difficult, since I'm quite sure Stillman was one of them. I have a witness who says he saw Stillman with another man, a gentleman, last Friday. That's the same night Carter was killed."

Tomlin rounded on Jasper. "What witness?"

"An old prison mate of Stillman's. It's my belief Stillman and this unknown gentleman went to Carter's home in search of whatever it was Carter had buried. That's why he'd given the location to his fiancée the night before. He knew he was in danger."

"*Your* belief?" Tomlin grunted a laugh. "And what does Miss *Leomorga* have to say about any of this? All the men have seen her here over the last few days. You even brought her to a murder scene."

Constable Wiley's idiotic name for her had caught on among some of the men. Jasper gritted his molars. "She was there to identify a body."

"Leave Miss Spencer out of this, Tomlin," the chief barked. "I mean that for you as well, Reid. I know she is like family—"

"Sir, that isn't the case," Jasper said, frustrated enough to interrupt. He received a chastising beady eye for it.

"You will keep her out of this. Do you have a problem with that, Reid?"

"No, sir." Unless Jasper wished to lose his post, there was no other answer Coughlan would accept.

"Good." He stood tall again, his knuckles white from

where he'd been leaning on them. "I will arrange the exhumation for tomorrow morning." He rubbed his temple and checked his watch. "I have a blasted dinner with the Home Secretary tonight, and I'll still have to get the paperwork completed, then alert the Strange family. So, Reid—you'd best hope you find something in that casket that leads to an arrest."

Jasper's pulse knocked in his neck as he threw open the door to leave Coughlan's office—and practically trod upon Constable Wiley's toes. The constable cleared his throat and scuttled away, pretending that he hadn't been listening at the door. Jasper glared at his retreating figure. The man was a gossipmonger and would surely repeat what he'd just overheard.

Should nothing be found once that casket was opened, Jasper would be a laughingstock. Comparisons were already being drawn between himself and Gregory Reid. Opinions regarding whether he'd earned his detective's warrant card or had it handed to him were also being settled upon. He couldn't afford a fiasco.

Back in his office, he found Leo pacing behind his desk. She spun around, biting her lower lip in a hopeful expression.

"Tomorrow morning," he said.

She exhaled and formed a rare grin. But it faltered. "What is wrong?"

Jasper braced himself. "You cannot come."

Leo balked. "Why not? I'm the one who worked out where Mr. Carter buried his mysterious treasure. And I spent all afternoon hunting down cemetery plot maps at the city records office."

"And I thank you for it. But Chief Coughlan is firm on

this," Jasper said, still slightly irritated that his interview with Stillman's wife and Tommy Welch had turned up little, while hers with Mr. Tipson had been a triumph. Not that it was a competition. At least he now knew Stillman had met with two men, both of whom belonged to the upper classes.

Leo tossed up her hands. "Once again, you take my discovery and leave me behind to twiddle my thumbs."

"Or you could take care of your uncle and aunt, who need you," he retorted—and instantly regretted it. Her eyes flared with insult and, worse, guilt. Hell, why couldn't he keep his damn mouth shut?

Leo sealed her lips tight and lifted her chin. "I'm getting tired of being told to stay home. If I had, you'd still be running in circles."

"You give yourself too much credit." The lie tasted bitter, even as he said it.

Leo had been the one to suggest Carter buried the item by means of his employment at the funeral service. She'd been the one to successfully question Mr. Tipson, and after looking closely at a hand camera in Carter's studio, she'd also suggested that the strange peephole in Miss Barrett's bedroom wall could have been just large enough for the camera's lenses.

"I am sorry." The words stuck in his throat for too long before releasing them. "This is out of my hands, Leo."

"Very well," she said tartly, then took up her handbag and the dark purple coat she'd hung on the peg stand. "Best of luck tomorrow."

As she started for the door, a foreboding slid through him. Jasper followed her, catching up in time to shove his hand against the door before she could open it. Leo stared up at him, incredulous. "What are you doing?"

He tucked his chin and met her challenging glare. "You gave up too easily. What are you planning?"

"Nothing at all. I'm going home to make supper for Claude and Flora."

"You're hurrying home to cook?" he scoffed. "Now I know you're hiding something."

She pursed her lips and tried to peel his hand from the door, finger by finger. He kept it firmly on the jamb, preventing her.

"Don't be daft. Let me go," she insisted.

"I'm not sure I should. In fact, I'm hesitant to take my eyes off you." The moment the words left his tongue, he heard how suggestive they sounded. Leo's hazel eyes pinned his, her lips popping open.

He tried to make up for it, fast. "Promise me you won't do anything rash or dangerous."

Her eyes slid away from his as she answered, "I promise. Now let me out. Or I'll scream, and Constable Wiley will come running with the notion I'm murdering you."

Jasper huffed a laugh and lowered his hand. "I'm sure that tempts you."

She cut him a wry look as she opened the door. "You've no idea."

Chapter Sixteen

Leo entered the north gate to All Saints just as dawn crested the trees. She'd left an hour ago, waking before Claude or Flora and leaving a note to say that she was visiting her family's graves. It wasn't an absolute lie. She would indeed go to their headstones, something she did at least once every year. But first, she would meander past block 17 to see if the exhumation was underway.

Jasper had said his hands were tied, and she could understand that—to a point. But this cemetery wasn't private property. Anyone could come here and spend the day, and if she just happened to be strolling past Mr. Strange's gravesite, well then, where was the harm in it?

She wasn't needed at home this morning anyhow. Their neighbor, Mrs. Gareth, had gotten on well with Flora the day before, and she'd offered to stay again while Claude spoke with the nurse who had responded to the listing in the *Telegraph*. She hoped this nurse accepted the position as Claude was desperately behind in his duties at

Spring Street, and the deputy coroner, Mr. Pritchard, would soon be hearing about it—if he hadn't already.

As Leo walked up the wide, flat lane to the four-spired stone church which stood like a sentinel to the graves beyond, her stomach grumbled. She'd wrapped some slices of bread and cheese taken from the larder for her breakfast, which she'd eaten on the nearly hour-long cab ride to Nunhead. The cost of the hansom to the outer reaches of the city was quite dear, but the less expensive omnibuses wouldn't begin operating for another few hours. She hoped the splurge would be worth it.

Her uncle paid her a wage every Friday, though he took it from his own earnings. The chief coroner could not agree to paying a woman for her services at the morgue, but she was welcome to assist on a voluntary basis. At first, Leo wouldn't accept Claude's offering, but he'd insisted, saying that unless she took it, he would not allow her to work with him. She mostly spent it at the market to keep the household running, as Claude took care of the yearly lease, the gas, the coal orders, and paying the nurse, whenever one was employed.

At the church, she turned down the path to the right, seeing again in her mind the plot map, which she'd scrutinized meticulously the afternoon before. It rose before her eyes again in sharp detail, each curving path and cleanly drawn, numbered block. Every block could hold anywhere between one to a dozen graves, all depending on the family's desire for either simplicity or extravagance. Barnabas Strange's purchased plot was in the southeastern corner of the cemetery. Leo's family's headstones were on the opposite side of the grounds, their simple granite markers in sharp contrast to some of the more ornate monuments topping the graves.

The Spencer family plot was slightly raised and surrounded by a square of curbing. Long ago, the Inspector had arranged for a bench to be placed inside the square, and that was where Leo usually sat whenever she visited. She never stayed very long, for she wasn't entirely sure what she should be thinking, saying, or doing. Not to mention, each time she sat there, looking at their headstones, she would feel undeservedly lucky that there was not a fifth headstone with her name chiseled upon it.

More so, she'd feel grateful to the faceless, nameless boy who had helped hide her. It made her sick to feel such disloyalty to her family.

Leo pulled her cloak tighter around herself as her breath fogged the air. Dawn's light broke meekly through the overcast sky, and without the sun's direct glare, everything still had a bluish tinge. The grass glistened with frost, and in the morning quiet, the chatter of birds was a near cacophony. A blackbird swooped from the branch of a nearby oak and, with a grating caw, flapped past her head. Leo jumped and let out a yelp, though she felt silly for it. Thankfully, as she closed in on block 17, there were no sounds of men digging or talking, so no one would have seen or heard her.

The groundskeeper must not have arrived yet to begin the task of reopening the grave. Neither had Jasper and his detective sergeant. However, stopping along the path, Leo cocked her head at an unusual sight—mounds of dirt were heaped around one of the graves ahead. A shovel had been speared into one of the piles. As she approached, her stomach dropped toward her knees. The grave, marked with a new, polished, black granite stone, belonged to Barnabas Strange.

The loose soil glittered with ice crystals, but with this year's temperate winter, the ground was only frosty, not frozen. Gravediggers were still digging several feet down, according to a few of the funeral services collecting bodies at Spring Street, though with more effort than they'd give in the warmer months. With hundreds of people dying every week in the city, milder winters were a blessing. So were the crematoriums that had started to become the answer to overcrowded burial grounds.

Leo smelled the freshly turned soil—and something more pungent.

As she stepped closer to the yawning pit, her attention landed on a metal stake driven into the ground. A length of rope had been tied around it and fed down into the pit. With a streak of alarm, she knew this was no professional exhumation. Someone had opened Barnabas Strange's grave during the night.

Leo crouched at the edge of the pit and peered into the hollow. It hadn't been a clean dig; the sides had been roughly scraped, leaving dirt scattered all over. Only the top of a tapered wooden coffin had been exposed. The lid was on, but it wasn't sealed. It lay askew, leaving small gaps at the top and bottom and revealing the silk-cushioned interior. *Blast it all!* Someone had gotten to whatever Mr. Carter had hidden in the coffin, and only hours before the scheduled disinterment.

A shiver along the back of Leo's neck announced a presence behind her. A person who hadn't yet announced themselves. She started to turn and stand, but a hard shove between her shoulder blades stopped her. With a short scream, she lost her balance and fell forward into the open grave. Her shoulder and hip struck the coffin lid as she landed on her side, the air driven from her lungs. Shock wiped out any pain for several moments, but soon, she felt it blooming in the back of her skull and throbbing through her arm and knee. Leo dragged in a shallow breath, choking on some dirt that came in with it. The world spun. She didn't know for how long she lay there—five seconds, ten, a full minute—before sense barreled back into her.

Pushing herself up, she grimaced from pain and a dash of horror. The knotted rope was gone. It had been drawn up, leaving her with no way to climb out. The tang of dirt and the sickly-sweet odor of a decomposing body filled the back of her throat. Taking her lacy handkerchief from her skirt pocket, she held it to her nose and mouth as she slowly stood. She reached, but her fingertips fell short of the pit's ledge.

No! She could not be found here, stuck in the open grave, by Jasper and his men when they arrived for the exhumation. It would be utterly humiliating! Desperate to climb free, she dug the toes of her boots into the wall of the grave to gain a foothold. But the soil gave way as soon as she pushed her weight into it, and she slipped back down again. With a frustrated grunt, she stamped her foot. Then instantly felt guilty. Surely, it was disrespectful to stomp on a dead man's coffin.

With the hankie still pressed to her nose, Leo looked at the sliver of an opening at the top of the coffin. The grave thief had left the crowbar he'd used to pry the lid up, as it would have been securely sealed before interment. The top of Barnabas Strange's head was visible. She didn't quail. A body was a body. Having been buried for over a week now, he would not be pleasant to look at. He'd be bloated, as his internal organs began to putrefy and produce noxious gases. Those gases were natural, of course, but were a wretched plague, especially years back when cemeteries were so overrun with bodies that four or more poorly sealed coffins would share a single pit. Gravediggers began to fall ill, and a few even died, when they reopened the graves to add another casket, exposing themselves to the gases.

The grave thief had dug a small notch into the wall of the pit on which to stand while he pried the lid off. The earth there had been tamped down, but there weren't any clearly defined boot prints. Nothing that might help identify a certain type of shoe the man had been wearing. So, she stepped there and then crouched to grip the casket lid herself. It was heavier than she'd thought it would be; the ornate brass fittings and the engraved breastplate added to the weight of it. As expected, Mr. Strange was a ghastly sight and smell, but even more upsetting was the lack of any object around him. It was just him in his burial suit.

Male voices drifted through the cemetery, and Leo squeezed her eyes shut. *Drat!* She lowered the lid and stood. There wasn't anything to do now but wait to be found. It was all too reminiscent of how she'd been discovered locked inside the morgue closet. Oddly enough, she much preferred being stuck down a grave than inside a dark, enclosed space.

The voices neared. Jasper's deep tenor, barking orders for Lewis to search the area, raked down her spine. He must have seen the piles of dirt and the shovel, just as she had. A few moments later, Jasper appeared above her, looming over the edge of the grave. His eyes sharpened on her as his mouth parted in shock.

"Leo? What the devil are you doing down there?" Anger flashed over his expression as he undoubtedly suspected what it looked like: that *she* had been the one to open the grave.

"This is not my handiwork, if that is what you're thinking, Inspector Reid," she snapped. "If it were, don't you think I would have brought a method to extract myself from this pit?" She raised a hand. "Would you please help me out?"

Muttering under his breath, he lowered himself, chest to the dirt. Leo gripped his extended arms, and though she expected a struggle to pull her up, Jasper hauled her free with astonishing swiftness. Once her knees were on the ground again, he helped her to stand. She pushed back her hat, the pins having loosened in her fall. Jasper wasn't alone. A man who must have been the groundskeeper gawped at her, and Sergeant Lewis was also returning from his search. His jaw dropped as Leo brushed off her skirt and tried to fix her hat again.

"What happened?" Jasper demanded. "Are you injured?"

She shook her head. "Not terribly. I was pushed from behind as I was crouching at the edge."

Saying it aloud made her feel exceedingly silly, and her face heated. Jasper's usual contemplative frown deepened into something closer to fury.

"Did you see who it was?" he asked, his voice rough and raspy.

"I think that is why I was pushed," she said. "To stop me from seeing him. He must have seen me coming and hid. Then, when the opportunity presented itself..." She shrugged.

Jasper glanced at Lewis, then lowered his voice as he turned back to her. "I told you to stay away. Why did you not heed my order?"

Heed his order! She barely refrained from pushing *him* into the open grave. Taking a deep breath, she gave him an overly benign grin. "I was visiting my family's plot."

"No, you were not."

"It doesn't matter now," she said, gesturing to the grave. "Mr. Strange's coffin has been breached, and if there was anything within it, it's gone. Except for the body, of course."

Lewis glanced into the grave and wrinkled his nose against the odor. "That's a lot of digging for one man."

"Not so much if the lad was spry," the groundskeeper offered. "The dirt hadn't settled just yet, so it'd be loose under the frosty crust. Easy enough to move, if you've an hour or two."

"He was cutting it fine, if he was still here past dawn," Leo said. Why not come at midnight and be gone well before the sun rose?

"Who else knew Coughlan had agreed to the disinterment?" Lewis asked.

Jasper whisked his hat from his head and stared out across the cemetery grounds. "Everyone at the central office, I imagine."

She kept to herself that she'd also been obvious at Hogarth and Tipson with wanting to know about Barnabas Strange and his plot number. Though, she didn't think Mr. Tipson had any reason to seek out the grave and open it. He hadn't even known Mr. Carter's studio had been ransacked. Besides, he was the furthest thing from spry.

The groundskeeper nimbly lowered himself into the pit and opened the coffin lid without hesitation. From this angle, Leo could see streaks of dirt on the snowy-white silk cushions around the body, as though a dirt-covered hand had reached here and there, lifting the body aside in a search.

"Want me to move him?" the man asked, as though the task of doing so would not trouble him in the least. Leo imagined he was quite inured to dead bodies, as was she.

Wanting to be sure there was nothing underneath Barnabas Strange, Jasper agreed to roll him onto his side. There was nothing there, however, and the groundskeeper got to work replacing the lid, then shoveling dirt back into the open pit.

"Well, that's that," Lewis said.

"Not necessarily. If he left in a rush, he might have left something behind. Or dropped something. Canvass the area from here to the west exit, through the trees in that direction," Jasper said, pointing toward the corner of the cemetery and a more secluded entrance path. "Miss Spencer and I will go toward the north gate and meet you on the street."

Her stomach flipped. If he wanted to be alone with her, it was certainly to chastise her without his detective sergeant overhearing. As they parted company with Lewis, Leo held up her hand.

"All right, I didn't come to visit my family's plot. I wanted to be here when the coffin was opened."

"Even though I told you in no uncertain terms that you weren't to be? This is my work, Leo, and I have orders to follow. If it looks like I'm letting you in on an investigation, do you think the superintendent is going to think twice about tossing me back to E Division?"

She cringed as they walked, their eyes scanning the ground for any evidence the grave robber might have accidentally left behind. "I hadn't thought of that."

"No, you hadn't." He groaned and slapped his hat back on. "Not that it matters now. I'll explain to Coughlan that the grave was already open, the body disturbed. Maybe… *maybe*…I won't be a laughingstock."

"Of course, you won't be a laughingstock," she said, getting angry herself now. "If anything, it proves that there was something valuable in that coffin. You were right to ask to have it exhumed."

He scowled at the grass, the frost glistening as it melted under the coming sunshine. "It doesn't matter. I was too late."

They walked quietly toward the church, Leo's mind's leaping toward everything they'd learned so far. There was one thing she kept coming back to.

"The hole in Miss Barrett's wall," she began to say.

"I've been thinking of it too."

She glimpsed sideways at him. "And the box camera?"

He nodded. "My guess is that either Miss Barrett or William Carter was taking photographs."

"Of someone in the guest room?"

"Or…of two people," he said, his eyes straight ahead.

Leo may not have been worldly or experienced, but she didn't misunderstand him. "Lewd photographs?"

Jasper tugged at his collar. "Possibly."

The ground seemed to suck at her bootheels, dragging her to a stop. "For blackmail purposes."

Jasper stopped too. He squinted against the rising sunlight, bright and unhindered by clouds. "William might have been a fringe member of the East Rips, but he was still a Carter. That family thrives on exploitation and blackmail."

For the first time in days, Leo began to feel as though she'd stepped onto the right path. "So, they take a secret photograph of someone in a…compromising position and then threaten to show it to others if they don't pay?"

"A wife, a husband, an employer," Jasper said, walking on toward the church and the front lane, though slowly, his eyes still peeled on the ground. "They might even have threatened to share it with the public."

"But the person didn't want to pay and instead threatened Mr. Carter."

Jasper continued with the theory. "William hid the photographs, as they were his only leverage. He then told his accomplice, Miss Barrett, where to find them if he was harmed."

"Why would he want her to dig them up?" Leo asked. "Why not leave them be?"

"Because they're valuable." He slowed his gait. "Or because they're evidence of some crime or could be connected to one."

Leo had to admit, the theory taking shape felt strong. But there were still gaps.

"Mr. Stillman knew about the locket. Why would Mr. Carter point his attacker toward Hannah, when he could have simply told Mr. Stillman where to find the photographs?"

Jasper shook his head and sighed as they passed the church. "I don't know. And we don't even know if there are photographs. For all we know, Miss Barrett had an obsession with a regular houseguest and spied on them."

Leo didn't believe that. Jasper didn't either, she was sure of it.

"We need to speak to Mr. Barrett again and ask him about the guest room." As soon as she said it, she knew what Jasper's response would be.

"We are going back to Westminster, where you will leave off this case. Leo—" He took a wide step and came to stand in front of her, forcing her to a stop. Jasper held her gaze, unwavering. "If the Carters are involved, then you are lucky you were only shoved into a grave and not killed."

"I'm not some helpless female, Jasper. Nor am I useless."

"I never said you were." His jaw tensed. "But it was a bit brainless to come all the way out here alone, before daybreak, just to spite an order I gave you."

Brainless! The insult plunged into her chest like a knife. "I am not brainless, and I don't take orders from you, Inspector Reid." She tried to step around him, but he held out an arm to bar her way.

"Can you not understand that I don't want to see any harm come to you?"

Leo drew back, surprised. She'd expected another order, another insult. The fire in her belly tempered, and her pulse slowed. It kicked back up a notch when Jasper's raised arm came forward. His thumb, encased in soft leather, swept along her cheekbone. Leo held her breath, stunned at his touch. His dark green eyes flared, and then quickly, as though he'd felt her frisson of shock, he dropped his hand.

"There was some dirt on your face," Jasper offered, touching his own cheek and then clasping his hands behind his back again. Leo rubbed the spot, realizing how disheveled she must have appeared after being pulled from a hole in the ground.

"Nothing is going to happen to me," she said, a strange tingling on her cheek.

"You're right, nothing is, because you're going to stay safely in the morgue." Jasper cocked his head. "You know what I mean."

At the head of the lane, flanked by two stone pillars, Lewis came into view. Jasper and Leo started walking again, increasing their speed to meet the detective sergeant and perhaps leave the awkward moment behind them. Lewis shook his head. He hadn't found anything in his search.

Needing to return to the Yard, Jasper invited Leo to share the police carriage. It felt strange to leave All Saints without seeing her family's graves, but she would have rather gone alone, and that was something Jasper would not have allowed, had she insisted on staying. So, Leo returned with them, and they parted ways at Whitehall.

"You're going straight to Spring Street?" Jasper asked her, as Lewis walked ahead toward the Yard's entrance.

He asked as if assuming she was going to run off and land herself in more trouble. She smiled tightly. "I have a stop to make first."

On the mostly silent ride to Westminster, Leo had contemplated the notion of indecent photography. Had Lewis not been with them, she might have shared her idea with Jasper. Then again, he might have become upset knowing that she hadn't ceased all thoughts about the case, as he so desperately wanted.

Jasper hesitated now, as though reluctant to leave her to her own devices. So, she moved past him; she wanted to reach Dita's home before her friend left for work. But then, Leo remembered her manners.

"Oh, and thank you," she said, turning back toward him briefly. "For pulling me out of that grave."

She said it just as two constables were passing by; they both slowed and stared in alarm. Jasper shook his head and smirked. "Let's try not to make a habit of it."

Chapter Seventeen

Nivedita and her father, Sergeant Byron Brooks, lived in a small terrace house in Covent Garden. It wasn't much different than Leo's home with Claude and Flora, except for the fact that every time Leo was welcomed inside, it smelled of something delicious. Unlike herself, Dita possessed culinary skill, taught to her by her mother. The late Mrs. Anika Brooks had been born to an East India Company captain who fell in love with and married a young woman he met while in the port of Calcutta.

Whenever Dita prepared Leo's favorite dish—spiced lentils and soft roti—she felt slightly envious that her friend had memories of learning to cook at her mother's side. Leo didn't know if her mother had cooked; she had a vague memory of an older woman speaking a strange language in her family's kitchen. But when she asked Flora once if they'd had a cook or a maid, her aunt had told her not to be ridiculous; they couldn't have afforded it.

So, Leo contented herself on Dita's memories of her own mother. When the front door to the Brooks' home opened, emitting a cloud of warm curry, onion, and spices, her rumbling stomach announced itself.

Dita laughed. "Did you burn the eggs again?"

"I wasn't home to try."

Dita yanked Leo inside and shut the door. "Where have you been so early in the day?" She gasped and grinned widely. "Or did you not return home last night?"

Leo scowled. "Of course I was home last night."

Disappointed, Dita waved her toward the kitchen. "My father is already gone. I'm following shortly. Here, eat this." She put a steamed rice cake into Leo's hand as soon as they stepped into the small kitchen. It was already topped with ginger chutney. She bolted it down happily as her friend gathered her things and then locked the door behind them.

"All right then, why do you look as if you slept on the ground last night?"

Leo had forgotten about her dirty cheek and Jasper's attempt to brush the dirt away. The memory of it stumped her for a moment, but then she got to the point of why she'd wanted to see her friend.

"I didn't sleep on the ground. I fell into a hole."

"How did you come to do that?" Dita exclaimed.

"It's a long and complicated story, but suffice to say, I'd like to ask you about the children you were guarding the other day at the Yard. The ones you said were caught up in a photographer's scheme."

Dita's chin dimpled in the center as she frowned. "What about them?"

"You said the person who was arrested was taking indecent photographs of the children?"

Dita walked fast by routine, but at this unsavory topic, she seemed to increase her speed. "Yes, that is what I was told. Why? What does this have to do with you falling into a hole?"

"It was a grave, actually."

Her friend came to a halt. "*What?*"

"We believe photographs of the same nature, perhaps used for blackmail, were buried with the man whose grave I fell into. And in truth, I was pushed, but that's too much to explain."

Dita peered at her more shrewdly. "*We?*"

"Inspector Reid and I. But please don't say anything to anyone."

"I won't," she promised as she started walking again, and Leo knew she would stay true to her word. "But you were pushed into a grave over some indecent photographs? Was Inspector Reid pushed in too?"

"No, he hadn't arrived yet," she answered, though things were sliding off course. "My question to you is where would I go to purchase this sort of photography?"

Dita slammed to a halt again. "Why would you want to do something so awful?"

"It's for the investigation, of course."

"But you're not a detective."

Leo arched a brow. "You're starting to sound like Jasper. But I am involved, Dita. It all started with the break-in at the morgue."

Her friend began to walk again, appearing dazed. "And finding illicit photographs is going to help?"

They had about fifteen more minutes until they

arrived at Great Scotland Yard, so Leo used that time to explain the details of the case to her friend. When she heard about the peephole and the box camera lenses that would match up against the hole in Miss Barrett's bedroom wall, Dita balked.

"A hidden camera taking photographs of people in…" She lowered her voice to a whisper. "*Sexual congress*? That would certainly be perfect for blackmail." She seemed to contemplate a moment. "Listen, I may only be a matron, but I hear things. The arresting officers who brought in the children mentioned that portrait studios and printshops sometimes sell the pictures. Not out in the open, of course, but in a back room. On the surface, they're just sitting people for portraits or printing leaflets, broadsides, and caricatures. But if you ask the right way, they offer something more."

"Where are these shops located?" Leo asked.

"You cannot possibly go!"

"I won't, of course," she said, lying through her teeth and feeling somewhat guilty for it. "The addresses are for Inspector Reid."

Dita didn't look convinced but sighed and said, "They mentioned Pall Mall and Covent Garden. Cambridge Circus and the Dials. And of course, Fleet Street has several printers."

Cambridge Circus? The busy traffic circle was where Hogarth and Tipson was located. Mr. Carter could have brought his photographs to a nearby printshop on his way to or from work.

Dita touched her elbow. "I worry about you sometimes. Are you sure this information is all for Jasper Reid?"

She danced around the truth. "I assure you it is for his case."

Her plan was only half-formed, and Leo knew that was a problem. If, and when, she found a shop willing to show her their illicit collection in some back room, what would she do? She couldn't very well ask if William Carter or Hannah Barrett had ever provided the photographs. She'd be tossed out on her ear.

Still, she was convinced Miss Barrett and Mr. Carter had been employing that peephole in some illegal way and that it played into the reason they were both dead. Finding evidence of their illegitimate enterprise could lead to the name of the person they'd mistakenly underestimated and tried to blackmail.

She walked Dita to Scotland Yard, then carried on to Spring Street, where she found her uncle in the postmortem room. He looked up from the cavity of an open chest on what appeared to be a middle-aged man.

"There you are. How was your visit to All Saints?"

For a moment, Leo forgot all about the note she'd left before dawn with her excuse.

"Eventful," she replied after her brain caught up. "I promise to tell you more, but first, do you need assistance with that?" She gestured toward the postmortem.

"Not at all. Look." He held out his bloodied hands. They barely quivered. "It's a good day. Not for this fellow, of course. Expired of a weak heart. The report will be simple. Why? Are you going somewhere again?"

The question tugged at her, pulling her stomach low. "I have been gone a lot lately, haven't I? I'm sorry."

Claude shook his head. "I didn't mean for you to apologize. I know things have been difficult with your aunt. Some of her comments..."

"It's not that. I'm not avoiding Aunt Flora, not on purpose at least. It has to do with the morgue break-in."

He blinked, his thick spectacles magnifying the motion. "You're not involving yourself in anything dangerous, are you?"

Being pushed into a grave by a potential murderer could be considered dangerous, but in the end, all she'd received were sore limbs and a dirt-streaked face.

"I'm being careful, I promise. So," she said, moving along swiftly, "you've no objection if I go out for another hour or two?"

He waved his hands as if to shoo her along and then turned back to the cracked chest of the corpse on the table.

Leo was grateful for the mild weather as she crossed Trafalgar Square and walked up Charing Cross Road, toward Cambridge Circus. It would have been a long way in the rain, but under the fair sky, it felt far less than the quarter hour it took before she entered the circle, where several streets joined into one central artery. She kept her eyes sharp for any shingles hung out for printers or photography studios as she walked around the circle, careful to avoid carriages and omnibuses.

To the east was the Seven Dials, a similar conjunction of streets. It wasn't the finest part of London, and Leo knew better than to tread there alone. However, it was very much the sort of place that might house a shop selling salacious photography. Ignoring the cautionary voice in her head—which sounded an awful lot like Jasper—telling her to stop, she turned in that direction. Her palms began to sweat as the businesses and buildings changed noticeably and with remarkable haste. Almost immediately, the middle-class appearance of Cambridge Circus eroded into that of a lower class. She started toward the center of the Dials, promising herself she would only go that far and then turn around if she hadn't seen anything.

But Leo slowed after a quick glance down a side street. A sign prominently carved with the word "Portraits" captured her interest. Looking over her shoulder, the corner frontage of Hogarth and Tipson across Cambridge Circus was still visible. Not a long walk for Mr. Carter to have made, to be sure.

Gathering her mettle, she turned down the side street. Shops selling tobacco, spirits, second-hand clothing, and one advertising herbal remedies and tinctures for one's longevity and good health dotted the pavement. The portraitist had a name painted on the shingle: Mr. Colin McDaniels. Still uncertain what to say once she entered, Leo pressed down her shoulders and let herself into the shop. A bell chimed overhead. The shop was spare, with some framed portraits of men and women, and a few children, displayed on the wall as well as on standing easels. A layer of dust had settled on the frames and the furniture, and the floor and carpets looked as if they hadn't been swept in a season.

There was no sign of the proprietor at first, and Leo was left to wander the shop. But then, a curtain to a back room swept aside, and a man appeared, tugging on the lapels of his coat collar, as if just having put it on at the sound of the bell.

"Ah, welcome, miss, and good day to you." His fair

cheeks had flushed from the rush to reach the front of his shop.

"Good morning," Leo replied. "You are Mr. McDaniels, the portraitist?"

He adjusted his thin bowtie, which was limp and spotted with grease. "That I am, miss, and what can I do for you? A portrait for your sweetheart?" He peered a bit closer at her, and his welcoming grin faltered. "If that's so, I've a mirror and comb for use, free of charge."

Leo touched her cheek, recalling the dirt Jasper had tried brushing away. She hadn't had a moment to stop and wash up.

"No, no portrait, thank you."

Mr. McDaniels flashed a pleased grin. "No sweetheart?"

His interest put her on her guard. She was a woman, alone, very near the Seven Dials. And though the photographer didn't appear violent on the surface, one never knew.

She pushed back her shoulders, prepared to tell him that it was none of his concern. But then, a different avenue presented itself. One that might lead her to what she'd come here to potentially find.

"Yes, I do have a beau." Her hands warmed in her gloves. "In fact, he is why I've come. You see he has… interests. I've been informed that this shop might accommodate them."

Mr. McDaniels lifted his chin. "I'm not sure I understand your meaning, miss."

She couldn't tell if he was baiting her. There was only one way to find out.

"I think you do," she replied, attempting to be coy.

She'd seen Dita do it before with Constable Lloyd and a few other men. Without practice, however, Leo felt like a marionette with knotted strings as she fluttered her lashes.

The photographer held her in a flat, unaffected stare. "I'm afraid I'm just a simple Irishman, miss."

Well, now she felt idiotic. Leo released the coquettish angling of her head. "I see. Very well then, forgive me for disturbing your breakfast." She touched her neck as if to indicate his grease-spotted tie.

He was caught between fussing over his tie and stopping her from leaving. "Wait, now, miss, if you'd just tell me more about his interests...*specifically*...I might be able to show you in the right direction."

He made a small gesture with his hand toward the curtain through which he'd come. *The back room.*

"I suppose you'd call these photographs artistic in nature," she replied slowly, tripping over the words. If she sounded doubtful, it was because she was. But Mr. McDaniels's flirtatious grin reappeared.

"If you'll follow me." He pulled aside the curtain and disappeared into the back.

Jasper's voice, commanding her to not, under any circumstances, follow, blared in her mind. But she was close. She could feel it. So, she ignored the voice and crossed the threshold, coming into a cluttered storage room filled with shelving. Mr. McDaniels turned on a frosted-green desk lamp.

"This beau of yours is a lucky gent to have a sweetheart willing to support his hobbies," he said with another sly grin. He unlocked a drawer and took out a file box. It was filled with photographs, all mounted on cards. They weren't uniform—she saw different sizes, different foils and engravings on the edges before the man set his arm over the top, blocking them.

"Now, what tickles his fancy?" Leo squirmed at the question, and when she failed to produce an answer, he rephrased. "What sort does he like to look at? Women? Men? Or..." He peered sideways at her. "Might you have an interest in sitting for a portrait yourself, as a *personal gift*?"

Leo couldn't stop the gasp of insult. "Absolutely not." She began to heat under her collar. This had been too hasty a plan. What was she doing in this back room, discussing lewd photographs with a stranger? She was about to beat a hasty path to the front of the shop and out the door. But then a thought came to her.

"Are there many photographers who specialize in specific topics?"

He nodded. "Aye. Quite a few."

She thought of the peephole and how those in the guest bedroom might not have known they were being watched. "Are most staged? Or are there some that are more voyeuristic in perspective?"

Mr. McDaniels touched the side of his nose, as if to say he understood her completely, then flipped to the back of the file box. Leo braced herself for what she might see. She was no shrinking violet, and dead bodies in all stages of decomposition usually failed to turn her stomach, but the first few photographs he spread out on the desk were a shock to her sensibilities.

"As you can see, the variety is colorful," he said.

It was an understatement. The subjects ranged from men and women together in various states of undress and positions, to women embracing in the same manner, and men together too. Leo's cheeks heated as she tried to focus on the details of the backdrop of these photographs and not on the people shown.

"See any prospects?" Mr. McDaniels asked after a few moments in which Leo felt entirely out of her depth.

"I'm not sure, I—" Her eyes stopped on a photograph. It was the mounting card she noticed first. Gold foil along the edges, just like the cards scattered over the rug in Mr. Carter's studio. Next, it was the busy floral pattern of the wallpaper, then the wrought iron poster bed, the privacy screen, and chaise longue. It was all an exact match to the Barretts' guest bedroom.

But it was one of the two men positioned together in an intimate manner that caused the hair on the back of her neck to stand on end.

"How much for this one?" Leo picked up the mounted photograph, and Mr. McDaniels cocked his head.

"I see now what sort your beau is," he said with a nod. "Me, I don't judge. I just provide. Two bob, miss."

She paid the man and left straightaway for Scotland Yard.

Chapter Eighteen

The first time Jasper had walked into Inspector Gregory Reid's office at Scotland Yard, he never imagined it would one day become his own. That first day, and for many more days afterward, he'd been too nervous to speak. Almost too nervous to breathe. He'd been unduly convinced that the Inspector would know who he was underneath the bruises, the split lip, and swollen eye. There was more evidence of the severe beating he'd received underneath his ratty clothes too, but Jasper didn't regret the injuries. Not one lick. He'd have endured that thrashing again and again if it meant getting away from where he'd been.

All this time, all these years, the Inspector had known the truth. Most of it, at least. And he'd still brought Jasper into his home. Into his life. He'd still given Jasper his name.

Jasper leaned his hip against his desk, arms crossed and looked out the window. He was at a loss. Chief Coughlan had given him a proper dressing down for the mess at All Saints. He hadn't cared at all that an unauthorized grave robber had gotten there before Jasper and Lewis—all he cared about was that not a bloody thing had been found inside the coffin.

"There might have been something there before," Jasper had argued.

"But there isn't now, and you've no idea who *might* have taken what *might* have been there," he'd scoffed. "It's over, Reid. Carter was killed in a housebreaking, Stillman in a mugging, and Miss Barrett was accidentally struck by an omnibus. You've no tangible evidence to the contrary, so you are done with it. Move on. Cases are piling up on your desk every day. Do your job and see to them."

He'd pointed to the door in dismissal, and Jasper had endured Tomlin's smug grin as he'd returned to his office. He hadn't been sacked, but Jasper could feel the ground shaking beneath him.

It was going to be a nightmare telling Leo it was over, especially now that they'd come upon a strong theory that Carter had buried photographs, perhaps intended for blackmail purposes. She wouldn't understand Coughlan's decision. The woman was so unreasonably stubborn it made his muscles tight with frustration. Why couldn't she simply be like other ladies? Though as soon as the question fired off in his head, he knew it would be impossible. It wasn't even what he wanted, really. He didn't know what he did bloody want, except not to find her in another grave or locked closet.

A knock preceded the opening of his office door.

"You're going to want to hear this, guv." Lewis closed the door behind him. Jasper twisted away from the window.

"Not if it has anything to do with the Stillman case," he said. "Coughlan's shut it down."

"Bugger that. You're going to want to hear it," Lewis said, though he started speaking more softly. "I was looking for anything we have on Tommy Welch in the convict office, like you asked, when I recalled that Stillman was a ticket-of-leave man. He was due to report in every week after his release from Wandsworth."

Most convicts released from prison early, usually due to good behavior, held tickets-of-leave, permitting them to live among the masses again and earn a living. But they were required to check in regularly with the convict office, so Scotland Yard could keep tabs on them.

"I asked Constable Fine in the convict office about Stillman," Lewis went on. "He says he didn't need to check the registry to recall that he showed up two Wednesdays ago, on schedule."

Jasper frowned. "All right. What of it?"

"Fine arrived at the office that morning to find a message on his blotter marked for Stillman. When he handed it over, wouldn't you know, Stillman couldn't read beyond his own name. So, Fine opened it and read it to him."

Intrigue straightened Jasper's back.

"It was a summoning to the Jugger on Friday night at eight o'clock. About some work," Lewis said, a sly grin forming. "I'll buy you a pint at the Rising Sun if you can guess who signed the message."

He didn't have the patience for games. "I'll buy you a pint if you'll just spit it out, man."

Thwarted, Lewis sighed. "You did."

Jasper went still. "*I* signed it?"

The detective sergeant lifted his palms up in surrender. "Constable Fine will attest to it."

Jasper slammed his closed fist onto his desk and cursed. What in hellfire was going on here? "I sent no such message. Did Fine keep it?"

Lewis shook his head.

"If it was left for Stillman on his scheduled day to report in at the convict office, the person who wrote it has access to the registry," Jasper said. The truth settled in like the drop of an anchor. "Someone here at the Yard is behind all of this."

"That grave was hit right after the chief arranged for a disinterment. Who do you know for certain overheard your request?" Lewis asked.

"Tomlin, of course." Jasper sighed. "And Wiley."

The desk constable had been listening at the door. Being a nosy parker, or so Jasper had thought. But then again, Wiley had just happened to be walking past Duck Island when he heard Mr. Gates, the bird keeper, shouting for the police.

Wiley was a peacocking simpleton. But involving himself in murders? Jasper couldn't imagine to what end. Though, he could easily envision him shoving Leo into a grave and snickering about it as he ran off.

"Send Wiley in. I'd like a word."

"He's not at his desk," Lewis reported.

"Very well, next time you see him."

The door to his office opened swiftly without a warning knock, and Leo, still wearing her dirt-streaked coat and skirt from earlier at All Saints, whisked inside.

"No Constable Wiley today? I almost missed being scolded and chased."

The apples of her cheeks were flushed, and her eyes glittered with excitement as she opened her handbag.

"We were right," she continued in a rush, pulling something from her bag and then slapping it onto the desk. When she pulled her hand away, Jasper was left staring at a photograph of two men, both unclothed and locked in an embrace.

Shock crackled through him, traveling like lightning from his skull to his feet.

"What in God's name—" He snatched up the photograph and stared at her, utterly baffled. "What are you doing with this?"

Lewis frowned. "What is it?"

Grimacing, Jasper handed it to him.

"Blimey," the detective sergeant breathed, dropping it back onto the desk with the image facing down.

"Honestly, the two of you." Leo took it up and held the image out for Jasper to see again. "Look at him."

He did, reluctantly. It was a photograph of the type they'd theorized Carter and Miss Barrett had been engaged in taking. After focusing on the men in the photograph, he understood Leo's reason for barging in. He took the photo from her.

"This is Mr. Barrett."

Hannah's brother was standing with another, unfamiliar man in a pose that could not be misconstrued.

"And that," Leo tapped the photograph "is the guest bedroom. Miss Barrett and Mr. Carter were secretly taking photographs of her brother and selling them to specialty shops."

Lewis scratched the back of his head. "Did he know about it?"

"More importantly, did he consent to it?" Leo asked. "Or might he have found out after the fact and tried to recover the photographs and glass plate negatives by any means possible?"

Jasper stuffed the photograph into his waistcoat pocket. "I think I'll ask him."

"Coughlan won't like that," Lewis said.

"He will if it leads to an arrest," Jasper replied, taking his coat and hat from the standing rack. But then he stopped. He turned to find Leo nearly upon his heels. "Where, exactly, did you find this photograph?"

She pulled back, her expression becoming opaque. "Does it matter?"

"You were supposed to go to the morgue."

"I did. Briefly."

Lewis cleared his throat. "Is there something I can do while you're out, guv?"

Jasper wanted to ask him to tie Leo to a chair. But, once again, she'd managed to bring in a valuable lead. Coughlan would pitch a fit if he knew it was her lead.

"Search for any records the Met might have on Samuel Barrett. And when Wiley gets in, watch him. Be careful. I don't know if we can trust him."

Lewis nodded and left. When Jasper stood in the open doorway another moment, staring at Leo, she sighed.

"I will tell you where I went and how I came to be in possession of the photograph on our way to Mr. Barrett's."

Jasper didn't want to waste time arguing. If he told her to go to the morgue or home, she would just find her way to the Barrett household on her own.

"And if he killed Carter?" Jasper asked. He was beginning to think it was a distinct possibility.

"Then you can arrest him while I fetch a constable."

"You always have an answer, don't you?"

Leo lifted a shoulder and walked past him. "You make it sound like a flaw."

They left the Yard, signaling a cab and giving the address for Great Chapel Street. As promised, Leo explained how she'd found the illicit photograph. Jasper's stomach sank like a rock with every subsequent word she spoke. Finally, when she described entering the back room with the portraitist to view the offerings, he hinged forward in his seat, unable to curb his tongue.

"Do you have any idea how bloody stupid that was? To put yourself in a room, alone, with a man like that?"

Leo glared balefully at him. "I knew that's what you would say. I could hear it in my head when he asked me to follow him."

"Then you should have listened," he barked before sitting back again.

"Mr. McDaniels might have been a bit slippery, but he wasn't a threat."

Mr. *sodding* McDaniels. Jasper would be looking into this shop and shutting it down.

"Samuel Barrett seemed to despise William Carter," Leo said, unconcerned about the potential danger she'd been in. "If he found out his private encounters were being photographed and sold, it would give him motive to kill William. But surely, he wouldn't need to hire anyone to hunt down his own sister and steal her locket. He could have simply taken it from her neck himself." Leo bit her bottom lip, as though having a troubling thought. "What if Samuel Barrett *knew* about this operation? What if…"

Jasper picked up on her idea. "What if it was the other man in the photograph who did not know? And he, and others like him, were being blackmailed?"

Leo nodded, but he wasn't convinced.

"To consent to selling these photographs would be a great risk for someone like Samuel Barrett. If they were to be seen by the wrong person, if he were to be recognized… there are laws against distributing pornographic photos, not to mention engaging in intimacies with a partner of the same sex. He could be arrested." Jasper shook his head. "I don't think he knew they were being sold in shops like the one this *Mr. McDaniels* owns, but he might have participated in a blackmail scheme."

The photograph in Jasper's pocket weighed heavy as they rode onward. He wanted to strangle Leo for daring to search out a purveyor of such things by herself. Impulsive and shortsighted, yet bold as brass.

"You should have brought someone with you," he grumbled.

"Like Uncle Claude?" she asked with a roll of her eyes.

"Like me."

"You're a police detective. Mr. McDaniels would have sorted that out the moment you stepped into his shop."

"I could have waited on the pavement. At least then you wouldn't have been alone."

Leo sealed her lips against another retort that was certainly banging to get out. Jasper shook his head and huffed a reluctant laugh, tapping his pocket. "I can't believe you bought this thing."

"That reminds me—you owe me two bob." She tried to

suppress a crafty grin. "And what was that back in your office, about not being able to trust Constable Wiley?"

He explained about what had occurred at the convict office with Stillman and the forged message Constable Fine had read.

"That explains it," she said.

"Does it? Enlighten me."

"Ticket-of-leave men can be arrested on any charge, or even on suspicion without proof, which would negate their condition for release from prison. That makes them vulnerable. Constable Wiley could have threatened Mr. Stillman with a return to Wandsworth unless he retrieved photographs that Constable Wiley himself was being blackmailed with. Photographs of a sensitive nature," she said, gesturing to Jasper's chest and the hidden photograph in his waistcoat pocket.

"You think Wiley was in photographs like these?"

He was aware that people's proclivities did not always run along standard, socially accepted lines, and he could not have cared less. Wiley's choices weren't any of his business. They weren't anyone's, and if Carter and the Barretts were exploiting people in this manner, then they were the ones who'd deserved arrest, not the people they tricked.

"It makes sense," Leo replied. "He could have easily gone through the convict files to find the perfect scapegoat."

The carriage came to a stop outside Mr. Barrett's home. Jasper opened the door and descended, then handed Leo down. They started for the black crepe door.

"I've been thinking about Miss Barrett giving her

notice at the hospital," Leo said. "The nurse at St. Thomas told me she'd been planning to leave London."

Jasper brought down the knocker. "Maybe she feared she was going to meet the same fate as Carter."

"Or maybe she'd decided not to do as he wished. Instead of digging up Mr. Strange's coffin to recover the photographs, she'd decided to cut and run."

There was no sound of Mr. Barrett approaching from within, so Jasper brought down the knocker again.

"Maybe he isn't at home," Leo said, but as she leaned over a wrought iron handrailing to peer inside the closest window, she gave a cry. "Oh, my goodness. Jasper, open the door. Open it!"

It wasn't locked, and they rushed inside to find Samuel Barrett sprawled face down at the foot of the stairs.

"Mr. Barrett?" Jasper stepped into the crimson-soaked carpet around him and crouched by the man's side.

His skin was ashen, and blood leaked from his lips. He was still breathing, though weakly.

Leo crouched across from Jasper. "He looks to have been stabbed in the back."

Three small slashes in Mr. Barrett's jacket had bled profusely. Leo met Jasper's eyes and shook her head. He wouldn't live. The copious loss of blood wouldn't allow for it.

Mr. Barrett gurgled a barely audible word—*"Father..."*—as blood filled his airway and sprayed from his lips.

"Mr. Barrett, can you give me a name? Who did this to you?" But Samuel's labored breaths went silent. His eyes stared, unfocused. Unseeing.

Jasper pressed his hand to the man's eyes, closing them. "He's gone."

Chapter Nineteen

Leo stared at Mr. Barrett's still figure. One moment, he'd been breathing. The next, he was dead. She'd seen countless corpses at the morgue, but she'd never actually witnessed someone's moment of death. The enormity of it sealed her to the spot.

Jasper, however, was not so immobilized. He drew his revolver from the holster under his coat as he shot to his feet.

"What are you doing?" she asked, her shock severed.

As he stepped around Mr. Barrett's body toward the sitting room, his revolver extended before him, she answered the question for herself: Whoever did this might still be present in the house.

Standing straight, Leo stole a look into the sitting room. The trinkets and picture frames that had been on the mantel had all been swept to the floor; the furniture overturned and slit open, stuffing torn out; the carpet shoved aside and left in a heap.

"It's just like Mr. Carter's studio," she whispered. "They were looking for something."

"Stay right next to me," Jasper ordered as he continued down the short hall to the kitchen in the back. This, too, had been razed, with cabinets open and cleared, and drawers and their contents scattered onto the floor.

"Mr. Barrett might have bled for some time," Leo said as they moved back toward the base of the stairs. "The lacerations on his back align with his spine and lungs. He may have been incapacitated while the killer ransacked his home. I highly doubt they're still here."

Jasper lowered his weapon and went to the front door to close it, to deter passersby from looking in. "He was calling for his father. I thought he'd said their father died when they were young—"

A sudden sound upstairs, like the clinking of glass, sent a bolt of alarm through Leo. Jasper raised his weapon again.

"Stay here," he mouthed as he started up the steps, revolver in front of him.

She gripped the banister's lower spindles, her pulse picking up speed. Jasper reached the landing and rounded on the open door to the left. He entered the room, disappearing from view. The moments stretched for ages. But then he reappeared, his weapon still raised. Jasper went to inspect the other two rooms—Hannah's and the guest room.

Leo waited, her worry mounting as no sound came from upstairs.

"Jasper?" she called.

He arrived at the top of the stairs, his revolver now lowered. "You should see this."

Leo didn't hesitate. She rushed up the stairs and followed him into the room to the immediate left. It was a workroom, though an unmade bed was tucked into a corner. There were metal tools and boxes of locks and all manner of hardware that she did not know the use of scattered over the floor.

"He explained he was a locksmith and kept his workroom in the house," she said.

"He kept something else in here." Jasper stood by a tall stand of shelves, all cleared of their contents. The shelves had been built into the wall, and they also appeared to be a front for a hidden door.

Leo pulled to an abrupt halt. It was a closet, big enough to walk into. The floor was covered in debris. A table had been overturned, boxes torn down from the closet shelves, but none of it had anything to do with locksmithing. There were photographs and mounting cards, along with what appeared to be glass plate negatives, some smashed, though others intact. That must have been the sound of clinking glass they'd heard; a few plates had shifted and fallen. Cording was strung between shelves, and while no developed photographs were clipped to it, attached were small metal clasps that would have once held them.

Leo stayed on the threshold, reluctant to enter any small space. She'd always hated them, ever since spending those interminable hours in the dark trunk in that attic. So, she crouched and reached for a stack of photographs and one of the glass plates. Nearby, a collection of bottles had been smashed, spilling a pale-yellow, sand-like substance. She read the label.

"Silver bromide. Isn't that a chemical used to develop photos?"

"His fingertips were discolored," Jasper said.

"Anyone working with silver or metal would have a grayish tinge to their fingers and under their nails," she said, thinking of how she'd ruled out the silversmith C.S. Longberger as being the John Doe whose bag Stillman had stolen. "I'd thought it was from his locksmithing business."

She stood. The phantom-like image on the glass plate in her hand displayed yet another intimate encounter, though thankfully the exposure didn't allow for a detailed image.

"You were right. Samuel Barrett was part of the scheme," Jasper said. "He developed photographs in this secret room. Which his killer then rooted out."

"Or he allowed William Carter to use this space," Leo said. "He wouldn't have wanted to risk Mrs. Hogarth or Mr. Tipson finding his work at their studio."

"But why would the killer come here today? He'd already dug up the coffin at All Saints."

She flipped through the photographs. "Mr. Carter buried *something* there. Though I wonder if something more had still been in this closet."

Jasper reached for the photographs in her hand. "You shouldn't look through those."

Leo whirled away. "I'm not that delicate, Inspector Reid." But then, her arm muscles locked, and a short gasp shuttled down her throat. "Oh, my."

She turned the photograph outward for him to view. He grimaced, as if seeing a woman in the nude was offensive. Perhaps it was, but it wasn't her lack of clothing that bothered Leo. It was her face.

"This is Hannah Barrett," she said. She'd only ever seen the young woman in death, but Leo wasn't mistaken about who the woman in the photograph was.

Jasper took the photograph. It was of three people. Two men and one woman. Truly, Leo's stomach cinched tight as he observed the image. What must he think of it? Goodness, what did *she* think of it?

Jasper tapped the photo. "This is William Carter."

Leo looked again at the young man with dark hair and an impressive, though ghostly pale chest. "How do you know it is Mr. Carter?"

The question lingered in the air, unanswered. Jasper shrugged belatedly. "Scotland Yard keeps its eye on the East Rips and the Carter family."

It made sense, but she also recalled Mr. Barrett's comment that William had never been arrested or jailed. Too slippery for that, he'd said. But she let it go in favor of a more pressing quandary.

"If Hannah and William are both in the photo, who is taking it?"

"Her dear brother, I imagine," Jasper replied.

Her brother had *watched* her with these men? The turning of Leo's stomach made her feel ill.

"Gracious." She handed Jasper the photo, eager to relinquish it. "I know I'm rather unworldly about such things, but I can't understand why anyone would wish to expose themselves in such a way."

He pocketed the photo. "It might not have been a wish. Sometimes people get caught up in things they regret afterward."

Jasper watched her for a moment and seemed to want to say more. But then, he cleared his throat. "I need to summon some constables. And you need to leave. I can't have the chief learning you were with me when I found Barrett's body."

Groaning, Leo followed Jasper from the room, down the stairs and back to the entrance hall. She didn't want him in trouble with Chief Inspector Coughlan, but she also despised being told where to go and what to do.

"I take it I'm to return to the morgue," she said as they again looked down upon Mr. Barrett's inert form.

A white piece of paper, sticking out from the breast pocket on his coat, was beginning to absorb some of his blood from the carpet.

"I'll come by later to let you know—" Jasper stopped speaking as Leo crouched, then balanced herself against the newel post to reach for the paper. "What are you doing?"

"Just looking." She pulled the paper free.

"That is, in fact, touching."

It was a business card for a Mr. Fordham Graves, a reporter at *The Times*. Leo had read his columns before, including one last week about the misuse of force by some constables in Blackfriars that resulted in the death of a suspected pickpocket. Up close, she noticed the card hadn't been absorbing blood from the carpet; rather, the blood had been pressed into the paper by bloody fingertips, leaving behind ridged swirls.

"Mr. Barrett was already bleeding when he reached for this card," Leo said, showing it to Jasper.

"What was he trying to do?" Jasper murmured, then looked up. Leo followed the direction of his eyes. They'd landed on the telephone, installed in the rear of the front hall.

"Mr. Graves's exchange number is printed on the card," she said. "Did he hope to place a call?"

"At the moment of his death?" Jasper took off his hat and scrubbed a hand through his hair.

She hardly ever saw him with his hat off, but each time she did, the shimmering golden streaks scattered through his dark blond hair drew her eyes. The fair strands didn't suit his somber disposition. He met her gaze, his dark green eyes piercing.

"This is becoming far too dangerous, Leo. I'm worried the man who did this," he gestured to the body, "is the same man who pushed you into the grave this morning. Which means he knows you're involved and that you know things he would rather you didn't."

A sensation crawled over her back, like there were eyes in the walls, another peephole perhaps obscured by the busy wallpaper pattern.

"If this person thinks I know too much, why was I pushed instead of stabbed?"

Jasper growled and stood. "I don't know. But for now…" He sighed, as if conflicted but resigned. "I want you with me."

Leo straightened with an odd uncurling in her stomach. He must have been truly worried for her safety if he wanted to keep her close more than he wanted to send her away. "Even if that means Chief Coughlan learns I was here?"

He scowled. "I'll handle it. And afterward, we'll go see Fordham Graves."

The Times, like many of London's other dailies, was located on a busy, industrial stretch of Fleet Street. It was nearing early evening by the time Leo and Jasper arrived. While waiting for Detective Lewis and a few of the constables to come to Great Chapel Street to see to Mr. Barrett's body, Leo had sent a messenger to the morgue to inform Claude that she was going to be away for the rest of the day. Her uncle would not resent her absence, though she did feel a pinch guilty for not being there, yet again.

However, if one of the last things Mr. Barrett wanted to do as he lay dying was call Mr. Fordham Graves, it was imperative they find out why. And if Jasper wanted her to stay at his side, well, she wasn't going to argue.

The man at the front desk of *The Times* took one look at Jasper's warrant card, tucked inside its black leather case, and leapt up to show them the way to the news department. The large room was filled with tobacco smoke, the blare of typewriter bars, and the dinging bells of carriage returns. There wasn't a female in sight, even though Leo had expected to see some lady typists. This was where Miss Hayes was employed, after all. But perhaps the society pages were typed elsewhere in the building.

The man leading them pointed out Mr. Graves. The reporter was hunched over a typewriter, furiously banging at the keys, while a cigarette smoldered in an ashtray by his elbow.

"Fordham Graves?" Jasper asked as he and Leo reached his desk. He'd raised his voice above the clamor of the newsroom and still barely caught the man's attention.

When Mr. Graves did look up, he was less impressed by the warrant card than the man at the front desk had been.

"What's this about, detective? Is there a problem with something I printed?"

Jasper put away his identification. "I'm not familiar with your work."

"I read your piece last week," Leo said. Graves looked pleased, so she clarified, "I thought it heavily biased. You cast quite a villainous light on the officers you accused of brutality, yet you painted the pickpocket suspect as a saint."

"Not a saint." His expression hardened. "Unfairly persecuted. He was just fourteen years old and dead before he even reached the police station. And there's been trouble with those same officers before. Two months ago—"

"I'm not here about any of that," Jasper interrupted. He held up the bloodied business card. "I want to know how you're acquainted with Mr. Samuel Barrett."

"I don't know a Samuel Barrett."

"He's five-foot-eight, about ten stone. Wears spectacles. He's a locksmith," Leo said. Then, thinking the reporter might have read the obituaries, she added, "His sister, Miss Hannah Barrett, was struck and killed by an omnibus just a few days ago."

Mr. Graves shot up from his chair, startling her. "I see." He gestured for them to follow him. He led the way into a small interview room, turning up the gas wall bracket and closing the door behind them.

Leo drew in a steadying breath. The room wasn't much bigger than a coat closet, and without a window, the air was stuffy and stale. For the second time that day, she was reminded of the hours she'd spent inside the steamer trunk in her family's attic on Red Lion Street. Sealed inside, she'd only been able to hear her own breathing, the slamming of her heart, and, for a handful of minutes, the voices of the men who'd just been downstairs, killing her family.

"Stay still. Don't move a muscle. Breathe through your mouth. Whatever you hear, don't come out." It was all the whispered instruction he had given her before shutting the lid.

Leo never saw his face; she'd blown out the candle when the attic door opened, and a pair of soles started scuffing up the steps. At first, she thought it might be Jacob coming to rescue her. But when she'd heard an unfamiliar voice whispering, *"Little girl?"* she'd known it wasn't her brother. She'd crouched on her knees, but her foot had moved, striking the tray holding the tea party set she'd been arranging for her doll, Miss Cynthia.

"He calls himself John Smith," Mr. Graves said, drawing Leo back into the present. The reporter looked suspicious. "Why are you asking about him?"

"He's dead," Jasper answered bluntly. It wasn't meant to be insensitive, just straightforward. It was the best way to deliver difficult news, as Leo had long since learned from her uncle.

Mr. Graves sank down into a chair, nodding solemnly. "I was worried they'd get to him."

"They?" Jasper crossed his arms but didn't sit. Neither

did Leo; her legs were far too tense to bend. "Whom do you refer to?"

"I can't give you names because I don't know."

"But you thought he was in danger?" Leo asked. "Why?"

"Because of what he wanted to sell me."

She exchanged a hopeful glance with Jasper, who asked, "Which was?"

"Photographs. The explicit kind," he answered with a furtive, apologetic glance toward Leo. "And before you ask, no, I didn't see them. He wouldn't show them to me until we settled on a fee, which I couldn't do."

"Why not?" Jasper asked.

Mr. Graves flipped up his palms. "My editor refused. Said our paper was too respectable an institution to run tawdry illustrations based on whatever the photographs would show."

Leo thought she knew why Mr. Barrett would have chosen Fordham Graves. "You write the police beat for the paper."

"And I'm happy to do it. The people of London are tired of the corruption and double standards at Scotland Yard."

Jasper's glare intensified. Leo had been privy to too many conversations with the Inspector over the years to be ignorant about police corruption. Some officers dipped their fingers into many pots, and that was just the way of it. Jasper's fingers were clean though. She trusted that, without question.

"Mr. Barrett approached you because the photographs were of someone associated with the police force," she guessed. He nodded.

"When was this?" Jasper asked.

"Last Saturday. I was here writing an article when he showed up. He said his sister had gotten involved in some blackmail scheme with her betrothed, but they had chosen the wrong person. The fiancé had gotten himself killed, and Smith worried he and his sister were next."

"Why not leave London? Why try to sell you the photographs?" Jasper asked.

"Smith said they *were* leaving. He hoped if the person was exposed publicly, it would create a distraction and give them some time to get away. But then, he came in a few days ago and told me his sister was run down. I got concerned. I couldn't buy the photographs, but there are others who might. I told him he had to be careful and that he should move the photographs and glass plate negatives to a safer location. He said they were already split up."

Leo frowned. "Split up? What did he mean by that?"

"The fiancé had put the glass plates somewhere safe. Smith—or Barrett, as that was his real name—had the photographs somewhere else."

Two different locations. She turned to Jasper. "That's why Mr. Barrett's house was ransacked even after Mr. Strange's coffin was dug up. The killer had found one set but not the other. And he would need both the negatives and the developed pictures to be safe."

"A coffin was dug up?" The reporter sat up straight. "This sounds like a good story."

"It isn't," Jasper said, then moved toward the door. "Thank you for your time, Mr. Graves."

"He wouldn't have had them in his house," he said as Jasper opened the door. "I told him anywhere but the house. Especially after his sister was killed."

Leo and Jasper walked back through the smoky clatter of the newsroom.

"If he took Mr. Graves's advice, then the photographs weren't in Mr. Barrett's hidden closet," she said as they exited and left the racket behind.

"Or maybe he didn't take the advice, and the killer now has both the plates from Strange's casket and the photographs." Jasper grimaced. "If so, he's certainly destroyed them by now. There goes the evidence."

"We cannot give up," Leo said. "There is a chance Mr. Barrett did move them from the house. If so, where would he have hidden them?"

"A place he would have had access to. A place he could easily return to," Jasper mused. "I'd say his work, but as his locksmithing business was at home—"

A locksmith. Leo paused on a step as they made their way to the ground level. "If he was a locksmith, well then, he could pick any lock he wished."

Jasper took a step back up toward her. "What are you thinking?"

"I'm thinking about the back door to the morgue. I found it open after returning from Striker's Wharf, remember? Someone was in the back room. I saw him run out the door, into the cemetery. What if it was Mr. Barrett finding a place to store his photographs?"

Jasper came up another step and now stood directly below hers. "Why would he choose the morgue?"

The answer dropped into her mind as if gifted from some magical source. "Because I gave him the idea."

He quizzed her with a look, but before she could explain, a voice carried down the stairwell. "Jasper?"

Coming from an upper floor, Miss Constance Hayes

slid her gloved hand along the wood railing as she descended. Her large blue eyes jumped with dubious curiosity from Leo to Jasper, and then back again.

She was the picture of perfection, with rose-tinted lips, a fashionable dress and matching shoes, a wide-brimmed Gainsborough hat dressed in plush, velvet ribbons, and a small, embroidered handbag looped in the crook of her arm. She practically radiated wealth and elegance and would draw eyes anywhere she went. It made her presence at a drab newspaper office all the odder—*and* interesting. Leo was certain she was not the only one affected by the heiress's choice to shun her rightful place in society to work instead. In fact, it was just about the only thing Leo liked about her.

"Constance." Jasper took a few steps up, passing Leo as he went to greet her. He kept his hands in his pockets until she held out her hand to him. He quickly grasped it and led her down the rest of the stairs. Leo turned first to head them off.

"I didn't realize you were going to be here," Constance said, her voice echoing through the stairwell.

"We're following a lead for an investigation," Jasper explained.

She canted her head and peered at Leo. "You're following a lead with Miss Spencer?"

"It involves the morgue," she explained, secretly enjoying the bilious press of Constance's lips.

"Does it? How unpleasant." She linked her arm with Jasper's and angled herself away from Leo. It was as effective as a door shutting in her face. "I'm off. Will you call on me tonight?" She rose onto the tips of her toes and whispered something into his ear.

Jasper listened intently, then nodded as she dropped back to her heels, still clinging to his arm. Leo fought a roll of her eyes.

"I'll come by after I call on my father," he told her, and it must have pleased her because she simpered before carrying on and exiting through the lobby doors.

"I'm not going to ask what she whispered into your ear," Leo said as they followed Constance's lead and exited onto Fleet Street.

"Good, because I'm not going to tell you." He tugged his coat collar up against a spitting rain.

Leo slowed as a familiar figure descended from a nearby carriage onto the pavement. Sir Nathaniel came toward them, his gait limping. The weather must have been *getting into his bones*, as he called it, his old injury from Africa making itself known. He tipped his hat to them.

"Ah, Miss Spencer and Inspector Reid, what brings you to Fleet Street?"

"Commissioner," Jasper greeted in return, his eyes skating toward Leo. She could read his reticent expression perfectly: He wished Leo wasn't with him.

"I've been following a lead on another murder connected to William Carter and Clarence Stillman," he answered.

I, when he'd just told Constance *We*. Leo bristled, even though rationally, she knew he could not credit Leo as a partner. She wasn't that anyway. Jasper had allowed her to accompany him because he feared for her safety. To tell the commissioner that would lead to the story about Leo being at All Saints and getting pushed into an open grave. So, she kept her lips sealed.

"Is this the Barrett fellow I heard about at the Yard just now?" the commissioner asked. Then, with a careful look at Leo, he added, "There is some…talk about what was found in an upstairs closet."

Remaining quiet would only lead the commissioner to believe such topics affronted her, when the true affront was being considered too delicate to be spoken to plainly. "Yes, Samuel Barrett and William Carter may have been blackmailing people with indecent photographs, taken without permission or knowledge," she said.

The commissioner swung a startled look toward Jasper. "Do you have evidence of this, Reid?"

"We're close." His short reply was laden with irritation. For Leo, no doubt.

Sir Nathaniel peered at her. "And how are you involved?"

She didn't have an excuse ready. Neither did Jasper, apparently. At their stumped silence, Commissioner Vickers raised a brow.

"It appears Gregory's penchant for solving a good tangle has been passed on to you as well, Miss Spencer." He tucked his chin. "However, there is no place for a woman inside the Met. You must allow Inspector Reid to conduct police business alone. Am I clear?"

The burn of insult and humiliation crept up her neck toward her cheeks. To be spoken to like she was a little girl, pestering Jasper to include her!

"Now, I'm late to my meeting with the publisher at the *Daily Chronicle*. The papers are either our friends or our enemies. Best to stay in their good graces." He sighed. "Keep me abreast of what you discover, Reid." He tipped the brim of his hat again toward Leo. "Miss Spencer."

And then, he was off.

"The utter gall," she hissed once he was out of earshot. "No room in the Met for a woman! As if I did not already know as much."

Of course she couldn't be a detective. She couldn't be a coroner either, though both of those positions suited her far better than any other available to women. She most certainly couldn't be like Miss Constance Hayes, typing society pages. She was gregarious and sociable, and always grinning. There was too much darkness in Leo for that. She could feel it sometimes—the burden of that darkness.

"You couldn't expect him to be pleased," Jasper said. "He isn't going to coddle you the way the Inspector has."

She turned her glare onto Jasper next. "I do not require, nor do I want, coddling."

He continued toward a cab stand. "Just tell me how you gave Mr. Barrett the idea to hide his photographs at the morgue. If they're there, we need to find them."

"Oh, it's *we* again, is it?" At his befuddled expression, she shook her head. "Never mind. I'll tell you on the way to Spring Street."

Chapter Twenty

The sky was the same bruised purple as a blackened eye when they arrived to find the front doors to the morgue locked. Leo tossed a look of trepidation toward Jasper before reaching into her handbag.

"Something must have happened with Flora," she said as she found the key and let them into the lobby. "Uncle Claude doesn't usually lock up until six."

Jasper sighed. He'd held his tongue for long enough. It was a sore subject with her, he knew, but he had to be blunt. "Leo, if he can't keep up with the work, the chief coroner will have no choice but to replace him."

He didn't want to think about what would happen to them if that came to pass. With Claude's palsy and Flora's deteriorating mind, Leo would be left to support them. She'd either need to find work…or a husband to provide for them.

Jasper kept on her heels, unreasonably irritated by that latter prospect as they entered the postmortem room.

"You're worrying for no reason, Jasper. He can keep up

with the work," she said, turning up the overhead gasoliers. Several sheeted bodies came into view. Jasper followed her as she passed them swiftly for the back room. "I've just been busy the last few days. Everything will go back to the way it was soon. Especially since I'm positive Mr. Barrett stashed his blackmail portraits in the crypt."

If her hunch was correct, then they'd soon find them. At last, they'd be looking upon the face of the person with the most motive to silence William Carter, Hannah Barrett, and her brother.

On the ride from Fleet Street, she'd reminded him of the day Mr. Barrett came to view his sister and arrange for her body's collection. Leo had stumbled over an explanation for why she was having him go through his sister's personal effects, piece by piece. What she'd intended was to find out if he'd noticed her locket was missing. In the process, she'd brought up the crypt, where unclaimed possessions were stored and accumulating dust. Her comment that hardly anyone ever went down into the crypt had likely given him the notion that it was where the much-coveted photographs might be safe.

If Leo's hunch was correct.

"Things cannot go back to the way they were," Jasper said after she'd lit the back office too and went directly for the door leading to the crypt. "You were sewing up cadavers after postmortems, and who knows what else."

Hell, she had to have a stomach made of steel. He'd seen plenty of bodies during the several years he'd been on the force, but sorting through internal organs and cutting into brains to decipher a cause of death? He didn't think he'd be able to bear it. And yet it didn't affect Leo.

He wavered between being disapproving of it and being impressed by her.

She placed her handbag on a shelf before lighting a pair of gas lamps with a lucifer match. Then pinned him with a glare. "Would you rather my uncle lost his position?"

"That isn't a fair question. You know I don't want that."

She handed him one of the lamps and then swung the door to the crypt open so fast he felt the breeze.

"Please, Jasper, let me decide how best to help my family." She disappeared onto the steps, and her voice grew muffled. "Wouldn't you do anything you needed to, to protect the Inspector? To help him?"

He started after her, ducking his head before entering the dark and musty stairwell. The walls were close, his elbows practically brushing them. He reached the bottom of the steps, their lamps flickering temperamentally and leaving most of the vast space in shadows. Gas had not been run down here, likely because of the lack of ventilation. There weren't any windows, and boxes and shelving and furniture and church pews had all been crammed between the arches propping up low, vaulted ceilings. An old confessional with its doors flung open leaned against the closest stone wall by the stairs.

"You're right. I would help the Inspector in any way I could," Jasper said. "So would you, even though he isn't your family. You care for him. Believe it or not, I care about Claude and Flora."

The gas light brightened her face as she held it higher. She met his gaze, and for once, her eyes weren't filled with remote poise or incisive cleverness. He saw doubt and a glimmer of distress.

"But they aren't your responsibility. They're mine. I could acquire another position somewhere, I'm sure, as a secretary or typist, or a switchboard operator, but how am I to take care of them on such meager wages?" She shook her head and closed her eyes. "Forget I said anything. I'm not going to burden you with my concerns."

She started away, but Jasper reached for her arm. He caught her wrist and brought her back toward him. Her arm went rigid under his palm but quickly relaxed.

"You're not burdening me. And you aren't alone."

Their lanterns flickered, lighting her pensive gaze. He had tugged her close. Too close. He should release her. But though his grip loosened and slipped, his fingers seemed to be ruled by a force other than his brain. He held on, his hand clasping hers. Finally, after a few heartbeats too long, he dragged in a breath and stepped back, letting go.

Haltingly, Leo moved a step in reverse too. "That…that means a great deal. Thank you." She coughed lightly and turned to face the vaults. "We should start looking."

Jasper started for the shelves and boxes nearby, and Leo took her lamp into another vaulted space, out of his view. Exhaling, an odd and stirring sensation crawled over his palms. What had possessed him to hold onto her hand for as long as he had?

He drew his mind away from the thought by opening the lid on a rectangular box made of corrugated board. The material was used to store files and evidence at the Yard, and many of these storage boxes looked to have come from the Metropolitan Police itself.

"Look under things, too, if they can be easily lifted," Leo called. He could see the light from her lamp bobbing through a collection of old church paraphernalia and unclaimed storage.

"This whole place needs to be cleaned out and organized. How do you find anything down here?" he called back.

"We don't. I was in earnest when I told Mr. Barrett that everything is just collecting dust."

Jasper shoved boxes back into their places after opening them but seeing no photographs. He was beginning to think Leo's hunch had been wrong when a box on a low shelf drew his attention. It looked like all the others, except for one thing: there was a smear in the dust on the lid.

"I might have something," he called, pulling the box from among its neighbors.

A hand had most certainly swept the dust away. Jasper set his lantern at his feet and lifted the lid. Inside was a pair of men's shoes, a moldering length of ivory neckcloth, and a small, rectangular paper box. He might have overlooked the little box entirely, if not for his having seen plenty of them scattered on the floor inside Mr. Barrett's ransacked hidden closet.

He brought out the small box, and lifting its lid, exhaled. A stack of photographs mounted on cards were stored within.

"Have you found them?" Leo's lantern shed light on the top photograph as she approached. It was of a man and a woman, neither of them dressed in even a stitch of clothing.

Jasper stared, unable to grasp what he was seeing. It wasn't the act that the hidden camera had captured on a glass plate negative that tolled through him and sank his stomach. It wasn't the nudity either. Those things couldn't shock him.

"No," Leo whispered as she stared at the top photograph. "Is that…?"

His pulse increasing, Jasper took the stack out of the box and began to flip through the photographs. There were five in all, each one progressively lewder than the one before it.

"Yes," he said, angling the photographs away from her line of sight. Leo's hand holding the lantern quavered. "It is."

The shutter of the concealed camera had captured Elsie Vickers while she'd been intimate with William Carter, as the top image had shown. Samuel Barrett joined them in three of the other photographs. Utterly nude and positioned in depraved ways, the images of the adolescent girl stoked a nauseating rage within him. God knew how, but Elsie had been lured into that bedroom and used by those two men, all while another young woman photographed the encounter, the opportunity to profit superseding any shred of human decency.

Leo lowered the lantern to the floor next to his own, and Jasper was grateful the images were no longer discernable. "It can't be. She's only seventeen, for heaven's sake. The commissioner…my God, if he knew…"

The wooden steps into the crypt groaned. When Jasper saw a man coming off the bottommost one, he dropped the box and reached for his police-issued Webley revolver underneath his coat.

"Don't, inspector." Benjamin Munson, the commissioner's deputy assistant, already had his own revolver trained on him. "Raise your hands high. Both of you."

Jasper lifted his hands, palms out, while stepping in front of Leo. "Munson."

Instantly, all the reasons why the deputy assistant would be here, holding them at gunpoint, unspooled in his mind.

Leo edged out from behind him. "They were blackmailing Elsie," she said before Jasper could. "How did you become involved, Mr. Munson?"

She sounded far too tranquil for being on the receiving end of a single-barrel revolver.

"There is no point in my explaining that, Miss Spencer." He took cautious steps closer, his aim firm and confident under pressure, as it should have been for a former military man.

Jasper eyed the Webley. "You shot William Carter and Clarence Stillman."

Though, why had Samuel Barrett had been stabbed?

"I need those photographs," Munson replied.

"Did Elsie turn to you?" Jasper asked evasively. His mind spun with possible ways to overpower Sir Nathaniel's assistant. Munson wasn't much in the way of muscle or brawn, but at this distance, his revolver's shot would hit its target. "Did she ask you to help recover the photographs?"

"Cooperate, Inspector Reid, and I will be sure neither of you suffer unnecessarily," he replied.

Leo produced a strangely belated gasp and huddled behind Jasper. It distracted him for the barest moment. It wasn't like her at all to cower or play the frightened female.

"If I were to guess," Jasper went on, choosing not to

respond to Munson's offer, "you agreed to help Elsie for a price: her hand in marriage."

It was why she'd been so upset when Jasper had last seen her. She didn't want to marry her father's assistant, but she wouldn't want those photographs to be released to the public—or perhaps to her father—even more.

Behind him, Leo had gone quiet. But not still. Jasper barely refrained from jumping when her hand slipped between the notched center of his frock coat. The tails split apart just above the buttocks, and that is where Leo's fingers now brushed. Jasper's throat cinched, and his body flashed over with heat, but as her hand moved slowly and smoothly along his left hip, he realized what she was trying to do.

"Enough," Munson said. "I don't relish killing a woman, but that is unavoidable now. If only you had kept your nose out of things, Miss Spencer."

"Let us discuss a different arrangement," Jasper said, his raised hands coming forward and together to help conceal Leo's fingers, creeping along his side, toward the black polished handle of his revolver. His temples began to dampen. She was either brilliant or mad.

"Take the photographs. The three of us walk out of here alive. I'll close the case, and you'll never hear a word about it again," Jasper went on. All bollocks, of course, but he needed to buy time.

"Why would you do that?" Munson asked.

"Do you think I want Elsie's secret exposed? I'll burn these photographs myself before they go anywhere."

Should the images make their way into the public eye, it would be a publicity nightmare for Sir Nathaniel and his daughter. He'd be scorned, his reputation tarnished irrevocably. And Elsie would be utterly ruined. Jasper didn't want that. And yet, he also couldn't burn the evidence.

Leo's palm grazed his ribs, and he tightened the muscles of his abdomen. It was the entirely wrong moment for it, but an answering tug came low in his stomach. It infuriated him. *She* infuriated him. What was she thinking? What did she know about handling a firearm? And yet, Jasper conceded that the Webley was their best chance at stopping Munson.

"Stop prevaricating, Reid. I know exactly what sort of copper you are, and you'd never allow me to go free."

"I would," Jasper replied. "If it meant keeping Miss Spencer alive."

With Leo standing so close that she'd practically adhered herself to his back, he found it wasn't a lie. *If* there was no other way out, he'd make the deal. But when the weight of her fingers fell upon the revolver's grip, he felt the smallest sliver of hope. It came with a surge of uncertainty. The woman had never fired a shot in her life. Hell, she might squeeze the trigger accidentally right now and send a bullet into his leg or hip.

"Unfortunately, I can't take that risk." Munson raised his revolver, preparing his shot. "My apologies, Miss Spencer."

The tinkling of a bell came on the heels of Munson's insincere apology. The morgue cat appeared at his ankle, rubbing up against his trouser hem. Just as quickly, Tibia swatted at him and hissed. Munson kicked his foot at the cat, his attention diverted.

"*Now*, Leo!" Jasper lunged, head and shoulders down like a battering ram. The bulk of his revolver vanished as she plucked it from his holster. Munson's split-second distraction cost him; when he fired his shot, it was hasty and untrained. Jasper collided with him, unscathed.

Munson barely stayed on his feet. They staggered backward, straight into the old confessional. Jasper pinned his arm against the corky wood and struggled to keep it there and take the revolver out of play. However, he had no control over Munson's trigger finger, which squeezed off a second, then a third, shot. Jasper jammed his shoulder into Munson's chest and, hoping to destabilize him, swept one of his ankles out from under him. Munson lurched, giving Jasper an opening to reach for the revolver.

But Munson slammed his forehead against Jasper's, hard. The blow stunned him, and a knee burrowed into his stomach. Jasper reeled backward but managed to cling on to Munson, and he brought the killer with him onto the stone floor.

A fist cuffed Jasper across the jaw, and then Munson was bowling him over, coming to sit astride him. Grabbing Munson's collar, he tossed him overhead, freeing himself from being held down—and certainly shot point-blank. Jasper scrabbled to his feet and turned to barrel back into the man. Munson had done the same, but in his haste to scrap with Jasper again, he'd paid no attention to the other person in the crypt.

Leo came up behind Munson and clubbed him on the back of the head with Jasper's Webley. After a muted *thud*, the deputy assistant's knees folded. He collapsed onto the floor, where he moaned incoherently.

Jasper kicked Munson's dropped weapon, spinning it away and out of reach. The man was writhing, still somewhat conscious. So, Jasper rolled him over and cracked a fist into his jaw. He went limp.

"Nicely done," Jasper said, his chest heaving as he tried to catch his breath. "Though, I thought you'd try to shoot him."

He took the patrolman cuffs, which he always carried, from his coat pocket and closed them around Munson's limp wrists before the man could rise to consciousness again.

Gingerly, Leo held out the revolver, as one might hold a dead rat by its tail. "I decided against discharging it. I was afraid I'd hit you instead."

He reclaimed his Webley, relieved yet impressed she'd entered the fray. It had been a risk.

He looked her over. "You aren't hurt?"

"No, and I think we have Tibia to thank," she said, forcing a half-smile to her lips. Her heart wasn't in it. She stooped to pick up the photographs Jasper had dropped, taking care to flip them face down. After a quiet moment, she stood again. "What do we do?"

Jasper took the photographs and tucked them into his coat pocket. He raked an unsteady hand through his hair, agitation climbing through him like ants. "I'll take Munson in and charge him with murder and attempted murder."

"But Elsie will be charged with accessory to murder."

"She committed a crime, Leo." He gritted his teeth. "If she knew what Munson was doing—"

"What if she didn't know?" she argued.

"I'll bring her in and find out."

Leo settled a hand on his arm. "Is there any way you can keep the photographs out of this?"

He stared at her, taken aback. "You're asking me to suppress evidence."

"I am asking you to think about what this will do to Elsie. Jasper, she will never recover."

"She should have considered that before allowing herself to be seduced by two men."

Regret curled through him instantly, and the flare of disappointment in Leo's eyes gave the feeling of thorns. He shouldn't have said it. He hadn't meant it. Elsie was young and impressionable, far more so than other young ladies her age. She would have been easily led, and Carter would have recognized that.

With a biting fury under his skin, Jasper grabbed Munson by the back of his coat and cuffed arms and hauled him up onto shaky footing. He needed to bring him in, book him, and then, he could question him.

He pushed the half-conscious man toward the stairs, knowing he should be grateful the killer had been caught. He would have been, too, if everything about it didn't feel so bloody wrong.

Chapter Twenty-One

The detective department was sedate when Leo and Jasper, and their prisoner, Mr. Munson, arrived. Being past seven o'clock in the evening, she should have expected it to be quiet. Unlike divisional officers, the C.I.D. operated during daylight hours and closed each night.

After what she and Jasper had just been through in the morgue crypt, the placid greeting they received was slightly dissatisfying. Constable Wiley shot to his feet, practically catching his thighs on the underside of the desk, when they turned toward the detective offices. He spared Leo a skeptical glare before looking twice at Benjamin Munson, his wrists bound and his face bloodied. "Isn't that the commissioner's assistant?"

Jasper shoved the deputy assistant forward, and the man staggered into the chair next to Constable Wiley's desk. He'd regained his senses, for the most part, on their brief walk to Whitehall Place, but he hadn't uttered a word.

"Benjamin Munson, yes. I've arrested him for the murders of William Carter, Clarence Stillman, and Samuel Barrett. Book him and then put him in the interview room. Keep him guarded at all times," Jasper said, forcing Mr. Munson to stay seated.

The man avoided eye contact, choosing to stare at a wall instead. He was acting far too complacent. Confident, even.

Detective Sergeant Lewis joined them, dressed in his coat and hat as if he'd been about to leave for the night. He eyed the commissioner's assistant and frowned. "This is our killer?"

He didn't sound convinced, and Leo had to admit, the man didn't seem overly villainous at the moment.

"I need you to go to Commissioner Vickers's home, Lewis," Jasper said, looking ill as he said it. "Bring in his daughter, Miss Elsie Vickers, for questioning."

Lewis looked at him, aghast. "The commissioner's daughter? You sure, guv?"

When Jasper nodded gravely, Lewis left on his task.

"Wiley, when you've finished with Munson," Jasper said, his tone flat and emotionless, "Miss Spencer will be in my office, waiting for you to record her statement."

He held out an arm toward his office. She started forward but then remembered Mr. Munson's pince-nez that she'd picked up from the crypt floor. She pulled the spectacles from her handbag, one of the lenses cracked from the scuffle with Jasper, and laid them on Constable Wiley's desk.

"In case he requires them to sign his confession."

She walked on toward Jasper's office, a rock in the pit of her stomach. It had been there since the crypt. It stemmed not just from the insensitive remark Jasper had made about Elsie, but from something else.

"How would Elsie have paid Mr. Carter and the Barretts?" she asked as she entered Jasper's office. "She wouldn't have access to any of her father's money."

He left the office door open, likely to keep an eye on Mr. Munson, and shed his coat.

"They likely didn't care how she got it, so long as she did." He hooked his coat on the stand and then exhaled. "I didn't mean what I said."

Leo lifted her chin.

"About Elsie," he clarified.

"I should hope not. Weren't you the one who so recently told me that sometimes, people get caught up in things they regret afterward?"

Jasper nodded. He touched the corner of his mouth, where blood had crusted from his split lip. His hair was mussed, an unruly lock coming to hang over his forehead no matter how many times he raked it back. His tie had been yanked loose too, the top button of his collar popped free, in the brawl with Mr. Munson.

A strange, unexpected warmth expanded in Leo's chest at his disheveled appearance. It dropped lower, into her stomach, as she observed him pulling two glass tumblers from a desk drawer and then a bottle of whisky. He poured a finger into each and held one out to her. She shook the notion from her head that Jasper somehow looked especially handsome after a fist fight and sipped the drink a little too quickly. She coughed, and he laughed.

"Punches harder than cherry cordial, doesn't it?"

Leo wasn't sure she liked it very much but kept it in

her hand. Her nerves were buzzing, her mind racing. "Do you think Mr. Munson had been following us?"

"I suspect so. Since leaving the Barretts' home, most likely." Jasper shook his head. "I should have noticed."

"Don't berate yourself," she said. "It all ended well."

He stopped short of rolling his eyes. "You could have been killed."

"So could you have been. Luckily, we're now safe at Scotland Yard, and the killer is under arrest. On top of that, he's concussed and sporting a broken nose—the least of what he deserves."

Jasper sipped his drink as he walked to a small, mirrored stand holding a bowl and pitcher in the corner of his office. He poured out some water, then cupped his hands in the bowl and splashed his face, gingerly wiping the corner of his lip. His eyes met hers in the oval mirror's reflection and lingered.

Leo raised her glass to her lips, slightly flustered. "What is it?"

"You returned his pince-nez."

She blinked. "You're right. I should have crushed them under my bootheel."

He turned from the mirror. "It's not that. I have a witness who saw Stillman at a tavern the night Carter was shot. He said a man joined Stillman. A man with spectacles and a mustache."

"Mr. Munson possesses both," Leo said, uncertain why Jasper looked concerned.

"This witness also saw Stillman and, presumably, Munson enter a carriage. There was a third person inside."

Leo took a seat in front of his desk, resting her handbag in her lap. "Elsie?"

Jasper started to fix his tie, his head shaking. "The person wore a top hat. It was a man."

"Is your witness certain?" she asked.

He fiddled with his tie another moment, and Leo nearly got up to help him. But she stopped herself. He didn't need her assistance, and after the way he'd held her hand earlier in the crypt, she was oddly apprehensive about standing too close to him again. Not because she'd disliked his hand clasping hers. Because she hadn't disliked it at all.

"He had nothing to gain by lying," Jasper said. "Hopefully, I'll get Munson to account for it when I speak to—"

A loud voice came from outside his office. "You there, constable! Where is he? Inspector Reid!"

Leo stood up as Sir Nathaniel barged through the open door to the office, displeasure gleaming in his eyes. "What is this I've heard? Munson has been arrested? I demand to know on what grounds."

"Sir Nathaniel." Hesitation slowed Jasper. He'd need to tell the commissioner about Elsie, and Leo felt a pang of anxiousness for him. "I've arrested Munson for murder and attempted murder."

The commissioner's mouth, set in a grim slash, wavered into amused disbelief. "You must be mistaken. This is Benjamin we are talking about. What evidence do you have?"

The question struck Leo as odd. Shouldn't he have instead asked whom his assistant was accused of killing? Stranger still was the timing. Leo glanced at the clock on the wall. She and Jasper hadn't been at the central office for more than ten minutes. And yet, Sir Nathaniel had somehow learned of the arrest. He was wearing his coat and top hat, and carrying his walking stick, as if just arriving.

Leo's eyes settled back onto the walking stick. Polished black, with a silver tip at the base and an ornate silver handle gripped in his palm. He employed it when his leg bothered him, he'd always said. Damp, cold weather made the old wound act up, worsening his limp.

"I know this must be difficult to hear, Commissioner, but your assistant attempted to kill me and Miss Spencer tonight," Jasper said.

Again, Sir Nathaniel scoffed. "Why on earth would Munson do that?"

"To retrieve what we had found before we could bring it here, to Scotland Yard," Leo answered, her heart beginning to pump harder than before. "Photographs."

At the barest hitch of the commissioner's chin, a notion began to swarm her mind. Her heart thudded faster even as it started to sink.

"What photographs?" His firm chin softened with an expression Leo could only describe as fear.

"Sir Nathaniel," Jasper started, still reluctant. He was about to tell him about Elsie's pictures.

Leo stepped forward abruptly. "Photographs of an unsavory nature." Moving swiftly, she approached Jasper and reached toward his waistcoat. He caught her wrist as her fingers slipped underneath the panel and brushed against his inner pocket.

"What are you doing?" he whispered.

She met his stare with imploring eyes. "We must show him the photograph, Jasper."

His brow furrowed, but his hand loosened from around her wrist. She plucked the card-mounted portrait of Samuel Barrett from Jasper's waistcoat pocket where he'd stored it earlier.

Leo walked toward the commissioner, taking time to watch his face before presenting it to him. With trepidation, he took the photograph. He jerked his head back in surprise or disgust, and then exhaled. The sound was poorly concealed relief.

"Goodness, Miss Spencer, what are you doing with material of this sordid taste?" He handed it to Jasper, rather than to her. Jasper kept his lips sealed. He was waiting for her to explain herself.

"This was a photograph we discovered in the morgue crypt tonight. One of them, at least. There was a box that had been stored there, in connection to William Carter's murder. I managed to pick up this one from the top before Mr. Munson arrived."

Her plan was still forming as she lied—something she was becoming rather proficient at, she admitted. It was hasty, probably reckless and stupid too, but this was the only way to find out if her suspicion was correct.

"Tell me what you know," the commissioner demanded. It came as no great surprise when he looked to the other man in the room for an answer rather than to Leo. Jasper cut his measuring stare from her, and she held her breath.

"Samuel Barrett, his sister Hannah, and William Carter were operating a blackmailing scheme," Jasper began. "They seem to have targeted Munson, who I believe hired Clarence Stillman to retrieve a stock of explicit photographs featuring your assistant."

Leo released her pent-up breath. Thank God, he'd understood. She wasn't sure anyone else would have, but his mind had always been incisive and quick. Just like the Inspector's.

"I had reason to believe Samuel Barrett used the morgue crypt as a hiding place for these photographs after his sister and Carter were both killed. He wanted them as leverage, with plans to go to the newspapers." He gestured toward Leo. "I asked Miss Spencer to show me into the crypt. That is where Munson set upon us, demanding we hand them over."

The commissioner's expression had pinched as he'd been listening. "And where is this box of photographs now?"

Leo wasn't sure if she was pleased that he'd asked or heartbroken.

"Still in the crypt, I'm afraid," she said. "We got rather caught up in fending off Mr. Munson and then bringing him to the Yard."

"There is plenty to do here tonight. Lewis and I will collect the box tomorrow," Jasper said. "Give it a thorough looking-through."

Sir Nathaniel tapped his cane against the floor. "Very good. It sounds as though you have your man, though I'm sorry to learn that it is Munson. I was fond of him, and I know my Elsie was keen for a betrothal." He grimaced sadly, and it looked so genuine that momentarily, Leo questioned herself. Though only until the commissioner said, "I'm sure the man will say anything now to avoid the noose. But evidence is evidence. Good work, inspector. As you say, you're busy here, so I will leave you to it."

He tipped his hat and left. Once alone, Leo let her

tensed shoulders droop. She turned to face Jasper and his inevitable displeasure at her deception.

He crossed his arms over his broad chest and peered down at her. Then said: "The walking stick."

Leo canted her head, taken aback. "Yes. The walking stick." Pleasure that he had come upon the same conclusion rippled through her. "It wasn't the bird keeper who left those impressions in the ground around Mr. Stillman's body. Sir Nathaniel was there when Mr. Munson shot him."

"He was there for Samuel Barrett too. Barrett muttered a word—*Father*—before dying. Not his father, as I'd assumed. The father of the girl from the photographs."

Leo's skin prickled. "He was telling us who killed him."

Jasper swore under his breath and stalked toward the office door, staring after the commissioner. "Stillman and Munson joined a third man in the carriage outside the Jugger. A man in a top hat." He grabbed his coat. "It wasn't Elsie who was being blackmailed. It was Sir Nathaniel."

Even though everything about this theory felt right, Leo couldn't be happy for it. Or relieved. Sir Nathaniel was the Inspector's finest friend. She'd thought she'd known him. Had trusted him. The betrayal was immeasurable.

"Don't bother to tell me to stay here. If you are following him, I'm coming with you," Leo said.

"Oh, I'm following him," he replied. To her relief, he gestured toward the door. "And if we're right, I'll need a witness when he confesses."

Chapter Twenty-Two

Sir Nathaniel had been given an ample head start, so they kept their pace brisk toward Spring Street. Jasper wanted to be wrong about the commissioner. The yearning stayed alive in the back of his mind and in his heart. But the more he sorted through the facts and connecting threads, the closer he became to certainty instead.

He'd forgotten about the commissioner's walking stick. He only employed it when the weather was cold and damp, as it had been the night of Clarence Stillman's murder. Paired with the inexplicable timing of Sir Nathaniel's arrival at the Yard just now, so soon after Munson's arrest, and his stark expression of terror when Leo took the photograph from Jasper's waistcoat pocket, he knew what they would find once they came upon the morgue.

Apprehension coiled through him as they neared the dirt lane between the former church vestry and the burial ground. Should he accuse Sir Nathaniel without proof, he would lose his position at the Met. He'd be ridiculed, and the Inspector would be disappointed. Which was why Jasper needed to be certain.

"You should know that this one time, I would very much like to be wrong," Leo said softly.

"So would I," he said. Then raised his hand. "Darken the lantern."

Leo had carried a patrolman's dark lantern from Whitehall Place. The oil lamplight had shone through the bullseye lens, lighting their way. Now, however, she turned the lantern's top, sliding a shield behind the bullseye glass. The light disappeared, obscuring the remainder of their approach.

It had been quick thinking on Leo's part to fib about the photographs having been left behind in the crypt, and then to show the commissioner the one of Samuel Barrett. The dread in Sir Nathaniel's eyes when she brought it forward, when he'd believed she was about to show him a photograph of his daughter, had been all the evidence Jasper needed. However, Chief Inspector Coughlan would require more.

When they turned onto the dirt lane, that evidence kicked Jasper squarely in the chest.

A man stood at the back door to the morgue, lit only by moonlight. From his tall stature to his long coat and top hat, it was most assuredly Sir Nathaniel. He appeared to be attempting to pick the lock. Disappointment mingled with fury as he and Leo approached. Jasper signaled to Leo. She spun the shield out of place, and light from the lantern illuminated Sir Nathaniel. He startled, holding up his arm to block the sudden brightness.

"I have a key, Commissioner, if you are looking for something inside," Leo said.

He fumbled with the lockpicks as he hurriedly stuffed them into his pocket. There was no excuse for being found in this manner, but that didn't stop him from trying.

"Why, Miss Spencer, it's you. And Inspector Reid," he said, greeting them with false joviality. "I thought I would come by and collect that box, as you said things were rather busy at headquarters. Save you the trouble."

"There is no box." Jasper reached into his coat pocket and held up the photographs of Elsie. At this distance, the commissioner wouldn't be able to see them in detail, but his expression still went cold and sober with understanding.

"How much was Carter asking for?" Jasper asked. "It had to have been a fortune for you to hire an ex-convict to retrieve them for you."

"I rather think you're out of line, inspector. I've no idea what you mean by all this."

Leo stepped forward, the lantern swinging its light. "There is no need to keep up the charade. We are aware you hired Clarence Stillman to recover the photographs that Mr. Carter was blackmailing you with."

"That is absurd," he spluttered with another bemused laugh.

"I have a witness who saw you collect Munson and Stillman at the Jugger on the night Carter was shot," Jasper said.

Tommy Welch's identification of the commissioner wasn't likely to hold up in court, given his prison record, but it worked to put Sir Nathaniel on edge.

"That is utter tripe and nonsense," Sir Nathaniel said. "You are crossing a line, Reid."

"Then I am in good company," Jasper replied. "You convinced Munson to clean up this mess with the photographs, and in return, you arranged for his marriage to your daughter. Promised to take him with you into the top echelons of society and government. And Elsie wouldn't complain, would she? Marrying Munson was her penance for putting you in this tight spot. I'm curious as to how she met William Carter to begin with. My guess is that you hired Hogarth and Tipson to arrange for your uncle's funeral services. November, wasn't it?"

The timing suited. His uncle's passing had been the reason he and Elsie were invited to Charles Street for their holiday supper.

"How dare you make these accusations?" he barked. "You have no proof, no evidence at all."

"I'm sure Mr. Tipson has record of it," Leo said. He glared at her, as though she was the one deceiving him. It ignited a new spark of ire under Jasper's skin.

"My detective sergeant is currently on his way to your home to collect Elsie for questioning," Jasper said. "I'm certain once I sit down with your daughter and show her these portraits, she will tell me everything. Including how she came to be betrothed to Benjamin Munson."

Sir Nathaniel's expression turned thunderous, and Jasper allowed his own anger to feed and grow. He'd respected Sir Nathaniel. Admired him. And yet he'd consented to murder—including theirs—to keep his reputation intact and unblemished.

"Stay away from my daughter, Reid."

"I'm afraid that's impossible now. How long do you

think Munson will hold his tongue when he is threatened with the noose?"

"You cannot trust a word from Munson's lips. The man is a killer, you said so yourself."

"What I would like to know," Leo said, her voice placid compared to the ratcheting tension Jasper felt, "is why Mr. Munson would agree to such a scheme. He is devoted to you, surely, and to Elsie, but committing murder for you? That is extreme, even for the most devoted servant or friend."

The commissioner pinned her to the spot with a glare. "Miss Spencer, I'm ashamed of you for joining Jasper in his outlandish accusations."

"And why," she went on, ignoring his chastisement, "was Samuel Barrett stabbed rather than shot? Mr. Munson possessed a revolver."

The commissioner shook his head, his composure beginning to break apart.

"I'm sure you read Constable Carey's report on Hannah Barrett's accident. Someone on that omnibus gave a good description of Clarence Stillman," Jasper pressed. As commissioner, he would have had access to it. Just as he'd had access to the files in the convict office. "That was one reason you decided to have Munson shoot Stillman. The other was that when he handed over the locket, the paper wasn't inside. He asked for more money before he would give it to you."

It was speculation, but Munson would likely confirm it. Perhaps in exchange for a reprieve from the noose.

"Hear me, the two of you—if you continue with this, you'll be sorry. Your promotion to the C.I.D. is already a subject of dispute, Jasper. And you, Miss Spencer…do you imagine whispers of your uncle's infirmities aren't already being heard?"

The warning cut deep, and if Jasper had held any doubt at all that the commissioner was guilty, he might have eased off. But he reasoned that this was exactly how Sir Nathaniel might have convinced Munson to kill for him.

"Chief Inspector Coughlan told you of the scheduled disinterment of Barnabas Strange's coffin, but the two of you were at a dinner with the Home Secretary that evening." Jasper frowned. "It wasn't until after your dinner that you were able to speak to Munson, telling him to get to the grave first."

"That is why he was still at All Saints when I arrived at dawn," Leo said. "He found the glass plate negatives but not the photographs. So, the two of you paid a visit to Mr. Barrett together. It wouldn't have been easy meeting one of the men in those photographs with your daughter. Might you have lost your temper?" Leo asked.

The commissioner sniffed, his fingers lifting and lowering as he regripped the silver knob of his walking stick.

"Tell me, Commissioner, if I were to take that walking stick, would I find a hidden sword sheathed inside?" Jasper asked.

Sir Nathaniel's scowl flattened. He didn't respond. It seemed he'd exhausted his denials.

"And if I were to ask the publisher of the *Daily Chronicle* if you met with him this afternoon, would he confirm it? Or had you simply followed Miss Spencer and me from Samuel Barrett's home?"

The commissioner turned his head to stare out toward

the darkened burial ground. His answer was unmistakable. It had been no chance encounter on Fleet Street. He'd wanted to know what Jasper and Leo had discovered. Why they had gone to *The Times*.

"I don't understand," Jasper said. "Why not just pay Carter the asking price and be done with it?"

Sir Nathaniel's leather-clad fingers drummed the knob on his walking stick, as though deliberating.

"Money isn't the only thing scum like Carter want. Connection, political influence, a lenient *associate* in a powerful position. Those are the things anyone in this city with the surname of Carter wants."

The commissioner's voice had deepened to an acerbic pitch; it was as though another man was speaking. Jasper reveled in the beginnings of a confession. The confidence Sir Nathaniel had in Munson had cracked, as had his trust that Elsie would remain steadfast.

"He wanted you in his pocket," Jasper said. William Carter had surely regretted his ambition when the commissioner failed to acquiesce.

"I refuse to be bought," Sir Nathaniel said through clenched teeth.

"But you find murder acceptable," Leo replied.

"Munson hired Stillman, and Munson killed Carter—*without* my directive. I wanted the photographs of my Elsie, that was all."

Jasper could see how this would be believable to a Grand Jury. One party was dead and couldn't speak for himself; the other was an underling without the clout the police commissioner possessed.

"Stillman was a madman," Sir Nathaniel went on. "He chased Miss Barrett into the street, and then later, he attacked me. It was hardly murder. Munson was defending me."

"You admit to being there, which makes you an accessory to murder," Jasper said. "And you withheld vital information in a murder investigation. The Home Secretary will not care for that, I imagine."

"It might have been wiser for you to have acted alone," Leo added. "Mr. Munson will sink you. So will Elsie."

"She won't." The commissioner clung to that hope with audible desperation.

"We'll see, won't we?" Jasper took his revolver from his holster and stepped forward. "Sir Nathaniel Vickers, I'm placing you under arrest for aiding and abetting in the murders of William Carter, Clarence Stillman, and Samuel Barrett—"

The commissioner pulled the silver knob on his walking stick, and a short sword flashed into view—just as Jasper had concluded. He took a deft swipe toward Jasper, the tip making a shallow slice near his shoulder. He staggered back.

"Commissioner, don't!" Jasper aimed his Webley, his blood seizing in his veins. He didn't want to have to shoot his father's friend. But he would if he needed to.

Sir Nathaniel held the sword in a defensive position. Then, he ran, heading fast toward the darkened burial ground.

Jasper gritted his molars. "Leo, stay here," he ordered before pursuing the commissioner. He darted into the burial ground, the moonlight guiding him as it shone dimly on his quarry.

The rows of headstones weren't neatly drawn, and as Jasper sprinted through them, he was mindful of the smaller stone stubs that often marked the graves of babies and children. If he caught his foot on one, he'd go down and lose momentum.

But then, a shaky light brightened the area around him. It reached toward the commissioner, who was leading by a few yards. *Damn it! Leo!* He didn't have time to stop and tell her to go back, and besides, the patrolman's lantern would aid him considerably.

Sir Nathaniel was strong and fit for his age, but his limp appeared to be slowing him, as were muddy patches and slushy snow. He must have sensed defeat bearing down on him, or perhaps he noticed the light from the bullseye glass growing closer. He came to an abrupt stop, then turned and brandished his sword again.

Jasper dug in his heels, his revolver ready. "There is nowhere to run, Commissioner."

He held out his arm to prevent Leo from moving past him with the lantern.

"Lower your weapon and surrender willingly." Jasper heaved for breath after the short burst of sprinting. "Don't force my hand. If you take one step forward with that sword, I *will* shoot."

He'd yet to fire his revolver in the course of his duties, and he sure as hell didn't wish this encounter to be the one to christen it.

Slowly, Sir Nathaniel lowered the short sword. Lifting his chin, his eyes slipped into the shadows, untouched by the candescent light thrown by the lantern. "You will tell my Elsie how very sorry I am, won't you, Jasper? Gregory too?"

A knot of foreboding electrified the base of Jasper's skull, lifting his hair on end. The commissioner's sword raised again with swift precision, only this time, he readjusted his grip and aim, leveling the tip with the bottom of his ribcage.

"No!" Leo screamed, starting forward. Jasper seized her arm—and Sir Nathaniel fell forward, driving his sword into the soft apex of his abdomen.

He collapsed to the ground in a lump between two tilted headstones. A cold swirl of sick rose in Jasper's throat as he holstered his revolver and ran toward the commissioner. The tip of the sword protruded through his back. Leo followed, the lantern illuminating the blood already darkening the thin layer of slushy snow. Kneeling on the ground, Jasper flipped him over, but he knew it would be too late. As a soldier, Sir Nathaniel would know where to position a sword to pierce a heart, and he had succeeded.

His eyes were open, and they were fixed in death.

Chapter Twenty-Three

The wide leather swivel chair creaked as Leo spun languidly in half circles. On the desk in front of her lay the thick file the Inspector had compiled on the Spencer family murders. She stared at the worn, closed cover, her arms wrapped around herself and her legs tucked up underneath her in the seat. The nerve to open the file still felt miles away.

She'd come earlier in the evening after having dinner with Claude and Flora on Duke Street. Leo spent an hour at the Inspector's bedside, reading aloud from last week's *Illustrated Police News*. Reading this week's edition was out of the question, as it was full of the commissioner's fall from grace—and his symbolic suicide. A soldier's honorable death, the ridiculous author of the article had written.

It hadn't been honorable. It had been the mark of a coward. His final act had been one of pure selfishness, falling on his sword to avoid facing the consequences of his actions and the annihilation of his career and reputation. He'd chosen to leave his beloved daughter to face the destruction of her own reputation alone. And he'd ended his life in full view of two people who had cared for him. Leo would never be able to sponge the image from her mind. It would always be there, in vivid detail. She wondered if she would ever stop questioning if there had been anything she could have done differently, said differently, to prevent him from doing what he had.

In the hours afterward, following the arrival of several constables, Chief Coughlan, and even Superintendent Monroe, Jasper and Leo had been separated. They'd each needed to give their statement of events to account for the death of the police commissioner. Their statements matched, of course, though the scrutiny had been intense. When Leo had been released from an interview room at Scotland Yard, she'd found her uncle and Dita waiting for her. Leo had refused to go home until Jasper, too, had been cleared of any wrongdoing.

By then, Benjamin Munson had done exactly as Jasper had intimated, confessing in full and pinning the blame wholly on Sir Nathaniel. It turned out, the commissioner had held a secret over Munson's head since their time together in Africa. Sir Nathaniel had discovered Munson attempting to desert during the skirmish against the Boers. Panicking, Munson fired his rifle, striking Sir Nathaniel in the leg. In a show of protecting Munson from a court-martial and perhaps even execution for attempted desertion, he lied to cover for him. But Sir Nathaniel made it clear that Munson was beholden to him for it, and ever since, he'd been his pawn of sorts.

When William Carter approached the police commissioner with one of Elsie's illicit photographs and demanded a princely sum of five hundred pounds, he turned to Munson. The offering of Elsie's hand in marriage had been extra incentive for Munson as well as punishment for Elsie.

The commissioner's death needed all the corroboration possible to make sense to the rest of the Met and to the ravenous public. When his leased rooms had been searched thoroughly, Hannah Barrett's locket had been found among Munson's belongings. His confession to the murders of Carter and Stillman, paired with Elsie's tearful confirmation after she'd learned of her father's suicide, closed the investigation with finality.

Reluctantly, Jasper submitted the blackmail photographs of Elsie Vickers to Chief Coughlan. He'd had no choice, Leo knew. Burning them to protect Elsie would only corrupt him, as Sir Nathaniel had been, at least to some degree. Chief Coughlan promised that he would do everything within his power to keep them private, but Leo hadn't been surprised when an illustration including details that only someone with access to the photographs could have had, ran alongside the *Illustrated Police News* article. Corruption was rife at the Yard, and she was sure someone had made a neat profit by giving an illustrator access, if only for a quick look.

So, she'd read the previous week's edition of the *Illustrated Police News* to the Inspector, happy to pretend none of the recent events had ever occurred. He hadn't opened his eyes more than once during her visit. Leo chose to believe he could hear her though, and before leaving, she'd taken his hand to give it a gentle squeeze. He'd applied the barest amount of pressure in return. He was still there. But quickly fading.

"You don't have to go through that."

Leo looked up, coming out of a daze. Jasper entered the study. Once again, he was wearing a fine evening suit. His hair had been neatly combed, though a gilded honey-blond lock of hair still sprung free from his attempt to pomade it back into place. It hung over his forehead, holding her attention for a fraction too long.

"Stopping in on your way out for the evening?" she asked, lowering her feet to the floor.

"Oliver is hosting a dinner party," he answered on his way to the desk. "I'm fetching Miss Hayes soon."

"Of course." She puzzled at the thorny irritation in her chest. A terrible mood had gripped her these last few days. She blamed the aftermath of the commissioner's suicide, instead of the mention of Constance Hayes.

"How is your shoulder healing?" she asked.

He rolled it. "Fine. The blade didn't cut deep."

No, it had been Sir Nathaniel's betrayal that had truly injured him. Leo had seen it in the deadened expression he'd worn for the rest of that awful night.

Jasper tapped the file and repeated what he'd said before. "He left it for you, but you're not obligated to go through it."

She ran her fingers over the worn spine of the folder. "If I don't, do you think he'll be disappointed in me?"

The Inspector had invested so much of his own time into the case, and he'd done it for her. Not for himself, or for accolades. He'd done it to give Leo answers.

"He could never be disappointed in you. Besides," Jasper arched a brow, "doing something just to please another person never ends in satisfaction."

Leo stood from the chair. "I won't tell you that you're

right; it would go straight to your head, and I imagine you've been the object of enough praise this week."

He grumbled under his breath as he cut a path toward the sideboard of decanters. "You are wrong. If anything, I am the object of contempt. The Met was already suffering from bad press, and now, with the commissioner's scandal aired, it's only worsened."

"I can't believe they would have rather let a case go only partially solved."

He reached for his favored whisky. "They were more than ready to pin everything on Munson. Chief Coughlan suggested I was too *ambitious* during the course of the investigation. Less is more, and all that rot."

Leo gaped. "That isn't fair."

Jasper poured his drink, then reached for the bottle of Grants Morella, which Leo had brought the Inspector the previous week. He overturned a small cordial glass.

"Fair doesn't exist," he said while pouring her a drink. "And if you chase it—"

"You'll be running forever," she said, finishing one of the expressions the Inspector had so often used.

Leo accepted the small glass from Jasper, who raised his to her in a silent toast before taking a long sip. She put her nose to the rim and inhaled the sweet scent of the cherry brandy liqueur. The strangest sense of loss came over her. It was absurd, considering they'd found the killer. Mr. Munson would go to the gallows for his crimes. How could she feel crestfallen knowing how close they'd been to becoming two more of his victims? Jasper didn't seem to be affected. He was, after all, about to dine out for the evening.

"I suppose things will go back to normal now," she said. "That must make you happy."

"I'm not sure happy is the word for it. But if by normal, you mean a new case will appear on my desk in the morning, and a new body—with any hope, one that hasn't been murdered—will show up in the morgue, well then, yes."

Crimes and dead bodies certainly seemed to be their sort of 'normal'.

Leo had assisted her uncle in the postmortem of Samuel Barrett's body, and predictably, he'd been stabbed three times by a short sword, perforating his left lung and nicking his heart. Thankfully, Sir Nathaniel's body had not been sent to the Spring Street Morgue. Jasper said it had been taken to the police hospital, where the police surgeon had seen to it.

"Have you spoken to Elsie?" she asked.

He frowned into his drink. "She didn't wish to see me. Her housekeeper said a cousin in Wales is taking her in. She's already left London."

It was the only way forward for her. Staying here would be out of the question. The newspapers would eventually begin to print the next story and scandal, but hers would not be forgotten. Leo knew that from experience. Even sixteen years after her own unwanted fame in the city's newspapers, people remembered her. Or at least, her story. Finally, she sipped her cherry cordial.

"I think the Inspector would be proud of how you stood up to the commissioner," she said. "Though, I am glad he won't ever know what his friend did."

Jasper was aware the Inspector wasn't responsive. According to what Mrs. Zhao had told Leo, for the last two days, he'd come to sit at his father's bedside for a short while each evening and morning.

After another sip of his whisky, Jasper met Leo's eyes. "He isn't waking up, is he?"

She shook her head. The doctor had come to the house on Charles Street a few times over the past week. He'd confirmed that the end was near.

"He's made his peace with it," she said, the taste of cherry cordial lingering on the back of her tongue. It reminded her of him, and she thought it always would. "He wants to be with them again."

Jasper nodded, but then his mouth twisted. His brow puckered. "I'm not ready to lose him."

Leo's eyes stung; the suddenness of it surprised her. She knew of Jasper's love and deep affection for the Inspector. But this was the first time he'd ever shown such vulnerability. He was about to lose the only father he'd ever known.

She reached for him, settling her palm on his forearm. "I'm not either."

But whether they were ready or not, changes were coming. Considerable changes. Once the Inspector was gone…what then? He had always been Leo's connection to Jasper, and his to her. She supposed, for a while, they would mourn him together.

But afterward, what then?

Her palm was still resting on his arm, the fine black wool soft and buttery, when the clock chimed the hour. Leo dropped her hand, and Jasper stepped to the side.

"You'll be late fetching Miss Hayes," she said, sipping the cordial again. She savored it as she blinked away the tears that had formed in the corners of her eyes.

"I'm not in the mood for a party," he sighed after tossing back the rest of his drink. Nonetheless, he started for the door.

"Don't do something you don't want to do just to please another person," she said, echoing his own advice from before. "It rarely leads to satisfaction, or so I hear."

He swung a teasing glower over his shoulder. "I don't think Miss Hayes would agree. But I won't stay long. I'll spend the night here. In case."

Leo scrunched her nose as it tingled. "I'll keep watch until you return."

Jasper allowed a rare, lopsided grin, then bid her a good evening. His attention drifted toward the thick file on the desk before shutting the door behind him. She took another look at it.

Jasper had said the Inspector would never be disappointed in her if she chose not to look through the file. She believed he was right. However, she might, in the end, be disappointed in herself.

She went to the desk and sat down again. She wasn't ready for so many things. To lose the Inspector, or for Claude to lose his position, or for Flora to lose her mind. But those things would all come to pass. It was all inevitable. So was this.

Leo finished the cherry cordial and swallowed hard, wincing at its sweetness. She set the glass to the side and reached for the file.

Method of Revenge

SNEAK PEEK AT SPENCER & REID
BOOK TWO

Chapter One
March 1884

Screams of wild laughter filled the dance hall, piercing Leonora Spencer's ears. She winced, the sound grating on her nerves, and knew she'd made a mistake.

The nightlife at Striker's Wharf had always been lively, but Leo didn't recall it ever having been this boisterous. As the other patrons raised their voices above the fast tempo of the piano, trumpet, and clarinet, all she could dwell on was how quiet the Spring Street Morgue would have been at this time of night. Leo worked there as an assistant to her uncle, a city coroner, and in fact, an evening in the morgue's office appealed vastly more than the popular dance club on the Lambeth wharves.

However, as it wasn't at all ordinary for a young woman to work at a morgue, let alone prefer the company of dead bodies to living ones, she kept the disquieting thought to herself.

Next to her at their table, Nivedita Brooks swayed in time with the music, her eyes turned toward the busy dance floor with longing.

"Go," Leo told her friend. "I can see it's torturous for you to sit here when there's a polka playing."

Dita cut her rapt attention away from the dozens of dancers. "It isn't torture to sit with you," she said, appearing offended. "Besides, I can't possibly take to the floor by myself. I'd need a partner."

Leo gave her arm a gentle shove. "I'm quite certain a number of gentlemen would appear as if out of the ether if you were to take one step toward that dance floor."

Thanks to a handful of favorable articles in the *Illustrated London News*, the club and dance hall was packed with a surfeit of men, many of them from the upper classes. In fact, the surge in popularity was so noticeable, Leo had started to think Eddie Bloom, the proprietor at Striker's Wharf, must have held some power over the paper's editorial choices. As the head of a criminal gang operating out of this area, it wouldn't have been out of the realm of possibility.

Despite Mr. Bloom's questionable business practices, and the establishment's mixed clientele, this was one of Dita's favorite places to go for music and dancing, and she had decided it was high time Leo threw off the mundane nightly routine she'd been keeping for the last several weeks.

Habits were easy and comfortable, and Leo had fallen into the practice of returning home from the morgue, preparing supper for her aging uncle and aunt, and then trundling off to bed with a book. The singular interruption to her schedule had been an evening she'd spent out, at a chophouse with a Scotland Yard constable—though she had yet to tell Dita. Her friend would have made too much of it, and Leo wasn't even certain she'd enjoyed herself enough to accept a second invitation...*if* the constable ever extended one.

"You could have your pick of dance partners," she told Dita now as she glanced at the tables surrounding theirs. "The gentlemen at the table behind you have been looking your way since we arrived."

The three men had been taking furtive glances toward Dita for the last quarter hour. She was pretty when she wore her blue wool Metropolitan Police matron uniform to her shifts at Scotland Yard, but she was downright stunning when she put up her hair and wore one of her brightly hued dresses for an evening out. Sunset orange silks and deep pink taffetas looked radiant against her darker skin, compliments of her late mother, who'd hailed from Calcutta, India.

Leo, however, with her dark hair and pale, ivory skin, preferred more somber shades. Tonight, she'd consented to the deep sapphire blue satin dress Dita had selected from Leo's limited wardrobe, the skirt fashionably gored, if unfashionably long-sleeved. She was certain none of the men at the neighboring table would be casting out their nets toward her. And in truth, she didn't care for any of them to attempt it.

Dita covered Leo's hand with her own. "Forget dancing. This is your first night out in ages, and I'm not leaving you to sit alone at our table."

"That never stopped you before," she replied with a good-natured grin. Dita would usually bring her steady beau, Police Constable John Lloyd, with them to Striker's.

They would spend half of the time on the dance floor, while Leo remained at the table. Dancing was not her forte, nor was she interested enough in it to improve.

"Perhaps not, but you weren't in mourning before," Dita reminded her.

Leo sighed. "I'm not in official mourning. I wasn't family."

Not exactly, anyway.

It had been two months since Detective Chief Superintendent Gregory Reid had succumbed to his illness. The Inspector, as Leo had always called him, had taken his last breath while sleeping one night at the end of January. It was just a week after the tumultuous case that concluded with his good friend, Police Commissioner Nathaniel Vickers, accused of murder. It had been Leo and Detective Inspector Jasper Reid, the Inspector's adopted son, who had closed in on the police commissioner's desperate plot to thwart a blackmail operation that had threatened to reveal intimate photographs taken of his seventeen-year-old daughter. The illicit photographs would have ruined Sir Nathaniel and Elsie publicly and personally, and he had decided there was no line he would not cross to prevent it—including lowering himself to murder. He'd even planned to have Jasper and Leo killed once they discovered the truth.

The only consolation had been that Gregory Reid had already been unconscious when his friend had been found out, and he'd remained completely unaware of his friend's decision to end his own life rather than face the humiliation and consequences of his crimes.

"He thought of you as family," Dita said, then sneaked a coy glimpse toward the table of men behind her.

Leo shook her head, amused. Her friend simply could not resist from flirting. Dita was correct though. The Inspector had thought of her as family.

For a short while when she'd been nine years old, he'd taken her in and cared for her after the murder of her family. The Metropolitan Police had been tracking down Leo's uncle and aunt, who'd been living on the island of Crete at the time, and in the meanwhile, she'd stayed with Gregory, who at that time had ranked as detective inspector. His home on Charles Street was an affluent address, a residence any other police inspector would never have been able to afford. However, Gregory had married a viscount's daughter, and the home had been bestowed upon them at their marriage.

When Gregory's wife, Emmaline, and their two young children died in a horrific accident while ice skating on Regent's Pond, he'd been distraught. A year later, he'd still been in mourning when he'd rescued Leo from the attic of the home in which her family had been killed. He'd treated her with all the tenderness and care of a father, and even after her uncle and aunt, Claude and Flora Feldman, arrived to claim her, he'd stayed a prominent figure in Leo's life.

She still felt the swift plunge of her stomach when remembering that early Sunday morning in late January. Heavy knocking had roused her from sleep just past seven o'clock. Throwing on her dressing gown and hurrying downstairs, she'd had the inkling in the back of her mind that it would be news of the Inspector. She'd been correct.

Jasper was standing on the threshold, his hat crushed in his hand. Even now, months later, her memory drew up the vivid image of his red-rimmed eyes and the anguish cutting through them. Grief had seized her too, crumpling her up inside like old newsprint bound for a stove. The grief hadn't relinquished her yet. The detailed memory of that moment never would.

All people could remember things, of course, but Leo's mind was particularly—and unusually—sharp. It would seal images into her mind, as photographic memories for her to draw up and inspect time and again. They never faded or became hazy. Significant moments, like the one of Jasper telling her the Inspector had died, seared most firmly into her mind, and stayed readily available for easy viewing. Other details—from what everyone was wearing at the butcher's last week when she was standing in line, to the contents of every postmortem report she'd ever typed at her uncle's morgue, to the names and faces of every officer at Scotland Yard—were stored away permanently and vividly too.

Once, Dita had likened her memory to magic, but Leo thought it more like a well-organized inventory room. Registers upon registers of memories that she could locate, draw down from an endless number of shelves, and look at again with clarity. However, just as her work at a city morgue tended to make others eye her strangely, so did having a perfect memory. So, she mostly kept the ability to herself.

Dita leaned over the table, set at the edge of the dance floor, and clinked her glass of wine against Leo's. "For tonight, at least, let's not discuss anything remotely miserable. We're here to have fun."

Leo sipped her drink obligingly, but her rebellious mind thought of the cherry liqueur that she and the Inspector had shared a love for. The last bottle of Grants

Morella she brought to him was likely still half full in his study. Or rather, Jasper's study.

Though he wasn't his legal heir, Jasper Reid had been listed as the main recipient in the Inspector's last will and testament. The home granted to the Honorable Emmaline Cowper's new husband when they'd married had come from her grandmother, not her father. So, when Emmaline died, the bitter viscount had been able to rescind the dowry but not the home.

Leo had always suspected maintaining the residence at 23 Charles Street had cost the Inspector most of his working wages, and now, Jasper had been given the home to keep up. Or sell. She wasn't certain what he would do with it.

At the will reading, Gregory's solicitor, Mr. Stockton, had given Jasper a bundle of papers detailing his inheritance, which included the home and some modest savings. For her part, Leo had been bequeathed an exquisite pair of drop pearl earrings and a matching necklace. The set had belonged to the Inspector's mother, and she'd given them to him with the wish that he might someday pass them along to his daughter.

While preparing for her evening out with Dita, tears had pricked Leo's eyes when she'd opened the worn blue velvet case and put on the pieces.

"Thank you," Leo said to her friend, touching the string of pearls at her throat. "For bringing me out tonight. I did need it." The cackling blare of a woman's laughter as she danced on the floor nearly shredded her eardrum. "Though a quiet restaurant might have done just as well."

Dita pursed her lips. "Careful, you're beginning to sound just as starchy as Inspector Reid."

She was referring to Jasper, who deplored not only Eddie Bloom and his club, but the fact that Leo frequented it from time to time. Jasper's disposition had always leaned toward grouchy and ill-tempered, though ever since his promotion to the Criminal Investigation Department at Scotland Yard, he'd turned even more austere and grumpy.

It had been weeks since she'd last seen him. With the Inspector gone, she had no reason to go to Charles Street anymore; she most certainly couldn't call on Jasper there. He was a bachelor, and she was unmarried. It didn't matter if the Inspector had tried to bring them together as brother and sister, or at best, distant cousins. The fact of the matter was that they were not related, and without the Inspector, she wasn't sure what they were to each other at all.

Oddly enough, as fractious as Jasper usually was toward her, their time spent solving the case in January had not been wholly disagreeable. And when he'd arrived at her home on Duke Street last month on the anniversary of her family's murders with an offering to accompany her to their graves at All Saints, just as the Inspector had always done, she'd been touched by his thoughtfulness.

In fact, she was beginning to think that the tight, unrelenting ball in the pit of her stomach might be stemming from not having seen him since then. It was unacceptable. She didn't want to miss Jasper when he was probably not missing her in return.

"Let's not speak of Inspector Reid or anything else too serious tonight," she told Dita as she tapped her glass against her friends' again. "Here is to a pleasant evening out, without a care in the world."

A scream, one of alarm rather than of gaiety, preceded a loud clatter at Leo's back. She swiveled in her seat to see a woman who'd been seated at the table behind theirs, convulsing on the floor, her chair overturned. Other patrons quickly closed in around her. And yet, one person was swiftly moving away, through the crowd. Leo pinned her attention on that person. The black cloaked figure hurried past the encroaching crowd and began to slip from Leo's view.

"Is she choking?" Dita asked as she left their table among shouts for help.

Leo kept her eyes on the retreating figure. The hood of the cloak was raised, obscuring the person underneath, but there was a distinct feminine quality to the person's movements.

"I'll be right back," she told Dita.

"Where are you going?" she called as Leo skirted the around the influx of people, craning their necks for a better view of the commotion. "Leonora!"

She carried on, reluctant to let the cloaked figure out of her sight. Instinct told her that this person had something to do with what had happened back at the table, whatever it may be. As Leo had no medical training for the living—her only experience being the handling of dead bodies—she wouldn't be of any use to the injured woman. However, no one else had seemed to notice this retreating cloaked figure. Pursuing the person across the club, she got a better look as the crowd thinned. It was certainly a woman. The cloak, embroidered with robin's egg blue threading, rippled as she rushed in the direction of the front doors, showing a dark skirt hem. Leo tried to hasten her pace but was caught behind a wall of shoulders moving into her path.

"Excuse me." The polka music came to a halt and her next impatient, "Excuse me!" came through loudly.

The men moved aside, albeit grudgingly, and Leo darted through. The hooded woman was gone. Leo passed the doorman and went outside, into a damp fog rolling in off the Thames. The wharf linked to Belvedere Street, but in this brume, she could barely see five feet in front of her. To go any further would be to disappear into the fog alone, and that would be far too risky.

Leo turned back to the doorman. "Did you see a woman come through here, just now? Wearing a dark cloak?"

He frowned, a deep crease cutting through his forehead, into the bridge of his nose. "Sure. She went that way." He nodded toward the street.

"What did she look like?" Leo asked. "Did you recognize her?"

"Didn't see a thing of her. Had her head covered. Why?" He looked back inside. "What's going on in there?"

The music had not resumed, and the noise of a panicked crowd began to overtake the club.

"A woman is hurt," she told the doorman on her way back in.

The gawking crowd created a blockade as she returned toward her table Employing her elbows, she physically parted arms and shoulders to force her way through.

By the time she saw Dita again, standing over the woman on the floor, a few minutes had passed. A grim pall enveloped the circle of patrons surrounding the immobile form. A pool of bloody vomit was on the floor next to the woman, and blood leaked from her ears, nose, and lips. Her eyes stared blankly.

She was dead.

"What is it? What is happening?" a loud male voice shouted from outside the circle. With another burst of commotion, he shoved people aside and lurched forward. He was tall, dark haired, and handsome. Leo recalled seeing him and the woman at the neighboring table as she and Dita took their seats earlier. They had been seated close, leaning together to talk and be heard above the loud music.

The man's eyes clapped onto the woman with horror.

"Gabriela?" He saw the blank stare of her eyes just as Leo had. "No! Gabriela!" The man threw himself to the floor and gathered her into his arms as he grated out a bellow of grief. Leo's heart clenched, and gooseflesh tightened her skin.

"Someone, call for the police!" a woman in the crowd cried out.

A loud murmur revolved through the room, and several distressed onlookers fled at the idea of the police's arrival. Another man pushed through, into the center of the circle. Eddie Bloom removed his hat, a dark purple bowler to match his suit, and stared at the scene. "I won't have bobbies in my place."

Leo gaped at him. "A woman is dead. You must summon the police."

Several people peered at her with curiosity, including Mr. Bloom and the husband cradling his wife's limp figure. The club's owner cocked his head. "This is my establishment, Miss Spencer. I give orders here, not you."

Leo jerked back an inch. He knew her by name? Though she wondered how, right then it wasn't her main concern.

Dita gripped her elbow, perhaps to signal a warning, but Leo ignored it. "By the sick on the floor and the leaking blood, which is evidence of ruptured capillaries, it looks to have been acute poisoning. If you refuse to call for the police, they will think you have something to hide, Mr. Bloom."

The murmurs around them hushed. All eyes turned toward the owner. He hitched his chin and peered down his nose at Leo, defiantly. But then, he snapped his fingers toward one of his uniformed waiters. "Go find a sodding constable."

Method of Revenge (Spencer & Reid Book 2) releases March 29, 2025

Also by Cara Devlin

The Spencer & Reid Mysteries
SHADOW AT THE MORGUE
METHOD OF REVENGE

The Bow Street Duchess Mysteries
MURDER AT THE SEVEN DIALS
DEATH AT FOURNIER DOWNS
SILENCE OF DECEIT
PENANCE FOR THE DEAD
FATAL BY DESIGN
NATURE OF THE CRIME
TAKEN TO THE GRAVE
THE LADY'S LAST MISTAKE (A Bow Street Duchess Romance)

The Sage Canyon Series
A HEART WORTH HEALING
A CURE IN THE WILD
A LAND OF FIERCE MERCY

THE TROUBLE WE KEEP

A Second Chance Western Romance

About the Author

Cara is the author of the bestselling Bow Street Duchess Mystery series. She loves to write romantic historical fiction and mystery, especially when the romance is a slow burn and the mystery is multi-layered and twisty. She lives in rural New England with her husband and their three daughters. Cara is currently at work on the rest of the Spencer & Reid Mysteries. The second book, METHOD OF REVENGE, releases in March 2025.

Printed in Great Britain
by Amazon